Benedict saw the spark[...]
and stood up.

'I have a feeling that [...]
upon the rival merit[...]
fashions—and I shall find myself very much *de trop*
among the silks and muslins!'

He bowed over the Duchess's hand with such an air
that for a moment Theo was afforded a glimpse of that
impudent, devil-may-care young gallant who had been
banished to India all those years before. Then he was
turning to her, the light still in his eyes.

'Goodbye, sweet coz,' he murmured. 'I need not say
be happy, for I'm sure you will be.'

The words sounded so final that she felt a sudden pang
at his going. She sprang to her feet, holding out her hand
impulsively. 'I shall see you again soon?'

His fingers closed around her hand. He looked at it for
a moment without speaking and then raised it to his lips.
'But of course,' he drawled, his voice softly mocking. 'I
am not so easily got rid of!'

Sheila Walsh was born in Birmingham and educated there until the bombing in 1941 forced her family to move. They settled in Southport where Sheila still lives. She is married and has two daughters. Her first Regency novel, THE GOLDEN SONGBIRD, won her an award presented by the Romantic Novelists' Association in 1974. She has since written seven further Regency romances, and has twice been shortlisted for the Romantic Novelists' Association Award. A HIGHLY RESPECT-ABLE MARRIAGE, published as a longer Masquerade earlier this year, won the 1984 RNA Award for the Best Romantic Novel of the Year. COUSINS OF A KIND is her second Masquerade Historical Romance.

COUSINS OF A KIND

SHEILA WALSH

MILLS & BOON LIMITED
15–16 BROOK'S MEWS
LONDON W1A 1DR

First published in Great Britain 1985
by Mills & Boon Limited

© Sheila Walsh 1984

Australian copyright 1985
Philippine copyright 1985
This edition 1985

ISBN 0 263 75108 2

Set in 10 on 11 pt Linotron Times
04–0885–66,660

Photoset by Rowland Phototypesetting Ltd
Bury St Edmunds, Suffolk
Made and printed in Great Britain by
Cox and Wyman Ltd, Reading

CHAPTER
ONE

THE AUTUMN afternoon was well advanced and looked set to fade into a watery sunset as the London-bound stage from Plymouth rattled through the village of Hatherton and came to a swaying halt in front of the local inn. The steps were hastily let down and a single passenger alighted.

The landlord hurried from the taproom the moment he heard the coach stop. Visitors were rare, uncommonly so at this time of year, and his mind was already busy listing the contents of the larder. From the kitchen regions wafted the aroma of one of Mrs Grimsargh's raised mutton pies, appetising enough to tempt the weariest traveller. There was also the best part of a cold ham, a couple of well-hung rabbits, and cheeses aplenty . . .

He flung open the door and was disappointed to find only a slight figure standing all alone on the flagged front waiting while a shabby corded trunk was unearthed from the boot of the coach. A young lady. She turned her head to smile at him as she heard the door, her plain round bonnet framing a face that showed a pleasing merry disposition.

Mr Grimsargh had an uneasy feeling that his wife would have something to say on the subject of unaccompanied females, though to be sure this one looked genteel enough for all that she was so oddly attired in a thick all-enveloping cloak more suited to a man. But there was no time to argue the matter; the coach was

ready for the off, the young lady's thanks having been
delivered most cordially in a clear light voice filled with
unusual cadences. He swallowed his misgivings and
begged her to come through to the private parlour.

'There's a cheery fire a-going in there, miss, on
account of we have a gentleman staying with us at the
present. Howsoever,' he added magnanimously, ushering her along a dim narrow passage, 'he'll be happy
enough with the coffee room, I daresay.'

'Are you sure?' The lady sounded anxious. 'I wouldn't
like to put anyone about.'

He assured her that she wouldn't be doing anything of
the kind. 'He is a very free and easy kind of a gen'lman,
miss, besides which, he en't here just now. He was away
to friends yesterday and as like as not he'll not be back
until late this evening, so come along in.'

He opened the parlour door so that she might enter.
Here too all was dimness apart from the glow of the fire,
but as he hurried to thrust a taper into the flames and
bustled around lighting the lamps, the room leaped into
cheerful life.

'You are very kind,' she said with a ready smile,
glancing around at the chintz covers against the dark
woodwork. 'What a very cosy room this is, to be sure!'

She removed her cloak and laid it over the back of a
settle before crossing to warm her hands at the flames. 'If
it wouldn't be too much trouble, do you think I could
have a pot of coffee?'

''Tis no trouble, miss,' Mr Grimsargh assured her,
thinking that she seemed more youthful than ever without that great heavy cloak—sort of delicate-looking in
her simple dark stuff dress. There'd been no mention
of a room, but unless she was to be met . . .? Mrs
Grimsargh wasn't going to like it one bit, holding
strongly as she did to the view that 'proper' young ladies
didn't roam the country without some kind of escort.
Still, there was no call for to starve the young lass.

'You'll be wanting more than coffee, I'm thinking, after your journey.' Inquisitiveness made him add, 'Come all the way from Plymouth, have you?'

'Yes.' Her mouth curved. 'There is certainly a most delicious smell coming from your kitchens. It is making me more hungry by the minute, but . . .' Her smile grew a little pensive, 'No, I really mustn't stay, for I very much want to reach my destination before the light goes. Do you know a house called Shallowford? The coach driver gave me to understand that it lies only a short way from here—and that I might be able to hire a gig . . .'

Her voice trailed away as the landlord turned to stare at her, the last lamp held up unlit in one hand while the taper burned away unheeded in the other.

'Shallowford?' he repeated, and as if to make quite sure, 'Lord Radlett's place?' Then, as she nodded, 'You want to hire a gig for to drive to Shallowford this evening—alone?'

'Why, yes. That is my intention.' She opened her brown eyes very wide. 'I am quite accustomed to drive myself, you know, and lack of company has never bothered me.'

'It en't that, miss . . , though I'm not saying it wouldn't raise a few eyebrows . . .' The landlord looked uncomfortable.

She looked amused. 'Well, then? Is it perhaps too far to reach before nightfall?'

'It en't that, either. Shallowford's no more than a couple of miles at most.'

'Yes, that is what I was told.' She waited, but again he seemed loath to continue. For a moment tiredness threatened to overwhelm her and a trace of exasperation entered her voice.

'I really must ask you to be more explicit. I cannot abide people who talk all round the point without ever getting to it.'

She regretted her sharpness almost at once and smiled

ruefully. 'I'm sorry, but it has been a long and wearisome journey. In fact, there are times when I feel I have been travelling for ever. All I want is to *arrive*! Can you understand that?'

'Course I can, miss. Very natural sentiments they are, too, I'm sure, only . . .' Mr Grimsargh told himself that it was none of his business, but she was such a very pleasant young lady. 'The thing is, ye see, his lordship is a bit of a high stickler . . . alus was. And I reckon as he might not be pleased, ill as he is, to learn of your arriving in such a skimble-skamble fashion, beggin' your pardon, miss, even allowing that you was expected?' It wasn't quite a question, but his very natural curiosity getting the better of him made it appear so.

'Oh. Yes, I see.' She uttered a short laugh, accompanied by an unconsciously weary gesture. 'It is a nice point. You see, I am expected—in a manner of speaking, though the precise hour of my arrival was necessarily vague, dependent as I was upon the somewhat unpredictable moods of the Atlantic Ocean.' Her laugh rang out again, mocking her own absurdity. 'I suppose I should have waited—sent word. Oh, what a coil! Well, there's nothing to be done now. I am here, and my grandfather will hardly turn me out of doors, I hope!'

A degree of comprehension was beginning to dawn upon the bemused landlord—the odd manner of her speech which he hadn't been able to place was at once clear to him. 'You'm from America!' He looked at her as though thunderstruck, and with her dark merry eyes confirming it, he wondered why he hadn't seen the likeness before. 'You'm never Mr John's lass?'

'Yes, I am.' Her voice was suddenly eager. 'Did you know my father?'

'Know him? Bless my soul, I should just say I did! Why, he's crossed this threshold more times than I'd care to count—him and Mr Geoffrey both—alus kickin' up larks, they were, but not an ounce of malice in them, you understand.' He sighed heavily. 'And now they're both gone—Mr Geoffrey killed at Waterloo and then your pa—' He busied himself with the last lamp so as not to seem too inquisitive. 'Sudden, was it?'

Theo Radlett felt the swift rush of anguish which she had not yet learned to master. She said tautly, 'Quite sudden. A kind of accident.'

'Ah!' said the landlord sagely. He waited for more, but when it failed to come, he cleared his throat and absently mangled the remaining piece of taper between restless fingers.

'That must have been a nasty shock for you, miss. But you'd others—family, maybe, to help you through?'

'No,' she said. 'I am quite alone.'

The landlord was by now in a dilemma and knew not how to resolve it. 'Well, I'm right sorry, miss.' He took refuge in speech while his mind grappled with his problem. 'We was all properly cut up when Mr John took off to America after that last difference with his lordship . . . Difference!' He chuckled. 'Proper blue the air was, so I heard! Beggin' your pardon, miss,' he added hastily, remembering to whom he was speaking. 'Course, the old gentleman had ever a short rein on his temper, but I don't reckon as he ever thought Mr John'd up and leave for good. Still an' all'—he sighed again—'it don't seem right to be speaking ill of him now, what with all the grief that's been visited on him. Taken to his bed and in a poor way, so they tell me . . .'

'Oh dear!'

Mr Grimsargh couldn't decide whether the young lady sounded sympathetic or apprehensive, but either way she ought to have matters made clear to her afore she went making bad worse . . . and it seemed that he'd have to be the one to do it.

'All in all, Miss Radlett,' he began nervously, 'things being what they are . . . and all taken into consideration

. . . I en't sure that it's such a good idea, you goin' along to Shallowford and surprisin' his lordship. Could give him a nasty turn . . .'

She put her hands to her face in a gesture of indecision. 'Do you really think so?' She looked out at the fading afternoon. It did not look welcoming. Common sense told her that the innkeeper was right, but with the end of her journey so nearly in sight the thought of any further delay was frustrating in the extreme. 'Oh, but I don't see how that could be. He is expecting me sometime, after all.'

'That's as may be, miss, but it's like this, you see—' He stopped abruptly.

From outside the window came the sound of a carriage rattling over the cobbles at a great rate, slowing as it swung into the stable yard, and a deep peremptory voice shouting: 'Sammy! Come along, you lazy young lummock—look lively!'

'Oh Lor! 'Tis Mr Benedict!' Somewhere in the depths of the inn a door slammed, and at the sound, Mr Grimsargh grew flustered. 'Forgive me, miss, but I must just have a word . . .'

She looked at him in surprise. 'By all means, sir. But if your guest wishes to have his parlour to himself, pray tell him that I shall not be in the least offended.'

It was too late. The door opened and a gentleman strode in, halted upon seeing that he was not alone and, noting the presence of a young lady, removed his hat unhurriedly, set it on the table with his gloves, and came forward, his drab driving-coat open and billowing gently as he moved.

He was a tall, loose-limbed man of some thirty summers, with a certain air of fashion about his dress, though it was marred by a careless want of attention to detail. His lean, rather swarthy face had registered momentary surprise upon finding the room occupied, but settled back almost at once into its harshly etched

lines. He lifted the quizzing-glass that swung from a
black ribbon about his neck.

'Ma'am.' He bowed, and the trace of irony in his voice
was echoed in the light grey eyes which he then turned
enquiringly upon Grimsargh, in whose face agitation
was writ large. The amusement deepened, and he said
softly: 'Do I intrude?'

The landlord became over-hearty. 'No! No indeed,
Mr Benedict! As if you could ever be guilty of such a
thing! It's just that . . . well, I wasn't expecting to see
you quite now.'

'Indeed, why should you?' The stranger cast a further
glance at Theo. 'As it happens, the business I had in
London took less time than I had expected, and since I
had no wish to suffer the company of my cousin, Beau,
or that young cub and his mama for one moment longer
than I must . . .' The stranger left the sentence in mid-air
as he shrugged himself out of his coat and flung it
carelessly over a chair. 'I thought perhaps a pint of your
best ale? However, if I am *de trop*, you have but to say.'

'I don't know about that, sir. You couldn't have come
more timely, to my way of thinking.'

Miss Radlett did not understand the curious atmosphere that had developed, but judged that it was time to
intervene.

'Indeed, sir, I fear it is I who intrude,' she said
pleasantly, moving across to the settle where her cloak
lay. 'I am aware that you have already bespoken this
room, so I will leave you to take your ease in peace.
Perhaps, landlord, when you have attended to Mr
Benedict's needs, we could finish making arrangements
in the coffee room—about the conveyance? I can
perhaps take some coffee while I wait.'

She smiled at them both, and with the cloak heavy
across her arm, turned to leave.

'One moment, ma'am, if you will.'

She hesitated, and the gentleman studied the heart-shaped face lifted to him, faintly blushing, dark eyes agleam with unspoken query, and resolute chin. A few chestnut curls escaping the confines of her bonnet lay against one flushed cheek.

'You have the advantage of me,' he began, and saw her unusually thick dark eyelashes quiver as her eyes widened in query. 'You clearly know my name,' he explained. 'Am I not to know yours?'

'I cannot see what purpose that would serve'—a polite smile and a decided coolness in her voice saying as clearly as words that she was not that kind of young lady. Again she turned to leave.

'Oh dear, oh Lor!' uttered Mr Grimsargh in the tones of a man much troubled and confused in his mind. 'Miss—I do think perhaps you should . . .'

'You do?' Theo threw the landlord an incredulous, half-impatient look, and then turned it upon the amused gentleman. Her chin came up with a certain hauteur. 'Well, I'm sure I don't see why I should, but since you are both set on it, then I will tell you, sir, that I am Miss Theodora Radlett.'

She wasn't sure what kind of reaction to expect, but the stranger certainly seemed to have been shaken out of his complacency.

'Did you say Radlett?' As she nodded, he stared at her, disbelief stamped across his harsh features. 'And are you travelling alone, Miss Radlett?' He appeared to choke on her name, his face a blank.

It was the second time she had been asked that question. Really, everyone was behaving in the oddest way! Theo began to feel irritated. She was tired, confused, and edgy about her forthcoming interview with her grandfather. She could do without the added unwelcome attentions of a possible madman.

'Quite alone,' she said firmly, and lest he should take any wrong notions into his head, 'Perhaps you know my grandfather, Lord Radlett? I have come all the way from

Philadelphia to see him, and if you don't mind, I would
very much like to do just that without further delay, so I
will bid you good day, sir.'

But before she could move he had flung back his head
with a great shout of laughter, which echoed and
bounced among the low heavy beams of the ceiling.

'Of course!' he cried. 'Theodora—Theo! Oh, it's rich,
Grimsargh—by God, it's rich! Don't you see, man!
Miss Theodora Radlett is from Philadelphia . . . and
Philadelphia is in America!'

'Mr Benedict, 'ave done, do, sir!' muttered the dis-
comforted landlord, who had stolen a swift glance at the
young lady and had surprised a look in her eyes that
reminded him irresistibly of her choleric grandparent. 'I
know well enough what's what—and what I say is,
there's no call to carry on like that afore Mr John's
daughter. Downright embarrassin', that's what it is!'

'Pray do not be thinking for one moment that you are
obliged to consider my feelings.' Unsure still whether he
was mad or merely insolent, Miss Radlett was curt, the
hold on her temper strained almost to breaking point. 'If
Mr Benedict is pleased to regard my name as an object
for mirth, I am sure he is at perfect liberty to behave as
he chooses. It is not for you or me to read him a lecture
on manners. Neither, however, do I intend to stay here
and endure his insulting behaviour.'

With this, she turned on her heel and marched, head
high, to the door. He was there before her, his hand flat
against the panel.

'Wait!' he besought her earnestly, though the laughter
still lingered in his eyes. 'I beg you, don't go.'

'Really, sir—this is beyond everything.'

'Yes, I know. Grimsargh is quite right. I have behaved
abominably and can only offer you my humblest apologies and crave a few minutes of your time in order to set
matters right.'

She hesitated.

'It is not enough? You want satisfaction?' He leaned closer, the irony back in his eyes. 'Well, here is my face for you. You may slap it, an' you will, without fear of retaliation.'

Miss Radlett's mouth quirked irrepressibly. 'Now you are being ridiculous!' She strove for dignity. 'Oh, very well, Mr Benedict, I accept your apology. The matter is forgotten. Now, if you will be so good as to let me pass.'

He sighed and removed his hand from the door with a gesture of resignation.

'As you will, Cousin Theo, though I'm bound to say I feel you are being over-hasty.'

Once more her eyes opened wide. 'What did you call me?'

'Cousin.' His mouth twitched. 'A small world, is it not?'

'I would that it were smaller,' she said crisply. 'There might then be room for one jester the less.'

He chuckled. 'Oh, cousin—I begin to like your style! My life of late has been woefully short of stimulating company. But in this instance I do not jest. Ask old Grimsargh, if you don't believe me, for he it was who misled you in the first place with his quaint way of addressing us all.'

But of course! Had not the landlord referred to her father as Mr John and *his* brother as Mr Geoffrey? She began to feel decidedly foolish.

'Then you are . . .?'

'Benedict Radlett.' He made her a mocking bow. 'Your father and mine were first cousins, which must make us cousins of a kind, wouldn't you say?'

Theo stared at him a moment longer before going through the formality of seeking the landlord's confirmation.

''Tis right enough, miss. If you had but met his lordship you'd not question it, for of all the Radletts it's Mr Benedict as has the family look.'

'I could wish that were more of a compliment,' drawled her new-found cousin. 'But I cannot deny the truth of it.'

Now that Theo had recovered from her initial surprise, she was not altogether displeased to discover that she had kin other than the ailing and reputedly difficult gentleman she had come so far to see. Mr Benedict Radlett might not have been her ideal choice as a relation, but aside from his odd manners and even odder sense of humour, there was something about his 'damn you—dare you' brand of impudence that she found curiously engaging. Her spirits lightened a little.

'So—we are cousins, sir,' she said, offering him her hand with a conciliating smile. 'I am very pleased to make your acquaintance.'

He held on to her hand rather longer than politeness demanded, studying the slim member with its practical squared fingers, and then looking up into her face. 'And I yours, coz,' he drawled. 'Though you are not at all what we were expecting.'

'We?' She eyed him with new interest. 'Have I more relations, then?'

Benedict laughed—a softly mocking sound. 'Oh, my dear—you have indeed!' His eyes met the landlord's vaguely troubled glance. 'Bring us some coffee, Grimsargh, while I make my American cousin *au fait* with her new family. Pray sit down, Cousin Theo.'

As the landlord moved to oblige, Theo allowed herself to be led to the settle, though she protested that time was passing and she had hoped that he might see her safe to her grandfather's house.

'Nothing would give me greater pleasure,' he assured her suavely, moving one of the dining chairs away from the table a little so that he might sit facing her. 'But tomorrow will be soon enough. Grimsargh?' The landlord paused on the threshold. 'Have a room made ready for Miss Radlett, will you, and—if I am not mistaken, your wife is baking one of her excellent mutton pies . . .'

'That's true enough, sir . . . and you'd be very welcome to it, I'm sure.'

'Good. And couple of bottles of your best claret, I think. My cousin and I can then get better acquainted over dinner.'

But Theo did not care for such high-handedness; she found Benedict Radlett's way of taking matters completely out of her hands totally unacceptable and she did not scruple to tell him so, springing to her feet again and standing over him. Grimsargh looked from one to the other and closed the door upon them, shaking his head and muttering about chips off old blocks. He left behind him an atmosphere charged with indignation, fuelled by Benedict Radlett's continuing to lounge in his chair looking up at Theo with maddening unconcern.

'Spoken like a true Radlett,' he said. 'We don't in general like to be bested. But in this instance you had much better be guided by me.'

'Well, I don't care to be,' she said, drawing herself up to her full height, which was hardly sufficient to intimidate him, and what advantage she did gain was set at naught by the entrance of a maidservant bearing a steaming coffee jug and cups, and a plate of pastries. By the time the tray was deposited and the coffee poured, she felt that much of the force had gone out of her argument, and she concluded a little flatly, 'If you don't wish to accompany me, then be good enough to say so and I will make other arrangements. But don't patronise me, sir! I am three and twenty, and have cut my eye-teeth!'

'I'm sure you have.' One eyebrow rose. 'A young lady intrepid enough to have crossed the Atlantic unaccompanied must be well up to snuff!'

Theo knew that he was being deliberately provocative, yet still she felt obliged to defend herself. 'As to that, I had little choice. The lady who was to have accompanied me was taken ill at the last moment.'

'But you were undaunted,' he drawled. 'And still are. Yet all I am suggesting is a little time in which to recoup your resources before facing a pack of strangers. Besides, Mrs Grimsargh's mutton pie is a treat not lightly to be cast aside, and her husband keeps a tolerable cellar. All this and a good night's sleep, and you will be feeling much more the thing.'

Theo was not by nature perverse, so that, had she stopped to think, it must have struck her as odd indeed that with so pleasing a prospect put before her she should behave in a manner that was quite wilfully perverse as she asserted that there was nothing wrong with the way she felt—she was as fit as a flea. This declaration showed so blatant a disregard for the truth that at any other time she would have blushed lest he should guess how every bone in her body was protesting of ill-usage from travelling so long on the coach. Her eyes dared him to challenge the assertion, but he refused to oblige her.

'Of course you are,' he murmured so soothingly that she longed to hit him. 'I daresay it is only the exigencies of your long journey that have made you a trifle crabby.'

'I am *not* crabby!' she protested, wounded by the injustice of his observation. 'Indeed, I have shown extraordinary forbearance with you until now. How would you react, I wonder, if a virtual stranger came along and proceeded to order your life in the most odiously high-handed fashion?'

'Oh, I should undoubtedly plant him a facer,' said her cousin with so much gravity that she found herself being obliged to smother a giggle.

'A typically male remedy,' she concluded unsteadily.

'Yes.' He nodded sagely. 'You know, I have always thought it a pity that girls were not initiated into the noble art of fisticuffs—so satisfying and immediate in its effect! I do urge you to try it sometime—much better than nursing a grievance.'

Theo was fast discovering that it was possible to be infuriated beyond measure while at the same time falling prey to an irresistible desire to laugh. In an attempt to quell the latter, she sought for some cutting rejoinder that might be guaranteed to prick his conceit. But again he forestalled her.

'I expect you will have been told many times that your eyes fizz with yellow lights when you are angry?' he observed conversationally, as though passing the time of day. While she was still robbed of speech, he added generously: 'Remarkably handsome eyes they are, too—quite your best feature in my humble opinion. Though I advise you to have a care, for they are also extremely eloquent. I trust you will restrain your present very evident impulse to grind me into dust beneath your feet. Have a pastry—they are quite delicious.'

As Theo waved the plate away and sought for the words that would adequately sustain her wrath, she made the mistake of looking full at him. It was her undoing, for there was about him such a deceptively meek air that her ever-ready appreciation of the absurd overcame her and she finally succumbed to laughter. 'Wretched man!' she exclaimed. 'To cut the ground from under me just as I was set to give you the father and mother of a trimming!'

He grinned lazily. 'It would have been breath wasted, sweet coz. I am well known for my incivility and would most surely have given you back as good as you gave— and more. And since your manners are clearly superior to mine, you would be bound to have come off worst.'

'Don't you underestimate me!' she flashed.

'Oh, I don't. Believe me, I don't.'

'I still mean to finish my journey this afternoon,' she insisted, determined now to prove her mettle.

He was looking at her in an oddly intent manner. 'Are you then so eager to meet your fate?'

'You make it sound ominous,' she said lightly. 'Is my grandfather such an ogre?'

'He don't readily inspire affection,' came the dry response.

But Theo refused to be discouraged.

'And my other relations? You were to tell me about them.' She frowned. 'Strange, but I had supposed that Lord Radlett lived alone but for his sister.'

'Great-aunt Minta? Oh, she's still there—a bit queer in her attic, but harmless enough. Then there is Geoffrey's relict and her skitterbrained son, Aubrey.' He saw Theo's brows lift. '*Her* son, not his, much to her chagrin, since he cannot inherit. You didn't know Geoffrey had married? No, I suppose you wouldn't. It happened only a few months ago, in the spring, when he was on the rebound from the army. How like Geoffrey to eschew matrimony all his life and then succumb to someone like Selina!'

'You sound very disapproving, sir. My late uncle was surely old enough to choose a bride without incurring censure?'

Benedict uttered a short bark of laughter. 'Too old, belike! Selina had buried one husband and was well up to snuff. The late Mr Fane had left her so purse-pinched that with a son to set up in the world, she was soon on the catch for his successor. Poor Geoffrey didn't stand a chance. He was heir to both a title and a fortune, and it was common knowledge that the old man was on the way out. Selina had but to play the brave little woman and turn her china-blue eyes on him, and every ounce of chivalry in him responded as to an order of command.' The sarcasm in his voice grew more pronounced. 'What Selina had not allowed for, of course, was Boney's escape from Elba and her new husband's quixotic insistence upon having one more go at him—with fatal results! To have been widowed twice within such a short space of time says much for the intervention of a benign

Providence, don't you think?'

'What a cynic you are,' said Theo pleasantly. 'I feel quite sorry for the poor lady already.'

'Save your compassion, coz. She won't love you any the more for't. In fact, the circumstances being what they are, she isn't likely to love you at all!'

She was about to ask why, but Benedict was speaking again, and the soft vehemence in his voice startled her. 'And then, of course, we must not forget Beau!'

It was the second time the name had been mentioned. 'Beau?'

His lip curled. 'Vincent Radlett, son of his lordship's second brother—a posturing dandy known to all as Beau. He would dearly like to add the title Viscount to his name.' Benedict eyed her sardonically from under straight black brows. 'Now, he *will* be pleased to see you, though he may do his damnedest to hide the fact.'

Theo moved her shoulders impatiently. 'I do wish you would stop talking in riddles. It may amuse you to be enigmatic, but it is, let me tell you, an excessively irritating habit!'

'My apologies.' He didn't sound in the least sorry.

'If you're trying to make me change my mind, Cousin Benedict, you won't succeed. I don't frighten that easily,' she added, as much to convince herself as him. 'And if I did, I have always held to the belief that the best way to conquer apprehension is to face its cause. So—do you mean to take me to Shallowford, or must I go alone?'

Benedict rocked back in his chair, arms folded across his chest, contemplating those fizzing sparks in the dark eyes as they challenged his cool scrutiny. She was not precisely a beauty, in the accepted fashion, he mused. There was a great deal too much resolution in her face (sufficient in truth to have carried her alone across the Atlantic Ocean), and more than a hint of the Radlett obstinacy about the wide mouth and firmly rounded chin. No milk-and-water miss, this—her qualities were of a more positive kind. From what little he had seen, he would judge her to be impetuous, good-humoured except when provoked, and a positive tiger in defence of her rights. Courage, she certainly had—some might even call it wilful foolhardiness! But there was a leavening of practical common sense there too, which he suspected would more often than not hold sway, and a very ready sense of humour—qualities that were likely to be tested to the full in the awkward days to come. He was suddenly intrigued to know how she would come to terms with her situation. His chair came down with a decisive thud and he stood up.

'Very well,' he said abruptly.

'You will take me?' she said eagerly.

'I'll take you.' He swept his coat from the back of the chair. At the door, he paused and looked back at her. 'I cannot, however, guarantee how his lordship will receive the news of your arrival. You should know that there is a strong possibility that he will refuse, point-blank, to see you.'

'But he sent for me—for us! I wrote to explain about Papa, and said that I would come.' She stared, uncomprehending. 'He is expecting me!'

'Correction, sweet coz.' The mocking drawl was back in Benedict Radlett's voice. 'What he is expecting—indeed, it would not be an exaggeration to say what has kept him clinging to life these past weeks—is the arrival of Theo Radlett.'

'Well then . . .'

'*Theo* Radlett,' he repeated with soft emphasis. 'His grandson and heir!'

CHAPTER
TWO

THE CURRICLE was travelling fast between high hedges, and with an evening mist drifting wheel-high across the road, Theo ought to have felt uneasy. But she was still busy turning over the extraordinary moment of revelation back in the parlour of the inn, her small soundless gasp of disbelief, followed by a moment of silence which only seemed to confirm her error. Then:

'Your letter to Lord Radlett,' Benedict said calmly, 'was something less than explicit—and was signed with ambiguous formality, "obediently yours, Theo Radlett".'

'And you all thought . . .? Oh, Lordy!' Her lower lip caught ruefully between even white teeth said it all. She felt her cheeks grow warm and took refuge in indignation. 'Well—the ambiguity certainly wasn't intentional, as you appear to imply.'

'Don't put words into my mouth, young lady.'

'I'm not! But you said . . .' She had met his quizzical glance and uttered a short vexed laugh. 'Oh, what does it matter! Honestly, it never even crossed my mind that no one here knew of my existence. I assumed Papa would have written to someone when I was born . . .' She broke off and began again. 'Yes, indeed, the solicitor's letter did begin "Dear Sir", but I never appreciated the implications and thought it of no particular consequence. I guess it was a little unthinking of me, at that, but at the time, there were so many things to be done . . .' The anguish of her loss welled up in her once more with frightening intensity. Benedict Radlett's out-line blurred, and she saw instead her father's image, grown skeletal with suffering, his voice a weary patient thread. 'Go home, Theo—to England . . . for me. I should have taken you years ago. Stupid things, family quarrels.'

It was very soon after his death that the letter had arrived from Lord Radlett's solicitor. Its imperative summons, though couched in the formal language of the lawyer, seemed to give added point to her father's wishes—as if it was all meant to be. But how different was the reality! Not only must she face a less than amiable set of relations, but she was likely to be accused by some of them of misrepresentation. According to her cousin, Lord Radlett would certainly accuse her thus.

'It was Geoffrey's death, you see, which forced his lordship's hand,' Benedict had told her with some relish before they left the inn. 'He became obsessed with the need to discover John's whereabouts and make his peace with him so that there could be no possible chance of Beau's inheriting the title. The news of your father's death came as an added blow to him, but he seized on your letter as proof that an heir *did* exist, and that buoyed him up no end! Selina, too, was hopeful of being able to bring an impressionable young man round her finger and cajole him into supporting her in the manner to which she had expected to become accustomed . . .' He paused, and then finished, 'Beau, understandably, was furious!' Again there was a hard edge to his voice as he mentioned the name.

'And where does Benedict Radlett stand in all this?' she asked.

'I?' He was instantly wary, as near to being discon-certed as she had seen him. 'Oh, I am nowhere, cousin. A mere onlooker, I assure you. I do but keep the peace.'

She had not pressed him further. But could it really be that simple? Superficially charming though Benedict was, he remained something of an enigma. He had very carefully told her about everyone else and very little about himself, where he stood in line to the title, nothing at all, in fact, except—and this more by what he had left unsaid—that he disliked almost every member of the family. She had never felt more alone . . .

The curricle, bumping over a deep rut in the road, jerked her back to her present situation. She peered over the top and saw the bright-yellow wheels skimming along perilously close to the edge of a deep ditch. She swallowed her unease, huddled into her heavy travelling cloak, and resolved thereafter to keep her eyes resolutely to the fore.

'Cold?' Her cousin's dry query invaded her teeming thoughts.

'A little,' she conceded. 'But I shall do well enough.'

He caught the bleakness in her voice and looked aslant at her pinched face buried deep in the collar of her cloak, her nose glowing faintly pink in the fading light. 'A curricle is hardly the ideal conveyance for a lady at this time of year—however adequate her attire.'

He did not add, 'but you *would* come,' though he might as well have done so. Theo resented the implied criticism, of both her behaviour and her dress, and her reply was in consequence stiffly formal.

'The cloak belonged to my father, and I value it the more for that. It may not be of the first stare, but I assure you it has proved invaluable throughout the course of my journey!'

'I do not doubt it,' he said softly. 'It seems exactly the thing for a sea-crossing.'

But not for impressing one's relations, his comment seemed to say. She wrapped it more closely around her in a gesture of defiance that went unnoticed, and fell to watching her cousin's strong competent hands on the ribbons, wondering a trifle nervously what would happen if some obstacle were to rear out of the mist into their path. A glance at his absorbed profile convinced her that he would cope admirably.

'We have spoken little about your father,' he said suddenly without taking his eyes from the road. 'You clearly loved him very much.'

'Yes, I did.' Still do, cried a small lost voice within her. Still miss him dreadfully.

'Was his death unexpected? He can't have been any great age . . .'

'Two and forty,' she said in a clipped unemotional voice. 'And yes—it was unexpected.' Benedict took his eyes off the road for an instant, and she met his look, chin high. 'You see, cousin—he was shot.'

'Was he, by God!' The road claimed his attention once more, but he was clearly intrigued.

'Do you mind if we don't speak of it now?' she said, her contained air of calm just failing to disguise an unconscious underlying pleading. 'I would rather know about Grandfather. Is he really dying?'

'So he would have us all believe, though like that famous monarch of yore, he is an unconscionable long time getting to the nub of the matter. It's my belief he hasn't the slightest intention of troubling the grim reaper this side of Christmas.'

Theo thought him shockingly unfeeling—and said so.

'Yes, but I am right, as you will soon discover for yourself when—or indeed if—you get to meet him.' His whip snaked forward to point his leaders, and he caught it again with a deft turn of the wrist. 'You know, I have a notion that your visit is going to precipitate events, one way or another.'

'That's a horrible thing to say!'

She thought he laughed softly to himself, and was about to remonstrate further when almost without warning a pair of massive stone gateposts loomed ahead. Upon seeing them, her cousin sent the whip whistling forward again and, with an audacity that made her gasp, executed a swirling right-hander which brought them around neatly between the open gates, the distance judged to a nicety.

Her gasp had not gone unnoticed, and this time there was no mistaking that he laughed.

'Fear not, sweet coz—I shan't overturn us!'

'I am vastly relieved to hear it,' she said tartly, annoyed to think that her nerve might have been tested and found wanting. 'Nevertheless, in the present conditions it would surely be more prudent to proceed with caution.'

'Yes, but then I am seldom given to prudence,' he said with a grin. 'As you will discover when you come to know me better.'

This time Theo declined to be drawn, and an injured silence prevailed. They continued to gouge a path out of the mist until, with another abrupt right-hand turn, the curricle came to a halt in front of a short flight of stone steps leading up to a massive door built of weathered oak.

'Welcome to Shallowford, Cousin Theo,' Benedict said, securing the reins before jumping lightly to the ground and coming to lift her down.

Theo glanced up with interest from the foot of the steps, but could see little other than the shadowy irregular mass of a large creeper-covered building. She heard the sound of bolts being drawn, the door swung silently inward, and a tall stooped man in a faded black coat moved stiff-limbed out the shadows, blinking a little to see the slight figure in the heavy frieze cloak being escorted up the steps.

'Mr Benedict—is that you?'

The butler's voice held an anxious quaver as he peered at the young gentleman's companion, and taking account of his lordship's dislike of strangers.

'It's me right enough, Purley. Have someone attend to the horses, will you? And there's a small trunk and a carpet bag to be brought in from the curricle. Come along in, Cousin Theo.' Benedict heard the butler's involuntary exclamation, hastily choked back—and he grinned. 'Yes, Purley—what do you say to this, eh? I have brought Mr John's daughter back with me. Won't that be a splendid surprise for everyone?'

His voice rang round the great vaulted roof, sending back mischievous echoes.

'Mr John's *daughter*, did you say, sir?' Purley repeated in a bewildered way. 'But I thought . . . we all thought . . . oh, my!' he said as the full impact of the words sank home, and it sounded rather like a cry for help. Theo's heart sank. If this was the butler's reaction . . . But then she saw he was looking at her more closely, staring eagerly into the strong youthful face as though peering back through more than twenty years of memory. 'Oh, my!' he said again, quite differently. 'Yes, indeed, miss . . . there is a decided likeness about the eyes.' He drew himself together with the dignity due to his privileged status. 'What a very great pleasure it is to see you here, miss, if I may say so—where you so rightly belong.'

'Why, thank you, Purley!' Theo smiled at him, deeply touched by the old butler's obvious sincerity. 'I'm sorry to have given you such a shock.' A reproachful glance put the blame squarely where it belonged, on her cousin, though Purley murmured incoherently that she mustn't be thinking any such thing. 'My father often spoke about you with affection,' she said. 'He told me of the many times you had helped him and his brother out of scrapes.'

'Did he say that? Well now!' The old man seemed much moved. 'They were such *good* boys . . . always funning . . .'

Benedict stemmed Purley's inevitable preamble towards maudlin reminiscence by asking if the family had yet gone in to dinner.

'I was on the point of announcing it, sir, when you arrived.'

'Good. So they will be in the library?' He took Theo's arm.

'But, sir . . .' Benedict shot him an impatient look. 'Your outer garments, sir . . . and the young lady will surely wish to refresh herself . . .'

'Later, Purley. We mustn't keep the family waiting.'

Theo resisted as he took her arm. He glanced down in surprise. 'It would be nice to be consulted, Cousin Benedict.'

'Why? You said you liked to get things over with.' He took her short exasperated laugh for agreement, urged her across the flagged hall where suits of armour standing like sentinels seemed to come alive in the flickering light of the candle sconces along the wall.

'It all seems delightfully Gothic,' she observed pleasantly. 'One is irresistibly reminded of one of Mrs Radcliffe's romances. I own I shall be bitterly disappointed if there is not at the very least a walled-up nun to be heard moaning on stormy nights, to say nothing of a clanking chair or two.'

He laughed. 'I wasn't aware that Mrs Radcliffe's fame extended as far as America.'

She gave him a prim look. 'We are not quite savages, cousin. I daresay you would be amazed to know how civilised we can be!'

'*Touché!*' He grinned.

They had by now left the hall and were walking down a wide and lofty corridor. Benedict came to a halt in front of a door and turned towards her, his eyes seeming to glitter with expectation. 'Well, cousin—are you ready to face the family?'

It was as though, now that they were here, he could not wait for a confrontation, and for a moment Theo's heart misgave her.

*   *   *

The library at Shallowford commanded a westerly aspect, but Gothic windows set deep in the walls conspired with thick velour hangings to resist the least penetration of its gloom on even the sunniest of days. Now, with darkness closing in, candlelight picked out the faded grandeur of heavy furniture and much Jacobean oak panelling interspersed with shelf upon shelf of tooled leather books.

From its position above the chimney-piece, a portrait dominated the room, the gentleman's flowing Cavalier tresses and frivolously plumed hat seeming curiously at odds with the severity of his expression. Of the four people present, only three were obliged to incur his displeasure, the fourth being immured in an embrasure beyond the fireplace, her presence betrayed only occasionally by the glint of her needle as it passed in and out of her embroidery frame.

A lanky youth of some eighteen summers stood immediately beneath the picture, one arm resting on the mantelshelf. He scowled into the fire, kicking pettishly at a smouldering log and sending sparks flying up the chimney. The gesture, though childish, was evocative of Mr Aubrey Fane's general discontent as he turned to address himself to his mother, who reclined on a sofa near by, her fair frail beauty displayed to advantage by the floating draperies of her widow's weeds.

'I don't see why we must needs wait on Benedict's pleasure,' he complained, in answer to her suggestion that dinner might be put back a little. 'When it seems to me that *he* comes and goes very much as he pleases!'

Selina Radlett gazed with troubled eyes upon her offspring, seeing his outburst as just one more demonstration of his frustration. And who could blame him, poor boy! At his age, Aubrey should be in London enjoying himself—and she with him—instead of kicking his heels in this desolate backwater, dependent upon the whim of a sick half-crazed old man.

Not for the first time she railed inwardly against the cruel fate that had led her to take Geoffrey Radlett for a husband. He had seemed the ideal choice back in those mellow autumn days—a jovial bachelor of mature years fresh home from a life in the army, with both title and fortune all but in his grasp. How could she have known that Boney would escape from Elba within weeks of their marriage, or that Geoffrey with quixotic stupidity would be off to fight him with hardly a thought for her feelings—like a small boy playing at toy soldiers!

'Must finish the bounder off for good this time, m'dear,' he'd explained with sweet reason in answer to her protests. 'Tell you what—I'll take you and Aubrey down to stay with m'father at Shallowford—time you got acquainted!' Dear God! What a fiasco that had been! The old man had taken against them on sight, but she had borne all without complaint, convinced that he was not long for this world—everyone had said that he was dying—and then she would be Lady Radlett. But it was Geoffrey who had died, and she was left in a worse case than before, with only the old man's heir on whom to pin her hopes . . .

Beau Radlett's heavy eyelids masked his malicious observation of mother and son. He stood at a table near the window idly flicking through the pages of the *Morning Post*—a slim middle-aged exquisite with ennui written large upon his lean, fastidious features. The country was not his milieu—only his uncle's relapse and an overpowering desire to see this puppy of an American, whose arrival was imminent, had kept him here thus far, but even such an inducement was apt to lose its appeal when weighed against present company. Poor Selina! Such a transparent creature with her china-blue eyes and that deceptive air of fragility—all pale curls and pale complexion and a tight avaricious mouth. How like Geoffrey to fall prey to such a one!

'There is time yet for Benedict to come,' she was

saying now, half hopeful, for though Benedict could be tiresomely sarcastic at times, he at least treated her like a woman. 'And if Beau would not mind . . .?' Her eyes lifted nervously in his direction.

'But I do mind,' he drawled. 'For my part, I shall oppose any attempt of Purley's to put dinner back. My uncle's cook has little enough to commend him at the best of times . . .' He broke off as the sound of voices penetrated the door.

It opened to admit Benedict Radlett, still in his driving coat, and at his side a slight figure enveloped in a ridiculously large cloak and unremarkable bonnet.

'My dear boy,' began Beau in pained tones. But Benedict put up a hand to command attention—and drew Theo forward.

'Permit me,' he said with undisguised relish, 'the pleasure of presenting to you your long-awaited cousin, Theo Radlett.''

Drat him! thought Theo, very nearly as disconcerted as they were by her cousin's perverse partiality for high theatrical drama—amounting now almost to farce. The silence hung palpably in the air while Beau (for it could be no other) lifted an ornate quizzing-glass to survey her, a flicker of something akin to exultation showing briefly in his narrowed eyes.

Selina Radlett's mouth opened in a soundless gasp. She half rose and then sank back against her cushions, and it was left to her son to voice the common thought.

'A girl, egad!' he stammered on a nervous giggle. 'Oh, how p-priceless! I'd give a monkey to see the old man's face when he learns of it. He'll go off in an apoplexy this time for sure!'

'The tone of your conversation is seldom elevating, Aubrey,' Benedict informed him with cutting coldness. 'In this instance I believe we can dispense with it entirely.'

The boy blushed scarlet, more embarrassed by his own outburst than any of them, Theo suspected. She could not but feel for him and offered him a sympathetic smile, but he only glared and fell into a sulky silence.

His mother had by now recovered her power of speech, and with it came an uncontrollable spurt of outrage born of disappointment. She had been cheated, for no one now stood between Beau and the title, and she could hope for nothing from him. She pressed a scrap of cambric convulsively to her mouth, her voice shrill, all her anger directed at Benedict.

'Oh, how could you? I expect you have known this all along, and have only now revealed it as a cruel jest at my expense!'

He looked down his nose at her. 'My dear Selina, you are being rather absurd—and not at all welcoming to Cousin Theo.'

'If we are to speak of being welcoming, Benedict,' said Beau, coming forward in his indolent way, 'I fear our cousin must find you equally remiss. Do take the poor child's cloak. She will feel much more the thing without it.' There was a faint smile in the heavy eyes as he extended a slim white hand to Theo. 'Our notions of civility leave much to be desired, my dear, but as family we need not be standing on ceremony. I am Vincent Radlett.'

She did not in general care for dandies, but in this instance she was grateful for his display of kindness, motivated though it probably was by selfish relief. She returned his smile as his fingers touched hers. 'I am pleased to meet you, sir. You are, I feel sure, the one they call Beau?'

He inclined his head graciously.

Theo undid the clasp at the neck of her cloak, and Benedict, waiting with ironic courtesy, lifted it from her shoulders. She loosed the ribbons of her bonnet and removed that also, handing it to him with an aplomb she was far from feeling, and smoothed her fingers over her sadly flattened bright chestnut hair.

Selina had by now recovered herself sufficiently to say a little sulkily, 'You had better come close to the fire.' Her glance encompassed the insignificant dark dress, and she used her most patronising tone, usually reserved for addressing members of the lower orders. 'I daresay you will be finding things very strange—wondering who we all are.'

'Not in the least, ma'am.' Theo drew herself up very straight, stung by the implication that she was probably simple-minded as well as dowdy. 'You must be my Uncle Geoffrey's widow.' Her speech was direct and incisive, and Selina would have done well to take note of the dangerous spark in her eyes as her glance swung from mother to son, coolly assessing. 'And you are Aubrey. How do you do?' She met the boy's hostile glance with equanimity and, unable to resist the temptation, added innocently, 'It is an unexpected pleasure to find a ready-made family awaiting me, and although I guess I'm not quite what you were expecting, I hope that some among you at least will not be displeased.'

A little colour ran up under Beau's pale skin, and behind her Benedict murmured irrepressibly: 'Rolled up, horse, foot, and guns! Bravo, coz!'

Far from reassuring her, this wry encomium and a growing coolness in the atmosphere convinced her that a very pardonable annoyance had led her to behave un-handsomely.

She was wondering desperately how to put matters right when a joyous chuckle came from the corner near the fireplace, where a shadowy figure, overlooked in all the excitement, stirred and resolved itself into a tiny cherubic lady—almost as round as she was tall, dressed all in black.

'I'm delighted to see you've a true Radlett head on your shoulders, John's child—and a ready tongue

withal. If my brother can only be brought to look beyond
the unfortunate obstacle of your sex, he may eventually
give up his notion of dying for the present and learn to
appreciate you!'

Her voice was surprisingly vigorous for one whose
hair was snow-white and surmounted by a black lacy
cap. Bright eyes cushioned in wrinkles twinkled with
malicious amusement.

'Aunt Minta!' Selina exclaimed crossly. 'I had quite
forgot you were there.'

'People frequently do, madam. But I do not repine. It
has afforded me much enjoyment over the years!' The
old lady moved nimbly enough towards Theo until she
stood quite close, looking up into her face. 'Yes, you've
a decided look of your father. John was a good boy.
Stubborn, of course, but we're all afflicted with *that* vice.
Are you stubborn, miss?'

Theo was beginning to feel that she had stumbled
pell-mell into a madhouse. She glanced at Benedict and
saw that he was enjoying her initiation. Her chin lifted a
fraction as she replied, as pleasantly as she was able,
'Only when driven to it, ma'am. I am, in general,
reckoned to be the most amiable of creatures.' Her eyes
dared him to question it.

The old lady saw the look that passed between them,
and chuckled again. 'Well, we shall soon see how much
like your father you are.' Her eyes clouded. 'It is hard to
believe that he is dead. I don't know if you feel up to
speaking of it, m'dear . . .'

Staring down into the flames, Theo had to subdue a
momentary sensation of panic. It had to be done sometime. Better perhaps to get it over. She felt rather than
saw Benedict come up behind her, and found herself
resisting an impulse to lean back against his shoulder for
comfort—an absurd impulse, when she scarcely knew
him.

'You don't have to, you know.'

The unexpected gentleness in his voice was almost her undoing, but she wouldn't cry, she told herself, and schooled her voice into steadiness.

'It's all right.' She half turned to look up at him, her profile delicately etched by the firelight. And then she looked around at the rest of them grouped in their various attitudes.

'I'm not sure how much you know about Papa's life?'

'Very little,' drawled Beau languidly.

'For many years he ran a very successful school for boys in Philadelphia,' she began.

'How quaint!' murmured Selina. Benedict frowned at her.

'He was ever bookish,' said Miss Radlett. 'And your mama?'

'She died when I was born. But that is neither here nor there. Last year, Papa decided that he would like to open a larger school in Washington, and we went there to look at a property. Only, while we were there, your General Ross marched in with his troops . . .' Theo's voice shook a little with the bitterness of the memory. 'They ransacked the place, and they burned the White House and the Capitol.' She looked around at their polite faces and wondered if any of them, with the possible exception of Benedict, had any idea of how it was. 'Feelings were running very high, as you might imagine, and a lot of men were fighting drunk.

'When Papa tried to reason with one of them, the man accused him of being a dirty no-good English bastard, and shot him.'

In spite of all her good intentions, tears blocked Theo's throat—they stung her eyes, and she blinked them away angrily.

'My dear child, this is too painful for you!' cried her great-aunt, much distressed. 'I should not have asked.'

Theo shook her head, swallowed several times, and said doggedly. 'There isn't much more, so you might as well hear it. It wasn't easy to get a doctor in Washington that night—and when one finally did arrive, he was of little help. The bullet was lodged in a difficult spot, and there was no way in which it could be removed. It was his opinion that my father would not survive until morning.' She looked up bleakly. 'In fact, he lived for almost a month in pain, and getting weaker and thinner every day until I prayed that he would die!'

There was a silence in the room. A log settled in the fire, sending up sparks. Theo shuddered, feeling suddenly empty of all emotion.

'I'm sorry,' she said. 'I ought not to have inflicted all that upon you.'

There were murmurs of 'No, no . . .' and embarrassed looks, only Benedict saying with a quick impatient gesture, 'Don't be nonsensical! Why should you not?'

She lifted her head. 'Because there is no one I despise so much as the person who dwindles into maudlin recollection, cousin.'

He looked slightly disconcerted, and then smiled wryly. 'I might have expected that, I suppose. But what happened to your school?'

'I continued to run it for a while, but it was difficult to find a good schoolmaster to replace Papa, and eventually I closed it, though I have kept the house for the present—until I decide what to do for the best.'

The door opened to admit Purley, and Selina looked relieved.

'Ah, good. We are ready to dine.' Her eyes once more raked Theo from head to foot. 'Unless Theodora wishes to change her dress.' For the life of her, she could not keep the waspish note out of her voice. 'I am sure we shall not regard the inconvenience, in the circumstances. Your boxes will have been taken up, no doubt . . .?' Purley inclined his head. 'We have put you in your father's old room. Hardly a suitable choice, perhaps, but then we could not be expected to know . . .'

'Selina, you are being confoundedly tiresome,' Benedict said.

Beau's voice cut in, bored—but with an edge. 'Let us not dwindle into wrangling, I beg of you!' He turned his heavy-lidded eyes to Theo, their expression unreadable. 'What is your wish, child?' He wafted a handkerchief airily. 'We are entirely at your disposal.'

She was all too aware of the tensions in the air. Only Benedict seemed unaffected. She shrugged off a threatening despondency, to say with determined cheerfulness, 'There is no need to hold up dinner on my account if you will accept me, travel-stained as I am.'

It was not the easiest of meals; the conversation, such as it was, being conducted in a kind of strained politeness, and hungry though Theo had thought herself to be, she now found her appetite had quite deserted her, and she wanted nothing more than to be alone to collect her disordered wits.

Selina displayed a similar want of appetite and watched impatiently as Aunt Minta ate her way steadily through each course with an obsessive dedication until there was nothing left to be consumed. Even then the old lady was slow to admit to repletion, and when several meaningful glances failed to move her, Selina took it upon herself to rise, gathered up her shawl, and indicated in the most patronising way that they should retire to the drawing room and leave the gentlemen to their port.

So it happened that they were all on their feet when a disturbance could be heard beyond the doors, which almost at once swung inward. A figure of bizarre aspect filled the opening.

In his prime, Lord Radlett had been a man of formidable proportions; even now, as he threw off the well-meaning support of his black-coated valet to stand swaying, shoulders back and leonine head thrust belligerently forward, there was a hint of unleashed power about him, though this was belied by the skin stretched paper thin over his prominent cheekbones and hooked nose. His hair, as snow-white as his sister's, grew with surprising vigour from a high forehead and fell, unconfined, until it touched the collar of a much-frogged dressing gown heavy with gilt embroidery that glittered in the candlelight.

But it was his eyes that held Theo—they blazed with a compelling, febrile intensity beneath soaring white brows, as they sought her out and fixed on her. She quelled her apprehension, telling herself that this was her father's father—she was flesh of his flesh in a manner of speaking. The thought should have uplifted her, but it failed quite dismally to do so. Unable to bear the tension a moment longer, she stepped forward smiling, hands outflung to him. There was no response, not a glimmer of acknowledgement, only a silence that stretched until, with a final fulminating glare, his lordship turned unsteadily on his heel and tottered away, leaning heavily on the arm of his valet, who had been hovering like a watchful crow. The doors had been left open, and as Theo watched the slowly retreating procession, her face felt like a mask that had been hammered into place. She was dimly aware that all interest was centred upon her, awaiting her reaction. But it was Benedict whose eyes she sought, and she found a look in them of fury mingled with something remarkably akin to compassion flung out to her like a lifeline. She held to it with blind gratitude while she salvaged what she could of her disordered emotions.

It was Great-aunt Minta who finally broke the silence, tutting audibly. 'How very like Edmund!' she exclaimed. 'He had ever execrable manners, you know. But I shall tell him exactly what I think—oh, you may be sure I shall tell him!'

Theo made a swift deprecating gesture, her voice husky. 'No, please—I beg you will not!'

'Such generosity,' murmured Beau in admiration. 'You are an example to us all, my dear. Pray accept my apologies in my uncle's behalf.'

Selina moved impatiently. 'What I want to know,' she said waspishly, 'is how a man so close to death as he would have us believe him to be managed to negotiate all those stairs.'

Her words could not have been more inopportune, for at that precise moment there was a sudden commotion among the hovering servants in the hall, and a skirl of fear was forced from her as Lord Radlett faltered, threw back his head, and then appeared to crumple without a sound. The distressed valet, unable to support his insensible master, was already lowering him to the floor as the servants all rushed forward.

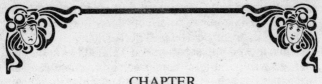

CHAPTER
THREE

IN THE dining room, Theo was the first to recover from the shock. She lifted her skirts and ran, while Benedict, having seen that Beau was unable or unwilling to act, wasted no more than a contemptuous glance on him before following hard on Theo's heels.

He found a scene of confusion which was clearly beyond the elderly butler's ability to resolve, upset as he so obviously was. Theo, already on her knees supporting her grandfather's head on her lap, was trying vainly to get someone to attend to his lordship's valet, who was in a state of near collapse at her side.

She looked up gratefully as Benedict strode into their midst and began to issue a number of tersely-worded instructions. Within moments one footman had been dispatched to summon the doctor, while several more lifted the valet and carried him away, unable to do more than protest weakly that his place was with his lordship.

With order restored, Benedict was able to give his attention at last to Lord Radlett, who lay ominously still, cradled in Theo's arms, his face betraying an alarming pallor.

'Let me have him now,' he said, his voice amazingly gentle.

She smoothed back the white hair from her grandfather's bloodless brow one more time before reluctantly surrendering him to her cousin. Relieved of the weight, her arms trembled and she remained kneeling, shaken to the core by the great surge of emotion that, unbidden, had suddenly possessed her for this man she scarcely knew.

'He isn't dead!' she declared fiercely.

'No, but we must get him to bed.' Benedict was quietly matter-of-fact, and his manner helped to calm her. She scrambled to her feet and watched him supporting Lord Radlett's lolling head firmly against his shoulder as he summoned one of the remaining footmen to assist him in carrying the unconscious Viscount to his room.

Theo hovered indecisively, wanting to be of use, yet conscious that she was very much the newcomer in this strange household. While she still hesitated, she turned and saw that Great-aunt Minta had come from the dining room and was also watching her brother being carried from sight. How long she had been there Theo did not know, but there was such a lost, uncertain look about her that she at once went to put an arm about the plump drooping shoulders. The old lady attempted a gallant smile, but her mouth went sadly awry.

Theo gave the shoulders a reassuring squeeze, but before he could speak, Selina came drifting towards them in a cloud of draperies, with Aubrey, his handsome face sullen, a few steps behind.

'Well,' she said in faintly aggrieved tones, 'that was all most unfortunate, though no more than one might expect in this house, I'm sure. And it has put Beau in a very strange mood. I believe he almost thinks himself master here already. He as good as told Aubrey that he had no wish for his company over the port.'

'I wouldn't have stayed anyway,' muttered the graceless young tulip. 'He has the most odious way of making me feel as though I were still in short coats!'

'That is nothing to how he will behave if Lord Radlett dies! I would not be in the least surprised if he turns us out of doors almost before the old gentleman is cold!'

'Ma'am—I beg you to mind your words.' Theo had felt Aunt Minta flinch, and rushed impetuously into speech without stopping to think. Selina, on the point of reproving her, encountered those dangerously flashing eyes, thought better of it, shrugged, and drew her wraps closer about her.

'Well, I'm sure I don't know why we are standing around in this draughty hall, when there will be a fire burning in the drawing room. Are you coming, Aunt Minta—Theodora?'

There was an offhandedness in her manner that irked Theo. She glanced swiftly at Aunt Minta, who seemed to have recovered herself somewhat, and the old lady, misinterpreting her look, patted her hand reassuringly.

'You go along, child. Poor Selina—try not to judge her too harshly. She is a very unhappy woman. It will be good for her to have you for company.'

It would have been ungracious for Theo to confess that she had no wish to bear Selina company—that upon brief acquaintance she found her vain and shallow and exceedingly selfish. Instead, she prevaricated.

'But what of you, ma'am?'

'I shall retire to m'bed.' The old lady straightened her back, and much of her former bluntness had returned. 'No, ye don't have to bear-lead me,' she snapped as Theo offered to see her to her room. 'I ain't so feeble that I need help. Go along with you now, and let me be.'

Feeling a general sense of rejection, Theo watched Aunt Minta stomp away bristling with outraged dignity, and then slowly followed in Selina's wake.

The drawing room proved to be much larger than the library. It was rather shabbily furnished in an antiquated style, but beneath the candlelight and with the flames licking round the logs in the huge hearth, the faded gold curtains and striped furnishings acquired a comfortable warmth, and it occurred to Theo that with a very little care and imagination the room might be made quite pleasant.

'Will the doctor be long coming, do you think?' she asked.

Selina gave a little shrug. 'I haven't the least idea. His house is no more than two miles away, but if he should be out to dine . . .'

'I see.'

Selina had settled herself on a sofa near the fire, and she watched Theo now as she wandered about the room, aimlessly picking objects up and putting them down again. Her initial assessment of the girl as an insignificant dab was rapidly undergoing a change, for in spite of a certain reticence of manner, due no doubt to the confusing nature of events since her arrival, there had been occasions during dinner and since when she had asserted herself in a way that showed a disturbing independence of spirit.

Nor did she care for Benedict's attitude towards the girl—a kind of camaraderie appeared to exist between them which, if they had truly met for the first time earlier in the day, must be nipped in the bud. If Benedict was to be of use to anyone, it should not be to this American interloper.

'Cousin Benedict seems very much at home here,' said Theo suddenly, as if reading her thoughts. The opportunity seemed heaven-sent.

'Yes, doesn't he?' Selina purred. 'Clever man!'

Theo looked at her in surprise. 'Why clever?'

Selina's blue eyes opened very wide. 'Lud, my dear! Wouldn't you think someone clever who appears out of nowhere, announces that he is Lord Radlett's great-nephew just home after years in India, and proceeds to make himself all but indispensable to the old man?'

'When was this?'

'Oh, I really can't remember. About two months ago, I believe.'

Theo found that her heart was beating uncomfortably fast. Her cousin was her only lifeline in this curious household. She didn't want him proved false. And yet, hadn't she herself found him enigmatic?

'Are you saying that Benedict is an impostor?' she asked, dry-mouthed.

'Heavens, no!' Selina tittered. 'There was never any question of challenging his credibility. Even Beau acknowledged him to be genuine, little as it pleased him to do so, for it was Beau who was partly instrumental in getting him packed off to India in the first place—more than ten years ago now. It seems that his youthful follies had become an acute embarrassment to his family . . .' Selina threw her what could only be termed a knowing look.

Theo said in a strained voice that she thought people were sent away only when they had done something dreadful, like killing a man in a duel.

The older woman's trill of laughter sounded almost offensively coy. 'Well, I'm not saying that it wouldn't have come to that, had he remained. You see, matters came to a head over some dreadful scandal involving the wife of a very high government minister who was hellbent on calling him out.' She sighed. 'I must say, I wish I had known Benedict then—he must have been a prodigiously handsome, wayward youth!'

Theo picked up a small figurine and examined it minutely, but her thoughts were elsewhere. She was seeing Benedict's lean saturnine features and trying to visualise them before time, experience and India had left their mark on him.

'I wonder what made him come back after all this time,' she said.

'Same thing that took him away, I shouldn't wonder,' offered Aubrey with a derisory snort as he sprawled in a chair opposite his mama. 'As for his turning up here . . . gave us some Banbury tale that Lord Radlett had heard of his return and had sent for him! I mean . . . as if anyone knowing the old man wouldn't spot that for a hum right away!' The boy's tone was scathing. 'More likely he'd reached *point non plus* . . . escaping the duns. It runs in the family, if Beau is any example.'

'Aubrey!' protested his mother faintly. 'You will give Theodora quite the wrong impression!'

'Well, why else would Benedict choose to kick his heels down here?' the youth continued doggedly. 'It ain't for love of any of us! No, it's plain as your nose . . . parents dead . . . arrives home with pockets to let . . . latches on to the only member of the family known to be full of juice, and sets out to turn him up sweet . . . and not without success!'

'Dearest, this is all pure conjecture.' Selina was gently reproving, without actually refuting her son's words. 'You really mustn't be vindictive about your cousins.'

'They ain't *my* cousins,' averred the boy sulkily.

'No. That, alas, is a circumstance we are seldom allowed to forget! As for the rest . . . ' She paused, sighed. 'It is certainly a fact that Lord Radlett has come to rely quite heavily on Benedict, even to the point of charging him with carrying confidential letters to his London attorney, as I am given to understand he did only yesterday.' She invested this last with deep significance.

Theo was in an agony of indecision. There was a growing certainty in her mind that Selina, for reasons of her own, was seeking to alienate her from her cousin, but how much of what had been said or implied was truth and how much fiction? For some of it must surely be true.

She said stiffly, '*I* had gained the distinct impression that Cousin Benedict has formed a very real attachment towards my grandfather, and I quite fail to see how he would stand to gain by pretending, when it is Beau, after all, who is his heir.'

'My dear Theodora!' This time Selina's laughter was a trifle shrill. 'You clearly do not appreciate the delicate nuances of the situation. Why do you suppose that you find us all so on edge? It is not simply a matter of the succession. Your arrival has resolved that much at least—the title goes to Beau.' She almost ground the words out. 'But not all the estate is covered by the entail. Shallowford and all that surrounds it came to Lord Radlett through his wife, and he may dispose of it as he pleases. It had always been assumed that his heir would get all, but he holds Beau in such aversion that Benedict could influence him otherwise!'

'Would that matter so dreadfully?' said Theo.

'Well, of course it would matter! Shallowford is a very valuable property . . . Beau would be furious. I daresay he will be praying that his lordship don't recover consciousness!'

'Tale-bearing, Selina?'

It was Beau's voice at its most silky. They spun round as though shot, Selina with one hand clasped convulsively to her breast, to find him leaning against the closed door. How long he had been there it was impossible to say, for engrossed as they had been, no one had heard him enter.

Selina was quick to recover, though she still looked ill at ease, and even in the candlelight it could be clearly seen that her face had lost colour.

'I was simply acquainting Theodora with the facts,' she said, bridling.

Beau moved unhurriedly into the centre of the room, only the faint lift of his eyebrows disturbing the bored countenance.

'*Facts*, my dear? Or a farrago of malicious conjecture? You do have a poisonous tongue when you've a mind to use it.'

The drawled insult was too much for Aubrey to stomach. He sprang to his feet. 'You have no right to speak to Mama like that, sirrah!' he cried. 'And if you weren't such a . . . a mincing fop and twice my age to boot, I'd . . . I'd jolly well plant you a facer!'

It was unforgivably rude, of course, but Theo found her heart warming to Aubrey. He did not want for courage, at any rate. She watched Beau put up his glass and look the boy over in silence for fully half a minute.

Then: 'Madam,' he said without moving, without expression. 'If you cannot control your son's outbursts, he would be better confined to the schoolroom. I shall speak exactly as I please in this house. I have always done so and it will take more than the temper tantrums of a miserable halfling interloper to induce me now to change the habits of a lifetime!'

The insult was cutting in the extreme. Aubrey squirmed, but he was not wholly crushed. 'You aren't *Lord Radlett* yet, you know,' he stammered, red in the face. 'And I, for one, jolly well hope the old codger recovers!' He rushed to the door and flung out, slamming it behind him. Selina uttered a single sob and pressed a hand convulsively to her mouth.

In the silence that followed, Theo sneaked a look at the dandy's face and found its expression chilling.

'I am sure we all hope so,' he murmured austerely, and then turned to Theo with his usual urbanity as though nothing had happened. 'Well, my dear child—I hope you were not too upset by the little drama earlier? If only his lordship had not attempted the stairs! I cannot think how Gorton came to permit it, but then, poor fellow, he was clearly not himself.'

The door opened again to admit Benedict. The lines of his face were sharply drawn, and he seemed preoccupied. Beau was the first to speak, his drawl concealing any hint of urgency.

'Well, my boy? Has Marston been?'

'He is still here,' said Benedict curtly. 'He has gone up to see Gorton.'

'And . . . and Lord Radlett?' faltered Selina, her eyes looking suddenly huge in her pale face.

'His lordship still lives, though Dr Marston is not optimistic about his chances, and I must say I agree. Without Gorton to attend him . . .' He shrugged.

'But there are others, surely?' Theo was unaware of the note of pleading in her voice.

Benedict turned to her a little wearily. 'None capable of acting without supervision, coz. And I'm not sure if they would take on the task willingly if they could, having been too often subject to his lordship's ill humour in the past. However, Dr Marston knows of a woman living this side of Hatherton who might be suitable.' He frowned. 'I can only suggest we try her out—at least until Gorton recovers—if he recovers!' He looked up, hard-eyed. 'However, it is for Beau to decide.'

'Must I?' The lace handkerchief, never absent for long, came into play. 'I do so dislike making decisions. However,' Beau added urbanely, 'if Marston recommends this person, we can only be guided by him.' He looked around at the others. 'I really do not see what more can be expected of us.'

'We could nurse him ourselves.'

The words were out before Theo had stopped to think. She found three pairs of eyes regarding her with varying degrees of incredulity.

'Well, why not?' she persisted. 'I would be more than willing to do my share.'

Selina shuddered. 'Well, I certainly wouldn't! And I think it is decidedly outlandish in you to wish to put yourself to so much inconvenience and . . . and unpleasantness for someone you don't even know!'

'He is my grandfather,' Theo said quietly.

'Small difference *that* makes! He never knew of your existence until recently and behaved abominably when he did!' Selina rose and flounced across the room. 'For once I agree with Beau. The matter is best left to those properly versed in performing such menial tasks.'

Beau inclined his head in gracious assent, pressed his

handkerchief to his nostrils, and avowed that the merest whiff of anything pertaining to the sickroom could be guaranteed to bring on one of his spasms.

In other circumstances his foppery might have amused Theo, but in the present desperately serious situation it struck her as vaguely obscene.

She said with some asperity, 'And what if my grandfather should recover consciousness and ask to see you?'

His hand stilled, the heavy eyelids lifted. 'Why then I should naturally lay aside all personal considerations and make the supreme sacrifice.'

'Deucedly obleeging of you!' mimicked Benedict with something perilously close to a sneer.

Beau's eyes were masked once more, but not before Theo had glimpsed a shaft of cold dislike that was disturbing in its intensity. A waspish note invaded the bland voice.

'I do my poor best. At least I cannot be accused of endeavouring to ingratiate myself with my uncle.'

An angry flush crept up under Benedict's skin. 'I know how I may take that, I suppose . . .'

'My dear boy, I care not how you take it. It is surely a matter for your own conscience.'

But Theo had had as much as she could take. 'Oh, do stop it, all of you! You're like spoiled children . . . utterly selfish! Not one of you cares a fig whether that poor old man upstairs lives or dies, except in so far as it affects your miserable lives!' Tears threatened to close her throat as she ran to the door, brushing past Selina, heedless of their astonished stares. 'I wish I had never come!'

In the corridor she almost knocked down Purley, who had with him a large untidy-looking gentleman. They were much taken aback as she fled past with only a muffled apology.

Benedict caught up with Theo at the foot of the staircase. He called her name, and when she paid him no heed, shot out a hand and took her arm in a bruising grip. She protested, struggled in vain to free herself, and finally demanded in tones of stifled fury that he release her at once.

'Temper!' he admonished, and swung her round to face him, but upon seeing the wild trembling of her mouth, her eyes sheening with tears, his voice softened.

'You are being very silly,' he said gently, as though reasoning with a fractious child.

Theo saw his face through a blur, brushed the tears away with her free hand, and, meeting his softened gaze, had to remind herself that he was probably no better than the rest.

'I had rather be thought silly,' she retorted with an undignified sniff, 'than callous and indifferent!' She glared at him. 'Now tell me I'm pretentious.'

'I wouldn't dare!' he murmured with such feeling that in spite of everything she felt almost ready to laugh. But her shoulders still slumped.

'Was I very bad?' she asked, biting her lip.

'No worse than anyone might be at the end of a long, tiring, and eventful day,' he said bracingly. 'And in this house it hardly signifies.'

She persisted. 'And you must allow the provocation to have been great?'

'Insupportable,' he agreed. 'But then I did warn you that you would do better to wait until morning.'

At last his words had the desired effect. A little of her former spirit returned, enough to prompt a rueful smile. 'So you did, sir. How unhandsome of you to remind me.' She smiled suddenly. 'No matter—I shall come about after a good night's sleep.'

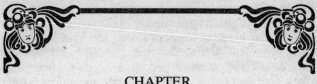

CHAPTER
FOUR

TIRED AS she was, Theo had little expectation that sleep
would come easily to her. Too much had happened too
quickly, and dominating all else was the memory of that
gaunt old man swaying on his feet, glaring at her with
something akin to hatred in his eyes.

But from the moment she was shown into her bedchamber, something very strange happened: a feeling of
peace washed over her that had nothing whatever to do
with the welcoming firelight, or the maidservant unfus-
sily attending to her needs. It was as though she had in
some curious way come home. And then she remembered Selina's words—'We have put you in your father's
old room, though it is hardly suitable in the circumstances'—and like a child she climbed into the vast bed,
laid her head on the pillow where he had once laid his,
and within minutes had fallen into a deep untroubled
sleep.

When she finally stirred it was to find pale sunlight
penetrating a gap in the heavy curtains to make watery
patterns on the counterpane. She lay for a moment
wondering where she was and, remembering, savoured
her pleasure anew.

And then a sound inside her room brought her
senses sharply into focus. She sat up abruptly to find
a wispy middle-aged maidservant, whom she vaguely
remembered as the one who had attended her on the
previous night, on her knees before the fireplace,
attempting to breathe life into a few feebly flickering

flames with a pair of ancient bellows.

The maid looked up nervously as the bed creaked.

'Oh, I'm ever so sorry, ma'am,' she said in a thin pale voice that accorded perfectly with her looks. 'I was just trying to get a proper fire going afore you woke, only when the wind's in a certain quarter, this chimney's a pesky nuisance, beggin' your pardon, ma'am.'

'That's all right.' Theo searched in the recesses of her memory. 'Maddie, isn't it?' She reached forward to rescue a shawl which was about to slip off the end of the bed, wrapped it tightly round her shoulders and sat up, hugging her knees. 'What time is it, Maddie?'

'It must be getting on for nine o'clock, ma'am.' Maddie abandoned the bellows and hurried to draw back the curtains.

'Heavens!' Theo cried, throwing back the bedclothes. 'You should have called me sooner. I had meant to be up long before now.'

'That's as maybe, but Mr Benedict said as I wasn't to disturb you if you was disposed to sleep on,' said Maddie, eager to exonerate herself of blame.

'Did he, indeed?' The light of battle was in Theo's eye as she padded across to the washstand and splashed some water into the basin from the ewer standing near by, dismissing the maid's offer of help. 'It would seem that Mr Benedict is in the habit of issuing a great many orders around here,' she continued, her indignation only partially muffled by the soft towel put into her groping hands by Maddie.

'I don't know about that, ma'am, but I do know that things has been a lot smoother-running since he's been around.' Something remarkably like a sniff accompanied her defence of Mr Benedict. 'And there's not many,' she added with deep significance, 'as would sit up all night along of the old gentleman the way he's just done, there being no one else what with Gorton worn to a thread and that Sarah Minchip not able to come till this morning.'

Theo turned from taking her first real look at the rolling countryside beyond the window and observed drily that Mr Benedict had clearly got a staunch champion in her. Maddie looked embarrassed.

'That's as maybe, ma'am. Anyways,' she concluded, her voice prim, 'though it's not for me to say, I reckon as Mr Benedict meant what he said for the best, you being tired an' all.'

Theo accepted the snub good-naturedly, but would make no decision about breakfast or anything else until she had been to see how her grandfather did. Hastily she donned a dress of blue dimity—the first that came to hand—and coiled her heavy chestnut hair into a knot at the back of her head. Then, with Maddie to direct her, she made her way to Lord Radlett's rooms.

She found Benedict sprawled in a chair beside the bed, legs stretched out and coat discarded. He rose unhurriedly as she entered and subjected her to a frank appraisal in the morning light that filtered between the half-drawn curtains.

'Well, Cousin Benedict?' she prompted at last, having returned his appraisal with interest, relieved to find him somehow less daunting with unshaven chin and crumpled shirt.

'Well enough, Cousin Theo,' he answered equably. 'You look suitably rested at all events. No need to ask if you slept.'

Her glance strayed involuntarily to the bed and then lifted to him, an unspoken query in her eyes.

'No, coz,' he said. 'I fear there is little change as yet.'

She stepped closer. In the half-light his lordship's face looked frighteningly unreal—like a grotesque waxen mask. At first sight he seemed not to be breathing, and for a moment, as the memory of her father's last hours came back with vivid clarity, her own heart felt squeezed beyond bearing. And then, inexplicably, the feeling grew into a wild consuming rage—she wanted to shake her grandfather into consciousness, to rail at him, to berate him for having the ill grace to contemplate dying when she had come all this way to meet him and make her father's peace with him.

Benedict watched the rigid profile with some curiosity; he could not hope to guess at the tumultuous nature of her distress, but she was clearly in the grip of some powerful emotion, her hands clasped tight to still their trembling.

'Have you had breakfast?' He spoke more roughly than he had intended, but the eyes she turned to him were blindly uncomprehending. He repeated the question, and she seemed to come back as if from a great distance.

'I'm sorry.' Theo shook her head, visibly pulling herself together. 'You will think me very rude. No, I haven't had breakfast.'

'Then you should. I'll get someone to sit with his lordship and we'll go down together.'

'Oh, but . . .' She met his half-impatient look with a rueful smile. 'The fact is, I am feeling a little foolish this morning. I made such a mull of things last night and must now do what I can to make amends, but . . . across the breakfast table . . .?'

He gave a decided chuckle.

'My dear girl, you don't suppose our beautiful relations put their noses beyond their doors much before noon? Especially Beau. That kind of magnificence is not achieved in a moment, I promise you.'

Thus reprieved, Theo allowed herself to be taken down to the sunny morning room, and having made an excellent breakfast selected from a quite extravagant quantity of covered dishes, she declared herself to be equal to anything.

'Well, then,' said Benedict. 'The morning is clem-

ent—we could walk for a while. If we keep fairly close to
the house we shall hear when Dr Marston comes. Do
you ride, coz?'

'Tolerably well.' She draped the shawl she had
brought downstairs with her about her shoulders as they
descended the front steps and walked out on to the wide
carriage sweep so that Theo might have her first real
view of the house. It was not a beautiful building, she
realised with a pang of disappointment—certainly not to
be compared with some of the splendid mansions she
had glimpsed during her journey from Plymouth.

'What you might call a Gothic pile,' observed Benedict, voicing her thoughts. 'The west wing is mainly
Tudor, but the rest has been added over the years with
scant regard for any particular architectural style.'

'How far do the grounds extend?'

'The estate in all comprises about a thousand acres.'

'Goodness!'

'Much of it is farmed by tenants, of course. You see
that row of poplars . . .' Benedict stopped, took her
arm, and swung her round, pointing into the distance. 'A
stream runs through there right across to the far side of
the estate. It was known as Shallowford Brook long
before this house was built.'

He glanced down at her in some curiosity. 'Your
father didn't talk about the place much?'

'Only occasionally, and then it was the small things,
you know—like the games he and Geoffrey played as
children and how they used to get out at night against
Grandfather's wishes by means of a secret passage . . .'

Her cousin's eyebrows lifted lazily. 'You clearly know
more than I do, coz. Did he say where this passage could
be found?'

'No. I guess there wouldn't have been much point. I
know that it came out well away from the house.'

'Fascinating,' he said. 'Perhaps one day we might set
ourselves to rediscover it.'

If I stay that long. But she didn't say the words aloud.

Benedict took her arm and walked her across the drive towards a path that led round the side of the house and through a small coppice. In the distance there was a horseman riding at a full-blooded gallop across the fields, putting his mount at the fences with a kind of reckless abandon.

'That will be Aubrey,' Benedict said off-handedly when she drew his attention to the rider. 'He always goes neck and crop at his fences. If he hadn't such a good seat, he'd have come to grief long since.'

'But . . . does Selina know how dangerously he rides?'

Benedict grinned briefly. 'I shouldn't think so. And I certainly wouldn't be the one to spoil the lad's sport. Apart from the occasional dalliance with village maidens, he has little enough outlet here for most of the very natural excesses to which striplings of his age are addicted. Small wonder he is frustrated and given to the sulks. I certainly wouldn't deny him the right to work off his spleen in the only way open to him.'

'Oh, what shocking indifference!' Theo exclaimed, and remembering what she had been told of his own inglorious youth, continued impulsively, 'I should have thought that you, of all people, might understand and . . . and try to help him!'

He had stopped in his tracks and turned her round to meet the rather uncomfortable glittering inquisition of his eyes. 'Indeed? And why me *of all people*, coz?'

Drat Selina and her spiteful gossip, she thought, feeling a slow blush creep into her cheeks. There was but one course open to her now. She looked back at him unflinchingly. 'Because I imagine that you will understand better than most the nature of those youthful excesses and their sometimes disastrous consequences.'

His fingers bit deep into her arms, his eyes narrowed to bright pinpoints of light, and Theo was very much aware of the fury lurking just below the surface. He would be a ruthless enemy, she thought with sudden perception, every ounce of her resolution being pressed into holding her own gaze steady.

At last he relaxed. A laugh, albeit harsh and with a hint of reluctance, escaped him. He loosed his grip, one hand slipping down her arm to enfold her own cold one, the other lifting to trace with feather-light finger the curve of her jaw.

'Oh, cousin!' he said softly. 'You, too, have a taste for dangerous living!'

She conquered a momentary light-headedness to say a little shyly, 'I'm sorry. My wretched tongue! I had absolutely no right upon such short acquaintance to . . . to fling your past in your teeth!'

This time his laugh rang out with unfeigned mirth. 'However reprehensible it may have been?'

'Oh, but I didn't *know* that, not for sure . . . and I do so abhor people who set their store by gossip.'

His finger moved to cover her mouth, effectively silencing her. 'Selina is undoubtedly a tattle-monger,' he said with acute perception, 'but in this instance I suspect she told no more than the simple truth.' His eyes brimmed with laughter. 'My past *was* highly reprehensible. I indulged every excess. One can scarcely blame my family for ridding themselves of such a disreputable youth!'

'Well, I think it was a dreadful thing to do!' she declared hotly, removing his finger. 'You don't solve a problem by ridding yourself of it . . . it simply becomes someone else's responsibility. If they had truly loved you . . .'

'Enough, my philosophising young firebrand! I refuse to be preached at. India suited me very well, and anyhow, what's past is done with.' Though he still smiled, there was something in his face that warned her not to proceed further. 'We have problems enough with the present.' He looked down at the hand he still held and drew it companionably through his arm. 'Time to go back, I fear, sweet coz. At least life promises to be more interesting with you around.'

There was a quick impatient step on the path behind them, and Aubrey came abreast of them. His reply to Theo's cheerful 'Good morning' was brusque, and he would have hurried past without another word had she not added pleasantly, 'I was watching you riding a while back. You are clearly most accomplished.'

He looked at her, surprised and a little suspicious. 'I get plenty of practice,' he said grudgingly.

'I wondered,' she persisted, 'if the stable had a horse to suit me, whether you would care to take me on a guided tour of the estate some time.'

Aubrey looked more keenly at her to see if she was joking, then at Benedict, and finally back at her.

'If you like,' he muttered. 'I daresay you'd be all right on the mare. I'll ask Hoskins.'

He slapped his riding-crop nervously against his leg a couple of times, then begged their pardon, uttered something about breakfast, and hurried on ahead.

'Very gracious!' observed Benedict drily. 'I hope you will not live to regret your magnanimity, cousin.'

'Oh, he's just very young—and probably rather shy,' said Theo, confidently, choosing to ignore the snort of derision which greeted this masterly assessment of Aubrey's character.

The sound of wheels on the drive effectively put an end to further discussion. A shabby black carriage came tipsily round the bend and was reined in at the foot of the front steps. The gentleman who emerged, his paunch seemingly cut in two by a tightly buttoned snuff-stained coat, was the gentleman she had glimpsed briefly on the previous evening in Purley's company. So this was Dr Marston. Theo experienced a slight sinking of the heart. At first sight he did not inspire confidence.

As she and Benedict approached, he reached back

inside the carriage, wheezing audibly and putting a severe strain upon his coat seams, to offer assistance to his passenger.

'That's the barber!' he urged encouragingly to a woman as stout as himself, though considerably shorter in stature, who was endeavouring to squeeze herself through the inadequate opening, and who at that very moment popped out with the suddenness of a cork, almost flattening him and laughing uproariously at his attempts to steady both her and himself. Then, noticing that they had an audience, she dug the doctor in the ribs with her elbow. His eyebrows, which sprouted incongruously to give him a look of permanent surprise, wobbled upward.

'Ah, well—here we are then, all right and tight!' He advanced, bag in hand, and upon being introduced to Theo, beamed at her and made some jovial comment about the stir her coming had caused.

She hardly knew how to reply, but it appeared that no answer was expected, for he went on almost without breath to commiserate with her about her father, and from there passed on to recall how he had brought Master John through many a childish ailment. 'A positive martyr to the croup he was as an infant. Why, I disremember how many times I was called to him and found him blue in the face, but we battled through—y'r grandma and Nanny Littlejohn, God rest them both . . . and myself, of course—and in the end, d'ye know he grew to be quite a sturdy lad. Still . . .' He must have caught Theo's feeling of impatience as she glanced appealingly at Benedict, for he cleared his throat. 'You won't wish be hearing of that just now, I daresay, eh? So, how is our patient this morning?'

Benedict said that there seemed to be little change.

'Still, as long as he's no worse.' Dr Marston blew his nose lustily. 'We've pulled him through before, and I've little doubt but that he's strong-willed enough to cheat

death again, especially now that we have the services of
Mrs Minchip. Eh, Sarah?'

The woman had returned to the carriage to extract her
carpet bag and now turned to them smiling and nodding.

'Are you sure he is competent?' Theo whispered
to Benedict as they all trooped up to Lord Radlett's
chamber.

'Well, I'll not say I wouldn't be happier to have
brought a man down from London, but his lordship's
always had Marston, and it isn't my place to say that he's
probably past his best.'

Theo frowned and reserved her own judgment until
she had seen how the doctor did, and was only partially
reassured by his examination of his patient, which to her
eyes lacked thoroughness. However, he was adamant
that he had seen many such cases, and that the next
twenty-four hours would be the crucial period. He departed, promising to return that evening, and leaving
Sarah Minchip in charge. But not for long.

Less than three hours later, Mrs Minchip was following him down the drive in the stable trap, driven by a
stony-faced groom who turned a deaf ear to her
screamed imprecations about brass-faced American
hussies who were no better than they ought to be.

'I did do the right thing, didn't I?' Theo pleaded, still
shaking from the effects of doing battle with the fat
woman, whom she had discovered comfortably en-
sconced in a chair near the fire mouthing lewd ditties to
herself with an empty gin-bottle beside her, while her
patient lay half off his pillows with his bedclothes in a
tangle.

Benedict, perched on a table near the bed, arms
folded, was eyeing her with something like awe. 'I am all
admiration,' he said as Theo confessed how she had, in a
rage, bundled the woman's things together and summoned a pair of footmen to remove her. 'The poor old
besom will probably have convinced herself by now that

you are some demonic manifestation of her befuddled gin-sodden imaginings.'

But Beau was less charitable when she presently sought him out in the library to make a similar confession of what she had done. With a peevishness that he was at little pains to conceal, he informed Theo that she had gone beyond the bounds of what was acceptable.

'You have not been twenty-four hours in this house and already you treat it as if it were your own! I thought you a great deal too forward from the first, but I was disposed to overlook any little shortcomings in view of your irregular upbringing. But now . . .'

Theo had been resolved to endure his censure, only too aware that she had acted precipitately, but his damning of her character was not easy to accept, involving as it did an implied criticism of her father.

'We will leave my upbringing out of this, if you please, sir,' she said passionately. 'I accept that it was not my place to dismiss Mrs Minchip, but if you had come upon her as I did . . . in short, my reaction was instinctive. However, I still believe I was right. My concern was solely for my grandfather . . .'

'Who, thanks to your meddling, is now without a nurse,' he interposed with thin-lipped sarcasm. 'Please God, he is not also without a doctor, since I doubt Marston will rejoice to find his authority undermined!'

Theo took a deep breath and looked down at her hands, which were clasped tight to stop them from trembling. 'I will undertake to nurse Grandfather,' she said, continuing before she had time to change her mind, 'And as for the rest, I believe that we should send to London for a doctor more competent to advise upon his condition.' She looked up with a touch of defiance. 'And Cousin Benedict agrees with me.'

'Does he, indeed?'

It was odd, she thought inconsequentially, that such a silly posturing dandy could look quite so menacing when he chose to do so. Perhaps it had to do with the absurd height of his collar points, which imprisoned his head in such a way that he must needs look down his nose at one with those heavy-lidded eyes.

'Benedict, of course, has his own reasons for wishing to keep my uncle alive,' he said in his most silky voice. 'But what are yours, I wonder?'

'I have none . . . beyond simple humanity.' In spite of herself, she stammered slightly.

Beau's lip curled. 'And if I do not give the scheme my blessing, I shall be dubbed *inhuman*, I suppose.'

'Don't be childish, Vincent!' Unnoticed by either of them, Great-aunt Minta had come into the room. She crossed to stand beside Theo as if declaring where her sympathies lay. 'Marston's getting older—we're all getting older, if it comes to that! Set in our ways. Takes the young to show us the right road.' She nodded at Theo, bright-eyed. 'You've done well, John's child—if you hadn't thrown that besom out, I'd have done it m'self!'

When Dr Marston returned later in the day, it was immediately evident that Mrs Minchip had already had her say and had given a wildly inaccurate account of her dismissal. It required considerable tact to acquaint the doctor with the truth and then to broach the delicate question of a second opinion without setting him all on end.

That this was amicably accomplished was due in no small measure to Theo. Benedict later teased her with having emptied the butter-boat over the old codger— 'Turned him up so sweet, coz, it was a privilege to witness it! I'll swear, by the end he'd taken the whole thing to be his own idea.'

Theo retorted that if it were so, then she was more than pleased, for her greatest fear was that Dr Marston might feel matters had been taken out of his hands; indeed, in those first crucial minutes soon after his arrival, she had glimpsed a faltering, an uncertainty, behind his bluster, which had prompted in her the impulse to bolster his confidence.

'No need to be sending to London,' he said gruffly. 'There's a very good man staying at present with the Grailys over at Long Winton. I was chatting with him a couple of days since . . . very impressed. Got a few too many new-fangled notions for my taste, of course . . . but then I'm too old a dog to be learning new tricks.' He cleared his throat. 'Matter of fact, had it in mind to suggest he take a look at his lordship . . . so, if you'd care for me to ask . . .'

It was agreed. Over the matter of Theo's decision to take over the nursing, he was less easy to convince. He threw Benedict a look best described as a plea for help, which Benedict out of sheer perversity dismissed with a shrug, and in desperation he resorted to bluster.

'Sentiments admirable, ma'am . . . commend you for them, indeed I do. But y're a gently nurtured young lady and your grandfather's an old man . . . there are things to be done for him . . .' He was floundering badly, harumphing in his throat. 'Ye won't wish me to be indelicate, I'm sure . . .'

Theo felt quite sorry for him, but there was a maddening, mocking glint in her cousin's eyes that hardened her resolve.

'Dr Marston,' she said crisply, 'you may be as indelicate as you please. I am not in the least squeamish. I nursed my father almost single-handed during the final weeks of his life, and I very much doubt that there is anything that you can tell me now about the needs of an acutely ill man that will have the least power to shock me.'

The doctor's grizzled eyebrows wobbled alarmingly, then he uttered a short bark of laughter. 'Well, well! By Jove, y're a true Radlett and no mistake! I can see there's to be no dissuading you!'

By the time he arrived on the following morning with

his colleague, Sir James Darcy, Theo had already super-
vised the removal of her belongings to the dressing room
adjoining her grandfather's room so that she might be
close at hand both day and night. In addition, she had set
about organising the household to meet Lord Radlett's
needs in a way that, had she not possessed a captivating
ease of manner, must have set many tempers on end.

As it was, with Purley already her willing slave, she
was able to gain the guarded approval of Mrs Hadley,
the housekeeper, and with their joint co-operation a
régime was well on the way to being established for
looking after his lordship which was designed to cause as
little disruption as possible to the smooth running of the
house. In this, Maddie was her staunchest ally, having
developed an earnest admiration for her.

Selina, jealous of the affection which Theo was
already in a fair way to enjoying and knowing it to be
something to which she could never aspire, expressed
the somewhat barbed hope that she would not wear
herself out in a vain cause.

'Not a bit of it,' Theo exclaimed cheerfully. 'To own
the truth, I am glad to be occupied. I have not been used
to inactivity and was in danger of becoming dull.'

She liked Sir James on sight. He was, she supposed, a
man between forty and fifty years, erect in his bearing
and with a keen eye and directness of manner that
appealed to her instantly. Beau, in an unexpected *volte-
face*, had insisted upon receiving him, which he did with
a gracious condescension that was largely wasted upon
Sir James, who had little time for empty pleasantries and
did not trouble to conceal the fact.

With his patient, however, it was a different story. He
asked a great many searching questions, and no observation was thought too slight for his consideration if it
might assist him in making his diagnosis. In this he
deferred to Dr Marston with a degree of tact that made
Theo think particularly well of him, for she suspected

that he was not a man who suffered fools gladly. He cast a particularly acute eye upon herself when her role was explained, but what he saw must have satisfied him, for thereafter he included her in any discussion as to treatment. He was also at some pains to reassure her that although there were as yet few visible signs of improvement, his lordship's pulse was surprisingly strong for a man of his years, and he had every hope of a happy outcome if she did but follow his instructions.

Sir James's confidence was contagious. Under Theo's ministrations the sickroom became less and less a place of gloom; she kept the curtains partly drawn back and would sometimes hum to herself as she sat sewing near the bed. Occasionally she would even talk to the unconscious man—about his son, and the life he had made for himself in the New World—of his struggle to bring up his daughter after his wife had died bearing her, and of how well the daughter considered he had acquitted himself in so doing.

Selina, putting her head round the door on the following afternoon, driven partly by curiosity and partly by sheer boredom, was astonished to hear a soft trill of laughter; more astonishing still, she realised that Theo was quite alone, sitting in a chair close to the bed with her arms resting on it in a most casual way.

Theo rose upon seeing Selina, surprise swiftly concealed, and beckoned her in with a smile. The older woman hesitated and looked uneasily towards the bed.

'It's all right,' Theo said. 'He isn't conscious . . . at least, I don't think he is, though he has opened his eyes once or twice, and although they didn't appear to be registering any kind of recognition, Sir James thinks it a very good sign.'

'But . . .' Selina went so far to close the door, but continued to lean against it, clutching the knob as though prepared for instant flight. 'I thought I heard . . . voices?'

'Oh, yes,' said Theo. 'I often talk to him. I was recalling my first proposal of marriage. I was only seventeen, and Mr Knight was a contemporary of Papa. But I fear his attachment was not in the least romantical. The plain fact was that he had several children in desperate need of a mother and he was much impressed by my many practical qualities!' She chuckled again, remembering.

It was quite clear that Selina thought her a trifle touched in the attic.

'But I'm not, truly,' she said, hastening to reassure her. 'Only it occurred to me that Grandpa might sometimes be aware of what was going on around him, and if that *were* so, a hushed silence could have the most lowering effect on him and send him into a fatal decline. Whereas a nice cheerful human voice just might make him curious enough to want to know who was speaking.'

Selina stared into the vital face of this extraordinary girl, her slim figure in its crisp sprigged muslin so full of life and eagerness . . . as though she really cared what happened to a crabby old man she didn't even know! She made an unconsciously helpless little gesture. 'Oh, I do wish I understood you!' she cried.

'As if I were some kind of freak!' Theo complained wryly to Benedict when she came down later to take her afternoon walk.

Selina had already regaled Benedict with a highly coloured account of what had happened, but he was for once tactful enough to refrain from contentious comment.

When, however, to her intense chagrin, her odd way of going on was made known to Sir James, his reaction surprised everyone. Far from rebuking her for showing a lack of consideration for his patient, he appeared to regard what she was doing rather in the nature of an interesting experiment and charged her with keeping him informed as to the outcome.

That night, when all had been done and Theo was making ready for bed, she brushed out her hair with extra vigour to combat a feeling of restlessness. More than once she had been tempted to have it cut in one of the shorter fashions, but vanity had prevailed. It was, she decided, staring into the darkened mirror, her only claim to beauty (though Benedict had once commended her eyes!), and besides, there was something very soothing about the long, repetitive, sweeping strokes of the brush.

Before climbing into bed she went back into the main bedchamber for one last check on her grandfather, comfortable in the knowledge that there was a footman within call in the corridor, should she have need of him.

It was as Theo leaned across to straighten the sheet that it happened; his fingers moved shakily to curl round her hand. The shock of it stifled the cry that rose in her throat, her pulse began to race, and she remained perfectly still lest she disturb him. With her hair spread across the sheets like a silken coverlet, she looked down into his eyes, open now, sunk deep in cavernous shadows.

'Marianne?' His voice was no more than a cracked whisper.

Without thought of deception, she returned a murmured 'Hush!'

His shaking fingers moved to bury themselves in her hair, 'Always . . . so beautiful . . .'

CHAPTER
FIVE

'HE WORSHIPPED your grandmother, of course,' said Great-aunt Minta.

She was standing at the foot of the vast bed in the morning light, watching her brother in a fixed way as though willing him to waken.

'I saw the likeness in you from the start,' she continued, 'but I hadn't realised how marked it was until I saw you with your hair down.' She sighed and shook her head. 'Uncanny.'

Theo felt drained. She had no idea how long she had remained at her grandfather's side through the night. She remembered easing herself into a sitting position on the edge of the bed—and there she stayed until her cramped limbs protested. He didn't stir when she climbed down, and in a panic she had to lean very close to assure herself that he was still breathing.

For the remainder of the night she remained curled up in the fireside chair, alternately dozing and starting awake. But he woke only once, briefly, just as dawn was breaking, and as she bent over him a film clouded his eyes, forming into tears that ran down into his hair while his mouth worked with childlike weakness.

And Theo, immeasurably moved, had wept too. She who had schooled herself to remain dry-eyed throughout her father's last unendurable weeks of suffering, because it was the only way she could help him, found herself utterly defenceless against the pitiable disintegration of this one-time giant of a man.

She was still sobbing in sporadic little bursts when Benedict came in. He stopped short at the sight of her curled miserably in the chair—looked frowningly towards the still figure in the bed and then back to her.

'Is he dead?' he demanded harshly, striding forward.

'No, oh no!' Theo pushed back the tangle of her hair and attempted a reassuring smile, but it was a woebegone affair confounded by eyes reddened with much weeping and an air of weary exhaustion.

She attempted an explanation, but he cut it short by sweeping her up in an inelegant heap, silencing her hiccupping protests by the simple expedient of pressing her face tightly into his shoulder as he carried her through to the other room. There he removed her dressing-gown and coaxed her into bed, soothing her as though she were a grieving child.

'Later,' he reiterated with a kind of rough gentleness as she tried again. He smoothed back her hair and tucked the blankets round her. 'I shall be here.'

She didn't argue. The pressure of her drooping eyelids had become irresistible, and as she drifted into oblivion she couldn't even be sure whether or not the faint pressure of his lips against her temple was real or imagined.

It was well into the morning when she woke, less refreshed than might have been expected, largely because of a thick-headed lethargy which was the aftermath of all that crying. And her mouth was dry as dust. She had already reached for her dressing-gown and was buttoning it up, when Benedict's shadow filled the doorway.

'So you're awake.'

She stifled a yawn. 'I think so.'

'Silly,' he said as she came close to him. 'You should have stayed where you were. You've earned your rest.'

'Nonsense. All I need is a good strong cup of coffee,' she maintained valiantly.

He laughed. 'I'll arrange for a fresh pot to be sent up at once.' He took her by the shoulders, holding her away a little, still smiling faintly. 'Very demure,' he murmured, eyeing the high ruffled neck of her now firmly tied dressing-gown. 'But with your hair loose, you look almost irresistibly alluring!'

She recalled that he had been responsible for removing it but a few hours earlier, and blushed scarlet. His smile broadened to a lecherous grin.

'Fear not, sweet coz. I do not ravish my relations!'

'So I should hope!' she exclaimed, and pushed past him.

'That's much better,' he approved. 'The light of battle is back in your eyes. For a while you had me quite worried!'

By the time Great-aunt Minta had arrived on the scene, Theo was dressed and in command of herself once more, and if she was a little quieter, a little paler than usual, the old lady was too preoccupied to notice.

'It's absurd, when he's so cross-grained, to say that I would miss him,' she mused. 'But we understand one another, d'ye see, and when you get to our age, that counts for a lot. Perhaps, if Marianne hadn't died when she did . . . she could handle him *so easily*!'

'I wish I had known my grandmother!' Theo said earnestly. 'Papa talked about her such a lot. Her death affected him deeply.'

Aunt Minta nodded. 'They were ever close—too close, belike. A boy scarcely out of short coats is at best a vulnerable creature, and a boy like John . . .' She sighed. 'After Marianne's death, the very sight of him, looking so like her, seemed to bring out the worst in his father. But although Edmund affected to favour Geoffrey more and more, it was John that he loved!'

'And yet he drove him away?'

'Oh, ay, but then, how often do stupid men seek to destroy that which they love?'

Theo did not know whether to tread further on delicate ground, but curiosity drove her on. 'Papa would never tell me what finally brought things to a head between them. But he never said anything bad about him, either. And . . . at the end . . . well, I didn't just come because of that lawyer's letter. Papa wanted me to come . . . to make everything right.'

'How like him!' The old lady gave an abrupt little snort of laughter. 'Strangely enough, it was that very quality of gentleness—which was Marianne's great strength—that Edmund saw as a weakness in John. Quite wrongly, of course. But because John preferred books and music to the more physical pleasures of hunting and shooting, and because he didn't care to womanise, Edmund taunted the boy constantly . . . and when he could neither bully nor shame him into changing his ways, he attempted to force his hand . . . informed him that he was buying him a commission in the Hussars . . . said the army would make a man of him. *That* was when John finally walked out!'

'Oh, yes, he would.' Theo was very quiet. She stood looking down at the crumpled, parchment-like face, now slack and impotent in unconsciousness, and tried to see him as he must have been in his prime. It would have taken great courage to oppose him. She wondered, when it came to the point, whether she would be able to forgive him for the unhappiness he had caused.

'Of course,' said Great-aunt Minta, getting to her feet with much puffing, 'y'do realise that if Edmund recovers, you're going to have your work cut out to deal with him? I'm not at all sure that even such a free-thinking young gel as yourself should be exposed to the kind of language he'll throw at you, even if you don't understand the half of it!'

Theo laughed. 'Well, we shall just have to see. Perhaps Gorton will be recovered before too long.'

Purley had kept the elderly valet informed about his

master's condition, having dissuaded Theo from visiting him in person.

'Put him all on end it would, Miss Theo, if you don't mind my saying so . . . having a young lady in his room. Very set in his ways, is Mr Gorton, and we don't want him suffering a relapse on top of all else, do we?'

'Certainly not, Purley,' she said with a smile. 'I shall, of course, be guided by you. I was only concerned lest he should feel overlooked.'

'Oh, I'll see that doesn't happen, miss. He's chafing at his confinement already, as is only natural, him having been with his lordship most of his life.' Purley shook his head. 'But he won't be taking up his duties again for a fair while, I'm thinking.'

'Well, we shall just have to try to keep his spirits up,' she said. Fortunately she had by then got her routine well established, and was able to view the prospect of a prolonged period of restricted freedom with equanimity. Sir James was delighted with Lord Radlett's steady progress and commended her care of him. He might have been a little surprised, had he witnessed her first coherent confrontation with her grandfather.

She had just returned from her promised ride with Aubrey, a thought-provoking experience, for although he had been taciturn to the point of rudeness for most of the time, she had twice managed to make him laugh, and came back convinced that beneath that sulky exterior there were all the makings of a much nicer young man.

She entered the room, still in her brown velvet riding-habit, with her cheeks glowing from the exercise, and her eyes beneath the small rakish brim of her hat full of a sparkling determination to find some way of helping Aubrey. She nodded absently to Maddie, who had been deputising for her, to indicate that she could go, and was a little surprised to receive by return a look of mingled relief and what could only be described as apprehension.

Theo swung round to the bed and saw that she was

being watched; his lordship's eyes, deep in their cavernous sockets, were not simply open—they were registering a startling degree of comprehension.

'Do you want me to stay, Miss Theo?' whispered
Maddie behind her.

'Get out!' The force in the snarled command surprised
them both. Theo hid her nervousness behind a quiet
confidence. 'Go along,' she said. 'We shall do better
alone.'

She made no attempt to move until the door had
closed. Then she took a deep breath and walked over to
stand beside him.

'Well, miss?' said the rasping voice. 'And who gave
you leave to issue the orders here?'

'No one, sir,' she replied as calmly as she was able.
'But I thought that if you wanted to come to points with
me, it would be better done without an audience.'

'Damned interfering malapert! *Miss Theo!*' The vitup-
erative fury of this last set him coughing, and as she
stepped forward to help him, he clawed the air with a
shaking hand. 'Get out!' he whooped. 'Send . . . Gorton
to me. Can't th-think what he's . . . about . . .' At this
point his voice gave out and he was gasping in a way that
alarmed Theo.

She poured a little of the cordial that stood on the
near-by table and came swiftly to his side, supporting
him with a firm arm about his shoulders and talking to
him in a calm unhurried way as she persuaded him to sip
it, chiding him for getting excited.

He lay back on the pillows at last, exhausted, and she
sat on the edge of the bed facing him.

'I'm afraid you can't have Gorton,' she explained
gently. 'He isn't very well himself just now, and must
rest.' She saw a shadow of distress pass over his face,
puckering his mouth, and instinctively she reached for
his hand, overcoming its initial resistance to her touch. 'I
know you won't like it, but in the absence of anyone

better, I'm afraid you must make do with me for the present,' she concluded with a wry smile.

His breathing was becoming less laboured, and the fierce, hawk-like face had lost most of that sudden alarming greyness. His eyes were unwavering as they fixed on her.

'Y're a . . . bitter *disappointment* to me, d'y know?' He ground the words out. 'Just like y'r father . . . to sire a girl!'

Passionate indignation rose like bile in Theo's throat, and was instantly quelled. What, after all, had she expected?

'Yes, well, we've neither of us got what we hoped for,' she said in a voice devoid of colour. 'But I'll try to make the best of it, if you will.'

He didn't answer, and after a moment she stood up. 'Now I must go and change out of my riding-dress, and you must try to rest.'

When she came back into the room presently she found he had fallen into a deep sleep. She called the footman in from the corridor to keep watch, and went downstairs. On the way she met Selina drifting in her usual aimless way towards the morning room, where luncheon was laid out. Theo wasn't really hungry, in spite of her recent exercise, but she didn't much care for her own company either, so she fell into step beside her.

'Aubrey tells me you have been riding with him?' Selina's voice echoed a faint suspicion. 'I'm sure I don't see why you should wish to do such a thing.'

'I simply thought it might be agreeable for us to get to know one another a little better,' Theo said, wondering why she should feel obliged to justify her actions. 'I wanted some exercise in the fresh air, and it has some-times seemed to me that Aubrey is lonely and irked by the inactivity of his life here.'

'Well, that isn't my fault!' Selina's voice was a little

shrill. 'Believe me, were I able to arrange it, we should both leave this house tomorrow and never return!'

'Oh, dear! Are you really so unhappy?'

To her consternation, Selina's wide blue eyes filled with tears. 'I h-hate every minute!' she sobbed, as they streamed down her face unchecked. It was as though a dam had been breached and all the pent-up emotions came pouring out of her in a torrent of incoherent intensity. Theo opened the door of a little saloon close to the morning room and whisked her inside. The room was dimly lit, and chill from lack of use, but there were several red plush chairs grouped under the window, and Theo guided Selina to one of these.

'Y-you have only been here a few days . . . you can have no idea what it is really like!' the older woman cried. 'N-no one ever comes to call . . . and if I go out, there is nowhere to go!' There was much more in similar vein, and with a sigh, Theo put her own problems to the back of her mind and gave her attention to Selina's distraught catalogue of woe.

'All I have for company is Beau with his awful sarcasm, which at its worst reduces one to shreds . . . and Aubrey. And he, like all young people, is selfish and totally wrapped up in his own misery!' She pulled at her handkerchief. 'If it were not for Benedict, I sometimes think I would go mad!'

Theo found it was possible to detach part of her mind so that she could make sympathetic noises while wondering just what kind of relationship existed between Selina and her cousin—and at the same time noting with an irrepressible twinge of envy that Selina was one of the lucky few who could cry without any distortion of her features. If anything, weeping gave her an added appeal, for with her pale golden curls framing her pointed face and those wide round eyes constantly filling and overflowing, she looked for all the world like a spoiled, vulnerable child—an illusion that her widow's weeds and the ridiculous scrap of black cap only served to emphasise.

'My dear ma'am,' she said with a bracing smile. 'You talk as though you were at your last prayers, when it is patently obvious that you cannot be a day above two and thirty.'

This appeal to her vanity had the desired effect. Selina's tears stopped as if by magic. 'Do you really think so?' There was a coquetry in her glance that made Theo realise how easily she would blossom in company—and how utterly out of her element she was at Shallowford. It made her more sympathetic than she would otherwise have been.

'I fear I cannot *quite* lay claim to that,' she confessed, preening, 'for Aubrey is almost eighteen, you know . . . and although I was a mere child when I had him . . .' Her eyes clouded and her mouth trembled anew. 'Oh, but of what use are my looks, incarcerated as I am in this great gloomy house!'

'Well, surely there is somewhere else you might go, if only for a visit? A friend . . . in London, perhaps?'

'Do you think I would not have done so long since, had it been possible? My dear girl, I have scarcely a feather to fly with! And Lord Radlett will support me only so long as I remain immured here as befits a relict . . . *a relict* . . . the very word strikes a chill into my bones!'

'Oh dear!'

'So you see, if I did decide to cut my traces, I don't know how I should go on. There is Aubrey to be thought of . . .' Selina's voice grew bitter. 'You would be surprised how elusive one's so-called friends can become when one is an impoverished widow twice over, with the added encumbrance of a son still dependent on one! And yet, if Lord Radlett dies, that is exactly the fix in which I am likely to find myself, for Beau will have none of me!'

The tears threatened to flow again, and Theo, feeling she could not take another moment of such wallowing self-pity, said quickly that her grandfather was not going to die—'And if we put our heads together, maybe we can come up with some scheme,' she added rather rashly; upon seeing the calculating look that flashed momentarily into Selina's eyes, she hoped she might not have cause to regret her own impetuosity.

'Do you know,' Selina said, pushing her sodden handkerchief into her reticule with a brave smile, 'I suddenly feel quite hungry.' She stood up and tucked her arm through Theo's. 'I must say it is very agreeable to have another woman in the house . . . gentlemen do not understand our problems.' With deceptive casualness, she added, 'It wouldn't astonish me if you might not in time come to wield considerable influence over the old man . . . I mean, he's bound to be grateful to you, isn't he . . . for your care of him?'

Theo was too choked with annoyance to answer, but her companion hardly noticed her silence, being occupied by several new and interesting trains of thought.

The luncheon was an informal meal, and they arrived to find Beau almost on the point of leaving the morning room, and Benedict and Aubrey helping themselves from a side-table groaning under the weight of a bewildering selection of cold dishes.

Beau asked with scrupulous politeness how his uncle did, and Theo replied with unaccustomed brevity that he was maintaining his progress. She saw Benedict look at her somewhat quizzically, and then at Selina, before returning to address himself to the contents of his plate. The mere sight of the food filled her with nausea, but for appearance's sake, she took a slice of ham and some bread and butter, and sat down at the table to pour herself a cup of tea. When he placed himself beside her, she threw him a quick brittle smile and then looked down as though absorbed in contemplation of the lonely slice of ham.

'Selina seems rather more animated than usual,' he observed conversationally, and she glanced up to see her, laughing with Aubrey, her plate piled high with delicacies. 'You, on the other hand, are less so.' He paused, and when she offered no comment, 'What should I make of that, I wonder?'

The ham was like sawdust in her mouth. She swallowed it and took a sip of tea, returning the cup to the saucer with a carelessness that produced a jarring clatter.

Benedict dropped the bantering tone and said quietly, 'Trouble with his lordship?'

She shook her head. 'We had words, but . . .'

'But?'

'Oh, nothing,' she said, not wishing to be pressed. 'We simply agreed to differ.' She watched Selina come to sit down, resentful of her ability to shrug off her misery so lightly.

'Ah well,' he said after a moment, 'when he realises all that you have done for him in the past few days . . .'

'No!' she said with such soft vehemence that he paused, his fork half-way to his mouth, to stare at her. The others, too, were watching in some curiosity. 'No,' she said again, low-voiced. 'I will not be put in that position! The very last thing I want is that my grandfather should in any way feel beholden to me!' Her angry gold-flecked eyes encompassed them all. 'I must insist that he should not be told!'

In the small silence, Beau stood up, flicked an imaginary speck from his immaculate blue coat, and made her a slight ironical bow.

'My dear Theodora—pray do not distress yourself. I am sure I speak for all when I say that your wish is our command.'

Selina bit her lip, as though she would have spoken

and thought better of it. Aubrey shrugged, and Benedict merely continued to look at her in an enigmatic way.

'You see? We are agreed,' Beau said smoothly, and turned to leave.

As he did so, Purley entered. He addressed himself to Beau, but it was to Benedict that the message was directed.

'If you please, sir, Mr Cartwright, his lordship's lawyer, has just arrived. He says, sir, that he is expected.'

Theo heard Benedict say 'Damn!' with some force beneath his breath. As Beau bent a coolly enquiring eye upon him, he pushed back his chair.

'Where have you put Mr Cartwright, Purley?' His voice sounded harsh.

'In the library, sir.'

'How very odd of him to arrive in this fashion,' murmured Beau. 'I suppose we had better see what he wants. The library, you say?'

'No need for you to be put to any trouble,' Benedict said, a shade too quickly. 'I'll deal with Cartwright. His coming is entirely my fault. I arranged it on Lord Radlett's behalf when I was in London last week—some trifling matter of business, but he would have it settled, and rather than argue with him . . .' He shrugged. 'In all the upset, I forgot to cancel the arrangements. If you will excuse me.' He nodded abruptly to them all and strode from the room.

'Well, really!' said Selina.

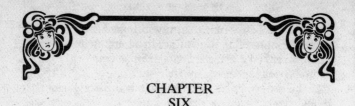

CHAPTER
SIX

IN THE library, a thin-faced spare gentleman, conservative in his dress and with a pair of spectacles perched on his nose, over which he tended to survey the vagaries of his fellow man with a censorious air, sat perched in an erect, faintly apprehensive attitude, as though he would rather be anywhere than where he was. He clutched a small portmanteau to his chest.

'Mr Cartwright.' Benedict shut the door and came forward to shake his hand. 'No, pray do not get up. Allow me to give you a glass of Madeira.'

The lawyer inclined his head, and in answer to a further enquiry assured Mr Radlett that he had eaten. Benedict handed him his drink and sat down in the chair opposite.

'Before we go any further, I owe you an apology, for I very much regret that you have had a wasted journey.' He explained what had happened, and the lawyer managed to look more disapproving than ever.

'Dear me. How very distressing . . . a severe relapse, you say?' He laid a tentative hand on the clasp of the bag. 'I have the papers, drawn up as Lord Radlett instructed me to do in his letter—also the codicil to his Will. Ahem . . .' He subjected Benedict to a frowning stare. 'I don't know how far you are in his lordship's confidence?'

'Given the somewhat radical nature of his proposals, I could hardly be other than fully aware of his intentions,' said Benedict drily.

'Quite so.'

'However,' Benedict continued, 'there is now an added complication. Lord Radlett's long-awaited grand-child has arrived—and is female!'

'Bless my soul!' Mr Cartwright's eyebrows lifted in thin crescents of astonishment. 'But surely, in that case . . .'

'You will need to take fresh instruction from his lordship with regard to the codicil. Yes, I realise that. The difficulty lies in knowing to what extent Lord Rad-lett may wish to amend it—if at all. And I very much doubt his being in any condition to take such a decision, let alone sign anything, within the next few hours. It could even be days.'

'Ah.'

'There is no chance of your being able to stay, I suppose?' Benedict asked.

'As to that, Mr Radlett, I have arranged to put up for tonight at the inn in Hatherton, and I suppose . . .' Doubt echoed in Mr Cartwright's voice. 'I could manage an extra day.'

'Well, there's always the chance that Great-uncle Edmund will rally sooner than we think,' Benedict observed with a grin. 'He's proved more than once that he's as tough as old boots! You may be sure I shall let you know if there's the least possibility.'

The lawyer's thin mouth quirked at one corner. 'You are most kind.'

Theo's insistence on concealing from Lord Radlett her part in his recovery was thwarted by Sir James, who upon his next visit found his patient so much improved that he was moved to comment with rather more animation than he was wont to show.

'A remarkable constitution,' he observed. 'I would not have believed such a degree of recovery possible. As it is, I have every expectation of seeing further improve-ment before I return to London at the weekend.'

The Viscount, banked up on pillows, his hawk nose very prominent, his deep-sunk eyes piercingly bright, fixed him with a glare.

'And finding yourself considerably plumper in the pocket, I've no doubt,' he growled irascibly.

'Grandfather!' exclaimed Theo, shocked by his ingratitude.

But Sir James only uttered a short bark of laughter. 'As to that, my lord, I have done little enough to merit reward! If anyone is deserving of your appreciation let it be your grand-daughter. I declare that I have seldom met with such a degree of imaginative dedication in anyone, let alone so young a lady! Or, for that matter, so much sensibility combined with good common sense.'

'D'ye say so?' snapped Lord Radlett.

'I do, sir—most emphatically.'

Theo knew that her grandfather's eyes were on her, but she would not meet them and moved quickly out of his range of vision so that he would not see how she coloured up. But it was less easy to avoid her cousin's quizzical glance, and she did not know whether to be glad or sorry when he finally took Sir James away.

The room was very quiet when they had gone, so quiet that the ticking of the boule clock on the mantelshelf seemed to fill Theo's head. She was annoyed to find that her hands were not quite steady as she tidied up the table used by Sir James, and a great deal of resolution was needed before she could bring herself to straighten the bedclothes.

A wasted, heavily veined hand shot out and the fingers closed round her wrist, pinning it to the bed with surprising strength as she tried to free it.

'So—I'm to be beholden to you, am I?'

'No!' she cried, and unable to release herself without hurting him, she made herself look at him, her thickly lashed dark eyes flecked with gold very close to his, so that they seemed locked together. 'You owe me nothing! I simply did what had to be done,' she said in a tight voice. 'I would have done as much for anyone.'

He grunted. 'Highty-tighty miss!' But he released her, and she moved quickly away, busy once more. But she knew he was still watching her.

'"A remarkable constitution," that prim-faced leech said.'

There was a note of complacence in the truculent voice. Theo caught a glimpse of him through the mirror; he looked for all the world like a sulky, lost, little boy hunched up against his pillows. Her anger dissolved on the instant. It was all too absurd!

'So he did,' she agreed, suppressing a quiver of amusement. 'And, seeing you now, I have to agree with him.'

'Ha! Can't think what Marston was about . . . bringing a cursed top-lofty nobody along to tell him something he ought to have known for himself! It wouldn't have happened if Gorton'd been here, let me tell you!'

Theo stood at the bottom of the bed, thinking that he looked more than ever like a fractious child, and with some trepidation she decided to treat him as one.

'Perhaps,' she agreed, 'but Gorton wasn't here, and if you weren't such a crusty old curmudgeon, you might be a little grateful that Sir James consented to give up part of his well-earned holiday in order to treat you! He is a very busy and highly regarded physician.'

His lordship glowered. 'Highly rewarded, too! You mark my words, I shall be expected to pay his fancy London charges!'

'Oh, Grandpa, really!' she exclaimed. 'As if that signifies!'

His brows came together with alarming suddenness, and she wondered if she had been wise, after all. But though her heart skipped a beat, she determined to face him out.

'Think I'm made of money, do you?' he snapped.

'I haven't the slightest idea,' she said lightly. 'But I

doubt that you're so purse-pinched that you can't pay a doctor's trifling bill.'

'Malapert!' he grumbled. His frown appeared to deepen. 'What was that you called me just now?'

Theo looked back unflinchingly. 'Grandpa,' she repeated. And then: 'It is what I used to call my other grandfather, but perhaps you don't care for it? Some people don't, I believe, and I shan't be in the least offended if you have other ideas.'

His mouth worked as though he had difficulty in expelling his words. When he finally succeeded, they fell gratingly on the ear.

'Come here, girl.'

Theo walked obediently to his side, and as he gestured irritably, sat on the edge of the bed, hands neatly folded. 'Such a charming invitation,' she said gently.

'Pshaw!' he retorted. 'Are all females in that America of yours so free with their manners?'

'I really hadn't thought about it,' she reflected. 'But Beau called me "forward" the other day, so I suppose there may be some truth in it.'

'Beau!' Lord Radlett almost spat the name out. 'You've little enough in common with that mincing park-saunterer! Still hanging around, is he . . . waiting for me to close my account?' He uttered a derisory snort. 'D'ye see what you've done, young woman? You and your father between you . . . saddling me with such a poor thing for an heir! But I'll thwart his ambition yet, damn me if I don't!' He was tiring fast, his breath labouring with every word. Theo stood up.

'You won't be able to thwart anyone if you don't rest,' she said firmly. 'And I don't want all my good work undone, so you will sleep, if you please.'

He could feel the awful darkness coming on him again, and his fear of losing her was out of all proportion to the brief span of their acquaintance. In his bitterness he had wanted to dislike her, but in a curious way it was as though her voice, her spirit, were in his head and in his heart, and the thought that she might not be there when he woke terrified him.

His hand reached out shakily to stay her. 'Haven't done with you yet . . . something I wanted to say . . .'

'It will keep.'

'No,' he said harshly. 'About this other grandparent . . . fond of him, were you?'

'Yes,' Theo said a little warily, wondering where the question was leading. 'We got along very well.'

There was a moment of silence, then: 'You won't go? Not . . . while I need you?'

The last few words were so indistinct that she had to bend close to hear them. Her reply came clear and steady.

'I shall stay for as long as you need me.'

Theo wasn't sure if he heard her, but the fingers biting urgently into her arm slackened their hold.

In the library below, Sir James had reverted to his more usual noncommittal attitude. Benedict pressed him to be more specific. Was he not as satisfied as his comments in the presence of Lord Radlett had appeared to convey?

Sir James pulled at his ear. 'It is true that his lordship has made far better progress than one could have envisaged—and to this end, there is no doubt in my mind that his grand-daughter's presence is of paramount importance. Whether or nor Lord Radlett acknowledges the fact, she has given him a lifeline to cling to, and as long as that association continues, there are at least some grounds for hope.'

Beau listened, his eyelids seeming heavier than usual; he crossed one leg elegantly over the other and narrowly regarded the gilded tassel of one gleaming Hessian.

'But you think it unlikely that my uncle will make a complete recovery?'

Sir James' thin face was inscrutable; clearly, he did not

care to be drawn, though he was obliged to admit that his lordship's age was against him, not to mention the ravages of past illnesses, and a temperament which he feared would not be conducive to restful convalescence. 'If, however, he can be persuaded to pass his days quietly and abstemiously, his life could well be prolonged for several years.'

Beau received this intelligence without comment, though his mouth tightened fractionally.

Benedict raised a droll eyebrow. 'Cousin Theo has admittedly worked wonders, but I doubt if even she is capable of performing miracles!'

In the days and weeks that followed, Lord Radlett seemed bent on proving them all wrong. There were setbacks, of course, but these he weathered with increasing certainty while remaining for the most part irascible, demanding, and totally selfish. There were many times, as Christmas came and went, when Theo's patience was sorely tried—times when her grandfather consistently rejected what he scathingly referred to as pap and demanded good red meat and a bottle of his best burgundy, and survived with no apparent ill effects.

One of the happier outcomes of his recovery lay in the departure of Beau, who soon accepted that there was little point in remaining and took himself back to town, a frustrated man. Benedict, too, once it was clear that his lordship's improvement was not temporary, disappeared for considerable periods.

Thus Theo and Selina were thrown very much more upon each other's company. The inclement weather restricted exercise, which did not trouble Selina, who did not ride and even in good weather seldom strayed farther than the rose garden. But the frequent snow squalls and lashing gales frustrated Theo and Aubrey, and the latter became broody as his mother chided him for being poor company.

Gorton had recovered sufficiently to take up very light duties, and in his austere way endeavoured to show his gratitude to Theo, but he looked so frail that the bulk of the responsibility for Lord Radlett still fell upon her. Ever-mindful of Sir James's precepts, she was inclined to indulge his whims in most things, and since he seldom cared to have her out of his sight, the strain eventually began to tell.

This was the situation Benedict found when he returned on a brisk February afternoon. In the presence of her grandfather, Theo happened to mention that she was going riding with Aubrey and brought down about her ears a blistering tirade of abuse against the boy and his parasitic mother. Her patience snapped and she began to defend them furiously, arguing that they had little choice but to remain.

'If you don't wish to be plagued with them, as you put it, the answer lies with you, for you have only to provide Selina with a house in London—a very small house would suffice—and an income to support it, which is no more than is due to your son's widow, I'm sure . . . and she would be glad to leave here!'

She stopped, appalled by her outburst and alarmed at the high colour suffusing her grandfather's face and his laboured breathing. 'Oh!' she cried, closer to tears than Benedict had seen her since the crisis days.

He rose from his chair, and took her arm. 'Go along,' he ordered, propelling her towards the door. 'Aubrey will be waiting.'

Theo dragged her feet, half glancing back. 'I shouldn't have shouted at him. Perhaps . . .'

'No perhaps. My dear girl, can you not see how much he enjoys bringing you round his finger? If all his self-indulgence to date hasn't killed him, he won't now die of a little plain speaking.'

When the door had closed behind her, Benedict walked across to the emaciated figure hunched belligerently in the chair by the fire, wrapped in rugs, and stood looking down at him, frowning.

'You don't deserve that girl, you know.'

'None of your business,' growled his lordship.

'In fact, I wouldn't blame her if she decided to leave,' Benedict continued remorselessly.

'She won't do that. I have her promise on it.'

His complacence exasperated the young man. 'Then the more shame to you. I sometimes wonder if you realise quite how much you do owe to Theo.'

Theo was very quiet as she and Aubrey took the road alongside the poplars and then struck out across the fields in the direction of Hatherton. And since it was she who usually initiated the conversation, a prolonged silence ensued.

Several times Aubrey glanced at her rather set profile before finally bursting out: 'You didn't have to come, you know! I never could understand why you should wish to in the first place, and if my presence bores you I can quite easily go off on my own!'

She seemed to come out of a dream, turning to him swiftly, her eyes very bright, almost as though she was close to tears.

'Oh, I say . . .' he began awkwardly.

'Forgive me,' she said with an abrupt apologetic laugh. 'For a moment I was preoccupied. Very rude of me.'

He stammered his own apology and they both laughed, releasing the tension. At Theo's suggestion, they put the horses to a brisk canter, and with the wind in her face, she suddenly felt much better.

'Aubrey, what would you most like to do—if you could choose?'

He seemed taken aback by the question. 'Mama hasn't been talking to you, has she?'

'No. Why should she?' Theo looked at him. 'There is

something, then?'

He shrugged. 'It isn't anything she knows about—only she supposes that I ought to wish to go to London as much as she does . . . to become a man of fashion!'

'But that isn't what you want?'

Aubrey threw his head up, staring straight ahead of him. 'There's no way by which I can have what I *want*,' he said bitterly, and then as though he couldn't stop the words rushing out: 'I want to join a cavalry regiment!'

Theo was surprised, but was quick to hide it. 'Well, then?' she asked.

'To buy into a *good* regiment is expensive—quite beyond anything I could hope for.' He turned towards her, and for the first time since she had known him she saw his face become truly animated. 'Oh, but I would settle for much less, except that Mama wouldn't hear of it. I say, you won't blab to her about this, will you?'

Theo assured him that she would not.

'She doesn't understand, you see . . . sometimes I'm so confoundedly bored and cross-grained I think I might run away and enlist!'

His cry was the cry of all young things throughout the ages eager to cut the leading reins and strike out for themselves—a mingling of frustration and recklessness that might just prove pressing enough to drive him into doing something rash. Theo hid her unease behind a brisk sympathetic manner.

'Yes, well, I'm very glad you have told me, Aubrey, and I do beg that you won't fall into a despair or rush into anything irrevocable, because if I have learned one invaluable lesson in my three and twenty years, it is that one can never guess what tomorrow may bring.' She smiled encouragingly at him. 'Why, only a matter of months ago I thought my life was quite hopeless—and now here I am with a whole new set of challenges!'

Aubrey was regarding her in a way that vaguely troubled her, with a kind of awed admiration that made her realise a little belatedly that he was at an impression-able age and she the only female, aside from his mother, within his orbit. She did hope that he wasn't about to develop a *tendre* for her! To give his thoughts a new direction she suggested a gallop to Mile End Farm and set off without further ado. He let out a loud 'Huzza!' and urged his mount in pursuit.

When Benedict came upon them later, crossing the hall, still glowing from their ride, still laughing and talking, he regarded them with an enigmatic eye.

Aubrey met that look and was at once embarrassed and a little put out. Somehow Benedict always managed to make him feel his lack of years. There was that indefinable air about him, the careless unconventional devil-may-care air that epitomised for Aubrey all the experience, the untold deeds locked in a past not quite respectable and shrouded in mystery. At this moment it only served to bring home to him his own inadequacy and lack of prospects.

The magic of the afternoon was at an end. He turned to Theo, flushed and stammering slightly.

'Th-thank you! I enjoyed that above everything!' He gave her an abrupt little bow and hurried away.

'I'm not sure that you should encourage that halfling,' Benedict mused, looking after him. 'He is fast develop-ing a severe case of calf-love.'

'Oh dear, I do hope not,' Theo sighed. 'Poor boy! He is so very unhappy already.'

'Boys of his age frequently are.'

Theo frowned at him. 'How very unhandsome of you! Only the other day you were voicing some sympathy with his situation.'

'Maybe then I was feeling in a charitable mood,' he drawled.

'And now you are out of countenance, I think.'

His laugh rasped slightly. 'Blame that plaguey grand-parent of yours. He is a man given to sudden whims, as you should know better than most. Nothing will now do for him but to see his man, Cartwright, as soon as maybe. So I must go to London to fetch him.'

Theo wondered why the news of his going should leave her feeling unaccountably flat, and shrugged the thought away. 'Should Grandpa be concerning himself with business matters so soon?' She could not help sounding anxious.

'No, but when did that ever stop him?' said Benedict drily. 'Incidentally, I hope you may find him a somewhat chastened character—for the present, that is. I have been ringing a peal over him about his treatment of you, and then Aunt Minta came in and I left him to her tender mercies.'

'There was no need,' she said quickly.

He came very close, tipping her face up to him with one finger placed under her chin.

'There was every need,' he said, and kissed her mouth lightly.

She protested, her hand flying to grasp his wrist, but the colour, already warm in her cheeks from her ride, warmed a little more, and her heart did a curious little flip.

'Cousin's privilege,' he murmured sardonically, and then they were apart again and he was resuming their conversation as though nothing had happened, and she was left with a curious feeling of frustration.

Theo found the reluctant penitent still sitting, staring into the fire.

'That scrapegrace of a great-nephew of mine tells me that I treat you badly,' he said without looking at her. She thought it was probably the closest he was likely to come to an apology.

'I daresay I shall survive,' she said lightly, removing her hat before going to her room to change her dress, for she had long since given up her occupation of the dressing room.

'I've had that sister of mine here, too,' the gruff voice continued. 'Gave me chapter and verse of your doings . . . made sense of much that had me confounded, thanks to your damn silly notions of secrecy! Why'd you do it, eh?'

Theo's step slowed, halted—but she didn't speak.

'Well?' His sudden ferocity made her jump. 'Ye could have turned your back on me that first day—and many times since. So why didn't you?'

Theo swung around to look at him. She saw the jutting profile, intensely proud, the now spare folds of skin quivering with the effort of keeping his head erect, and she ran across the room to sink beside his chair, her skirts billowing round her.

'Because Papa would never have forgiven me for leaving you,' she cried unsteadily. 'It was for him that I came, and through him, I believe, that I have come to feel as though I am a part of you'—her own chin jutted—'whether you like it or not!'

'Coals of fire, eh?' he growled.

'If you like!'

The two pairs of dark flashing eyes clashed and held. His voice grew harsh.

'I've no doubt you think I treated your father shabbily?'

'He never permitted me to believe it,' she insisted.

'But you thought it, none the less,' he said. 'Well, I did! He was *so* like your grandmother! She ought not to have been taken from me so soon . . .' He shook his head wearily. 'Every time I looked at John I saw her, and cursed him for reminding me! And when I saw you that first time . . . just for a moment, I thought . . .'

'Please, Grandpa—it doesn't matter any more!' she cried, shaking her head, agitated by the thought that he might seriously distress himself, and a strand of hair, worked loose by her afternoon's exertions, slithered from its pins to lie against her shoulder.

His hand moved shakily, like the tentative hand of a blind man, to touch it, his uncertain fingers seeking for the pins that held the knot in place and then pulling them out one by one so that it all came spilling down about her face. She sat very still, close to tears, as he fumblingly explored its silkiness.

'So like her!' he muttered. 'D'ye know, many a time I thought it was she who was there with me . . . when I was lost in that damnable no-man's land . . . her voice sounded different, but it was so clear, that voice . . . so young and fresh and full of hope, that I stopped being afraid . . .' He glared at her. 'I daresay you think grown men shouldn't be afraid?'

'I know Papa was,' she said huskily, 'during the worst times. And yet he was *so* brave for so long!'

Lord Radlett uttered something very like a groan of pain. 'Minta told me,' he said in a voice thick with emotion. 'Damned ironical, meeting a violent end, the way he did! Gentlest boy I ever knew. Damned ironical!'

'Yes.' Theo felt suddenly too drained to say more. Her foot was fast going to sleep, but with the communion between them so complete, she was reluctant for the moment to end. It was so quiet that the ticking of the clock beat a steady rhythm in her head.

'Well, God be thanked, I now see my way clear,' he said suddenly. 'I mean to do right by you, child. There's much to make up for, and little enough time to accomplish it, but we have already made a beginning.'

Theo thought of Benedict's visit to London, the lawyer and all the repercussions that were bound to ensue. She moved restively and stood up, wincing over the cramping numbness in her foot.

'You don't have to do anything for me, truly!' she pleaded. 'That isn't why I came.'

'I know, I know!' he said with a faint rumble of mirth. 'But ye can't stop me if I have a fancy to make you dance to my tune!'

CHAPTER
SEVEN

THEO WAS in the drawing room with Selina when Benedict arrived from London, bringing with him the prim-faced lawyer. They went straight away to the Viscount's room, and remained closeted there for so long that she began to wonder if the business had been concluded and the man had gone without her knowing.

She would not admit to curiosity, but the time seemed to drag, and the sight of her companion struggling with a half-completed reticule, the instructions for which were clearly set out in the *Lady's Magazine* before her, did little to soothe her. She was driven more than once to peer out of the window rather than watch, yet even here, there was little to engage her interest. A capricious wind soughed round the corners of the house with seasonal fervour, buffeting the newly burgeoning trees beyond and moving like an undulating shadow over the avenue of yew trees that bordered the long walk.

'Oh, what's the use? It isn't as if I shall ever use the wretched thing!'

Theo turned in time to see Selina throw the offending work as far as it would go. She walked across and picked it up.

'It's very pretty,' she said encouragingly. 'And very unusual with this white and gilt threadwork.' She sat down beside Selina to study the pattern. 'Of course you must finish it. See, it isn't so difficult.'

'The material came from a spencer I had once. It was vastly becoming!' Selina sighed, and watched Theo's nimble fingers making sense of the incomprehensible instructions. 'How fortunate you are. I never was the least use with a needle!' She sighed again. 'I can't think why I ever began it, except that it was something to pass the hours.'

It was at times like this that Theo found her patience most tried by this butterfly of a woman. To be sure, she had had an unfortunate experience and was clearly the sort of person who needed company (preferably male), as surely as plants need light to thrive, but it seemed to Theo so poor-spirited to sit and sigh and do nothing positive to alter things.

'Did I tell you?' she said with determined brightness. 'Gorton is well enough now to resume his full duties, so I shall have more time at my disposal. Perhaps, if you would care to, we can send away for some material and make one or two new dresses for spring?'

A light sprang into Selina's eyes, but it was quickly quenched as she reflected bitterly on the unlikelihood of her being able to afford one new gown—let alone several.

'Oh, fustian, as Grandpa says. You leave that part of it to me. The dresses in this magazine are out of date, of course. We shall need to purchase a new one, but still . . .'

Theo began to leaf through the magazine, stopping here and there to examine a pattern with a critical eye, and this kept them both absorbed until Purley came in to say that his lordship would be very much obliged if Miss Theo would step up to his room.

She found Lord Radlett sitting up in his bed, supported by a quantity of pillows and wearing his most elaborately frogged dressing-gown; a quizzing-glass dangled from his neck, and a snuffbox (its contents expressly forbidden by the doctor) was defiantly clasped in one hand. Theo was convinced that it was no happy accident that a stand of branched candles had been placed near enough to the bed to highlight the leonine head with its awesome profile. As she dropped a deferential kiss on the noble brow, she wondered if Mr Cartwright had been suitably impressed. Intercepting a droll look from her cousin, she was obliged to smother a grin.

The lawyer, who had been writing at a table near the window, stood somewhat ill at ease as she came in. With the introductions and preliminaries at an end, Lord Radlett got down directly to the purpose of his visit.

'There is no need to waste time with a lot of flim-flammery,' he said impatiently as Mr Cartwright cleared his throat in expectation. 'The plain fact is, I've decided to settle a sum of money on you now, rather than leave it to you in m'Will.'

Theo opened her mouth to protest.

'Tch! Tch! Don't interrupt me, child. Gets me muddled. Cartwright here can fill you in on all the details later.' He frowned at the lawyer. 'But in essence it's to be an allowance to be paid monthly. It should keep you very comfortably in gewgaws until such time as you marry.'

'No, please!' Theo cried, agitation making her less than careful how she spoke. 'This is not necessary, and I don't want . . .' She covered her burning cheeks with the palms of her hands.

'Grandpa, you are more than generous, and I'm sure you mean it for the best, but I cannot accept such an arrangement!' She saw his brows draw together ominously. 'Oh, I beg that you will not be offended, dear sir, but I have no need of it. I have money left me by my father . . . more than sufficient for my needs!'

'Humgudgeon! First time I ever heard you say anything so cork-brained! Damme if I care what John left you—you may dispose of *that* as you please.' He thus dismissed her argument as being of little worth. 'I'm concerned with providing for your future in my own way. Can't expect to move in first circles without money behind you, like it or not.'

Theo looked to her cousin, who shrugged, and then to the lawyer, whose thin-nosed expression clearly indicated that he considered her undeserving of such generosity. A feeling of helplessness engulfed her.

'I wasn't aware that I might be expected to move in first circles,' she ventured.

'Well, of course you will. Got to have a bit of a whirl before ye settle down!'

A need to assert herself was struggling for supremacy against her by now natural instinct not to upset him, fuelled by the growing suspicion that he was seeking to manipulate her.

'And do you mean to pick my husband for me, also?' she asked with deceptive meekness.

'No need,' said his lordship complacently. 'Y're a sensible girl.' His glance flicked to Benedict. 'I am confident you'll choose wisely.'

He was matchmaking, Theo realised with sudden horror! The old rogue thought he was being subtle, but she could have little doubt of his intentions. And Benedict? Was all this being arranged with his connivance? He was being suspiciously bland about the whole thing. Oh, it was iniquitous! She began to know exactly how her father must have felt.

'I also intend to leave this house to you in my Will,' continued Lord Radlett, blithely unaware of the fury fulminating in his beloved grandchild's breast.

'No! Oh, Grandpa, pray don't go on!'

She didn't care that they were all looking at her. She crossed swiftly to the bed and sat down beside him, so that it was just the two of them, her hand in his.

'Please listen to me, because what *I* want should be important, too,' she pleaded. 'I believe I know why you are doing what you are doing, but really you mustn't. It isn't at all necessary, and you cannot deprive Beau and everyone else of what is their due simply to assuage your conscience, you know!'

'Don't be impertinent!'

'I don't mean to be, but you are putting me in an impossible position. Beau is your heir . . .'

'Beau will get his due,' he said harshly. 'The house in Grosvenor Square will be his, and a fine property in Warwickshire that will provide a more than adequate income. Give him more, and he'll only squander it on gambling. He'll get the family sapphires, too—more's the pity. I'd have liked you to have those. If I know Beau, he'll pledge 'em within a week—or have 'em copied in paste and sell 'em!'

'But what about everyone else?' she persisted doggedly. 'What about Selina?'

'Not your concern, miss!' he snapped discouragingly.

But she was not to be put off. 'Grandpa—you do mean to provide for Selina? Oh, it would be too unjust if you did not!'

He snatched his hand away, and she saw that it trembled. 'I'll not be preached at by a chit of a girl—not even you, m'girl! I shall do as *I see fit!*'

'Let be, Theo.'

Benedict had come up behind her. His voice was quiet, but more than usually incisive.

'Oh, but . . .'

His hands came down hard on her shoulders and he lifted her bodily to her feet.

'I said *enough!*'

She twisted her head round, her eyes blazing into his. 'How dare you presume to tell me what to do! You are too free with your advice, cousin.'

'And you are allowing emotion to cloud your reasoning,' he returned with maddening calm. 'Where is your excellent common sense, sweet coz?'

A moment more she glared at him—and then, reluctantly, uttered an abrupt little laugh. 'Oh, well!' she said.

Lord Radlett watched the exchange with interest—and what he saw did not displease him. In better humour once more, he said, 'That's all settled, then. Cartwright has only to finish drawing up the papers—damned long-winded creatures, lawyers—and we shall be right and tight.'

Mr Cartwright looked pained, and suggested that it might be a help if he could work quietly somewhere. Theo, resigned for the present, though by no means defeated, took pity on him and said she would find him a quiet place.

But Lord Radlett hadn't quite finished with her. 'Let Benedict do it,' he said. 'I have one more small piece of news for you.

Her heart sank as he glanced pointedly at the other two and waited for them to leave the room.

'Now, then.' He reached into his pocket with the air of one about to bestow a great treat. 'I want you to read this, if you please.'

Theo took it from him, made suspicious by all that had gone before. She read it at first without taking in the sense of it. Then she read it again: *It would give me the greatest pleasure to have your grand-daughter to stay with me for a few weeks. I confess I am quite longing to see John's child. He was, as you know, ever a favourite with me, and now that all my own girls are married I find myself very much at a loose end* . . .

There was much more in similar vein. She looked up at last, feeling rather dazed. 'Who is Drusilla?'

'The Duchess of Bury . . . an old friend of mine,' he said. 'You will like her.'

'Will I?' Theo gave him a measuring look. 'How very obliging of your Duchess to extend me an invitation just at this particular moment! I wonder how she came to know I was here?'

He looked at her with bright appreciative eyes. 'I wrote to tell her, of course. Benedict took the letter—brought the reply back with him. Sounds quite keen, wouldn't you say?'

'Oh, really, Grandpa! She could hardly refuse you.'

'Gammon! Drusilla ain't like that! And it would be just the thing for you . . . Season coming up. Time you saw a bit of life beyond these four walls . . . and I can't take you m'self.'

For the life of her, she couldn't be angry with him this time. She sensed that he desperately wanted to show his appreciation to her in a positive way, and she had to admit that the idea appealed to her.

She folded the letter and waved it under his nose. 'You are a wicked old man!' she said. 'I suppose you reckon that if you persist long enough, I shall tire of arguing—like water wearing away a stone!'

'Something like that,' he admitted with a chuckle. And then, more seriously, 'But you'll go? I would like you to enjoy yourself. Not much gaiety in your life of late . . . and now that Gorton is recovered . . .'

'You mustn't expect too much of Gorton, Grandpa,' Theo said anxiously. 'He'll never be quite the man he was, you know.'

'Tch! You leave Gorton to me, child. We understand one another.'

Benedict put his head round the door. 'I've put Cartwright in the yellow saloon.' He looked from one to the other. 'I listened outside for sounds of violence before venturing in.'

'Y're an irreverent pair, the two of you,' grumbled his lordship without heat.

Benedict laughed. 'I take it you've won?' And then, quizzically to Theo, 'You disappoint me, sweet coz . . . to cave in without a fight!'

'I may yet come about,' she said valiantly. Her eyes sparkled suddenly. 'But London would be fun!'

'By the way, sir, while I was in London I encountered a distant relation of ours—or so he claimed to be. A Comte de Varron?'

'Impossible,' said Lord Radlett with surprising vehemence. 'The Comte and his family perished during the Terror.'

'Are you sure that no one survived? A child, perhaps?' Benedict suggested. 'This man is about forty, so he would have been a boy of fifteen years or so at that time.'

'I tell you they butchered the whole family,' said the Viscount harshly. 'I should know. I was there.'

'Grandpa!' Theo stared, half appalled, half fascinated. 'You don't mean you actually saw them guillotined?'

'Haven't thought about it for years now,' he said obliquely. 'Damnable affair. Came devilish close to getting my own head cut off! I'd gone to try to get them out, d'ye see . . . another twenty-four hours and we'd have done it, too.' His voice dropped. 'Helen was so beautiful, even more beautiful than your grandmother . . . she was her sister.'

'So Madame de Varron was English,' said Theo. 'How dreadful!'

'Well, this present Comte is quite definitely French—and something of a philanderer, I fancy,' drawled Benedict. 'He was most anxious to contact you, sir.'

'I'll have no truck with any damned impostor!' It may have been a trick of the light, but Theo thought that a flicker of alarm showed momentarily in her grandfather's eyes. 'I hope you didn't give the fellow any encouragement? I give you fair warning, I won't meet him if he does come here!'

Benedict raised one eyebrow. 'Oh, he won't do that. I convinced him that you were much too ill to receive anyone at present. He may prove persistent, however. He is endeavouring to trace a family heirloom . . . *La*

Cascade Diamant. Some kind of diamond necklace; quite priceless, so the Comte seemed to think, but I expect if you knew the family so well, you must remember it.' He waited for some reaction from his lordship, and getting none, added, 'It vanished apparently at the time of the tragedy and hasn't been heard of since.'

'Well, what more d'you expect—with the *canaille* looting everywhere?' growled the old man. 'Probably got chopped into little pieces!'

'I expect you're right,' Benedict said. 'I just wondered, as you were there . . . whether you might have some idea what became of it.'

'None whatever,' snapped his lordship. 'And if I had, you wouldn't catch me telling some greedy, hoaxing jackanapes!' He shut his eyes. 'Now I'm tired. You may go away, both of you.'

'Well,' said Benedict, as he walked downstairs with Theo. 'What was all that about, I wonder?'

'You thought he was being evasive, too?' Theo said. 'It is certainly very odd. I do remember Papa once telling me that his father used to go to France quite often after his mother's death, though I had no idea he was actually there at the time of the Revolution!' Her cousin was quietly thoughtful. She glanced at him. 'Oh, but . . . you don't think he really does know something about the necklace?'

'I don't think anything at present,' he said equivocally. 'But I feel that a few enquiries might be in order. What I confess does worry me is that if the Comte pursues his quest with his present zeal, he will sooner or later meet up with Beau, who might be more than a little interested on his own account.'

Theo, however, had more important things on her mind than elusive diamond necklaces.

'About the money . . .' she began.

Benedict stopped in his tracks and turned her to face him. 'Let the old man do things his way, Theo. It's how he wants it.' And when she again protested that she couldn't take so much, 'He can afford it, believe me. If you're afraid that it smacks of payment for services rendered'—she moved under his hands—'then I can set your mind at ease. He had already had papers drawn up along similar lines before he even met you.'

'Truly?' She looked steadily into his eyes.

He shook her slightly. 'Would I lie to you?'

I wish I knew, she thought, her throat tight.

'You remember when Cartwright came down here—oh, well before Christmas—before you were even on good terms with your grandfather? Well, most of it had already been decided then. Truly.' He looked quizzical. 'I told you right at the start that his dislike of Beau outweighed all else.'

'And the visit to London? The extremely generous allowance?'

Benedict took her arm and they began walking again. 'Oh, that is certainly a demonstration of his growing fondness for you—a way of saying thank you, if you like. You surely don't begrudge him that?'

She lifted her shoulders in a faint sigh. 'It would be churlish indeed to do so. But he is making it very difficult for me to return home to Philadephia.'

His fingers tightened on her arm. He looked down swiftly. 'Do you then wish to? I confess we all rather hoped you had come to think of this as home.'

'We?'

His eyes were unreadable. 'Well, your grandfather certainly believes it.' He paused, before saying with soft irony, 'And I should naturally be desolated were you to leave.'

'Would you?' She wondered again about his part in the scheme of things. He had certainly made himself indispensable to her grandfather, yet one would not think altruism to be a facet of his character. Could a scapegrace youth change so much? It seemed unlikely, so what was he hoping to gain? A fortune by way of a rich bride, belike, she thought, recalling the fleeting impression she had received in her grandfather's room. Yes, that would fit the character much better. She shied away from the thought, and turned her attention elsewhere.

'I don't know how I am going to break the news to Selina,' she confessed. 'I would not blame her if she succumbed to hysterics on the spot!'

'I shouldn't worry about her,' Benedict said with an off-handedness that made her indignant. 'She wouldn't concern herself about you.'

'As if that made it any better!' she cried.

'Well, then,' he said. 'I repeat, don't worry about her. His lordship hasn't quite finished playing God yet.'

Further than that he would not be drawn, and Theo was left with her dilemma. With unaccustomed cowardice she kept to her room for the remainder of the afternoon, but when dinner time drew near she knew that she must face Selina, who would be curious about the events of the afternoon. Since no miracle solution had revealed itself, she was resigned to the prospect of a stormy scene.

When she entered the library, however, she found Selina sitting on the sofa beneath the censorious gaze of the Cavalier surrounded by a sheaf of closely written documents which spilled out over the seat. Benedict and Aubrey stood close by, and there was such a curious atmosphere that she at once feared the worst.

'What has happened?' she cried, running forward.

'The old codger's gone queer in his attic, that's what!' said Aubrey as his mama raised dazed eyes to Theo and thrust at her the letter she held clutched in her hand.

I stand accused of dealing less than adequately with you and your son. While refuting the charge absolutely, I have no wish to compel to remain under my roof one who is so glaringly unappreciative of my generosity. Therefore, please find herewith enclosed the lease of a small property in Upper Wimpole Street made over in your name together with an agreement that you shall be paid six hundred pounds a year, except in the event of your remarrying, at which time all monies will cease. With this gift I consider all obligations towards you to be fully discharged.

Lord Radlett's signature was shaky, but had been executed with a defiant flourish.

Theo looked up, and encountered a sardonic smile from Benedict.

'What did I tell you, coz?' he said.

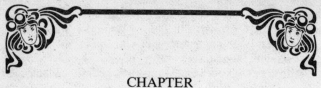

CHAPTER
EIGHT

LONDON WAS all and more than Theo had hoped for. She had been loath to leave Shallowford when the time came, for the air had just taken on that first velvety mildness, the poplars and chestnut trees were newly tipped with green, and the rooks were courting noisily in the elm tops while primroses starred the grass beneath.

But London held an equal magic. Here too were trees, set in great sweeping parks; elegant rows of terraced houses and even more elegant secluded squares where gracious mansions stood in discreet splendour. And in Grosvenor Square, almost opposite the unoccupied town residence of Lord Radlett, lived the Duchess of Bury.

Any qualms Theo had entertained about meeting the Duchess were dispelled the instant she and Benedict were announced. No one could have been less formidable than the petite pretty lady who rose from a sofa near the window and hurried forward, hands outstretched in welcome, her musical voice full of pleasure as she declared that she would have known her anywhere for her father's daughter.

Benedict too was not forgotten in the enthusiastic warmth of her greeting.

'Do come along and sit down, both of you.'

Her skirts rustled gently as she led them across a vast expanse of carpet, the like of which Theo had never seen; from its exquisite texture and colouring she supposed it must be Persian. All the hangings and upholstery in the room were of cream and gold, a luxurious background with which her hostess harmonised so admirably that Theo wondered in awed amusement whether the effect was accidental or deliberate.

At all events it made her own sensible brown twill travelling dress seem indescribably dowdy by comparison. But not by so much as a flicker of an eye did her hostess allow her to suspect that she found it so.

'Now, tell me first of all how your poor grandfather does.'

Theo said that he was very much better than they could have hoped for, but her tone was unconsciously pensive, so that her grace was moved to make encouraging protestations. Theo knew that Benedict was looking at her curiously, but she could not put into words her quite illogical unease as she had bidden her grandfather farewell; illogical because he *was* so much better, the hands gripping hers no longer shook, and he now spent a good part of the day up and dressed and in the sitting room which adjoined his bedchamber.

'I shall write,' she had said with sudden urgency, bending to kiss the now slack folds of his cheek. And she had made Gorton promise that he would let her know if anything untoward happened; not, she had added hastily, as much to convince herself as him, that anything would.

'I cannot tell you how overjoyed I was to receive your grandfather's letter, my dear,' the Duchess was chattering on. 'I had been feeling thoroughly moped before it arrived.'

'It is more than kind of you to have me,' Theo said.

'Nonsense, child! It is you who are doing me the kindness.' She sighed, though her eyes twinkled. 'You can have no idea how one's spirits are sunk by the realisation that with all of one's chicks having flown the nest, nothing is left to one but to dwindle as graciously as may be contrived into old age!'

This was so patently a nonsense that Theo and Benedict exchanged amused glances and said so in chorus.

The eyes twinkled ever more appreciatively. 'Well, perhaps not quite yet! Especially now that you have come, my dear Theo—I may call you Theo, may I not?' And upon receiving eager assent: 'We shall have so many delightful things to plan—dressmakers to consult . . .'

It was on the tip of Theo's tongue to say that she had already made several dresses in anticipation of her visit, but a few moments in the Duchess's company had served to convince her of the total inadequacy of her poor efforts. Theo, not by nature extravagant, began to think she might very easily grow to enjoy herself for a while at least.

Benedict saw the sparkle of expectation in her eyes, and stood up.

'I have a feeling that the conversation is about to turn upon the rival merits of the Season's anticipated fashions—and I shall find myself very much *de trop* among the silks and muslins! Your grace's obedient servant.'

He bowed over the Duchess's hand with such an air that for an instant Theo was afforded a glimpse of that impudent, devil-may-care young gallant who had been banished to India all those years before. Then he was turning to her, the light still in his eyes.

'Goodbye, sweet coz,' he murmured. 'I need not say be happy, for I'm sure you will be.'

The words sounded so final that she felt a sudden pang at his going. She sprang to her feet, holding out her hand impulsively. 'I shall see you again soon?'

His fingers closed round her hand. He looked at it for a moment without speaking and than raised it to his lips. 'But of course,' he drawled, his voice softly mocking. 'I am not so easily got rid of!'

Smiling, she reclaimed her hand but the imprint of Benedict's kiss lingered on her skin long after he had gone.

'Such a charming young man!' said the Duchess approvingly. 'Lud! How he broke hearts as a youth! But I confess I like him better now.'

Theo slept fitfully that first night—and wished more than once, as the intermittent rattle of carriage-wheels disturbed her rest, for the peace of Shallowford. But by morning her natural resilience had asserted itself and she could not wait to begin. It had come as something of a disappointment to discover that the Duchess was not an early riser.

'But, my dear child,' she had explained with a trill of laughter. 'Country hours would wear one to a thread in no time here!' And as Theo's eyebrows lifted in surprise, 'Yes, I know. At your age I, too, could burn my candle at both ends, but now, alas, it is necessary to conserve. Only wait a few weeks, and you will understand.'

But on that first morning Theo woke with the dawn, and as she watched the sun rise she could remain in bed no longer. By the time Maddie came in, she was up and dressed and contemplating taking a walk. Maddie expressed disapproval. Only her attachment to Miss Theo had persuaded her to come to London, which, as she knew well from having it dinned into her as a girl, was nothing more than a hotbed of sin and debauchery. And the thought of her idol walking the streets of such a place without protection shook her prim provincial soul to the core.

'It isn't proper, miss—that's what I say,' she insisted when, smiling, Theo declined her company. 'Not proper and not safe, either . . . and what am I to say to her grace when you don't come back?'

'But I have every intention of coming back, Maddie,' Theo pointed out reasonably as she donned her one good pelisse, which was a pretty shade of amber, and tied the matching ribbons of her bonnet in a rather dashing bow beneath one ear.

'Ah!' There was a wealth of meaning in that brief exclamation. 'Intentions are all very fine . . .'

'Oh, do stop, Maddie,' Theo cried, half laughing. 'I am going, and there's an end to it! I don't intend to be away very long, but if I should fail to return, I give you full leave to say *I told you so!*'

A pair of footmen stood like wooden sentinels in the cool marbled hall. Not a flicker of expression crossed their faces as she bid them a serene 'Good morning' and waited for them to open the door, but she received the distinct impression that they were equally disapproving. Ah well, they would no doubt put it down to her odd American ways!

Outside, the traffic of the previous night had vanished. The square was deserted, but wore a calm quiescent air of expectancy as though it knew that all too soon the merry round would begin again. The air was full of spring with a fresh impudent breeze tugging at Theo's skirts as she chose her direction at random and began to walk briskly.

To her delight her steps led to a park, and here she wandered contentedly for a while, heedless of the dew that soaked her feet and the hem of her dress. There was much activity in the branches above her head, but the only human sign was a lone horse-rider galloping in the distance.

Theo's mind turned to Aubrey. Perhaps, if the Duchess could provide her with a mount—and Aubrey too if he wasn't able to talk Selina into purchasing one for him—they could resume their rides here.

It was now more than two weeks since Selina and Aubrey had come to London, and she supposed she would have to find time to call on Selina before too long. She was obliged to own that the visit would be more in the nature of a duty than a pleasure. It might have been supposed that Selina would be overjoyed at the change in her fortunes, but after the initial flush of triumph had died, she had compared her lot with Theo's and, like a small child envious of another's larger bag of sweetmeats, had found it wanting.

At last, reluctantly, Theo retraced her steps, still with the world very much to herself. Only as she once more approached Grosvenor Square did she see anyone. A gentleman, very elegant in olive green riding-coat and buff breeches and mounted on a bay hunter, came cantering towards her. And because the sun was shining and he was prodigiously handsome she was half smiling to herself as he approached. Their eyes met, and he doffed his hat in gallant salutation, returning her smile in a most charming lopsided fashion.

Theo blushed and quickened her step. Lordy, how forward he must have thought her! But for all that, her mouth curved—it really had been a very pleasant walk.

There were repercussions, of course. Bracegirdle, her grace's butler, looked down from his imposing height, carefully averting his eyes from her sodden hems, and informed Miss Radlett with exceeding politeness that had he been aware that she was wishful to take the air so early in the day, arrangements would have been made accordingly. Maddie scolded her and made her change her dress and shoes at once before she took an inflammation of the lungs, and most certainly before she took one bite of the breakfast which would be brought up to her at any minute. And the Duchess was scandalised.

Theo was summoned to her unbelievable pink-and-gold boudoir, where she found her grace reclining upon a day-bed fashioned like a huge shell, amid a sea of frothy pink lace.

'In London, dear child, a young lady does not go out alone,' she said in gentle reproof, dipping a sponge finger delicately into her cup of chocolate. 'Still, I daresay it won't signify this once, as *no one* is about at such an hour!'

Theo thought of her charming gallant and lowered her eyes demurely against the memory, as she regretfully gave her promise not to do it again.

The next few days passed in a whirl of activity. The first grand ball of the Season was still several weeks away, but already people had begun leaving cards and there were invitations to soirées and receptions delivered almost daily. It would be as well, said the Duchess, to waste no time if they were to secure the services of the very best mantua-makers and milliners before they became rushed off their feet.

Thus Theo presently found herself being pinned into silks and muslins and the flimsiest of gauzes, and soon a bewildering collection of gowns began to accumulate— morning dresses, walking dresses, half-robes, redingotes, and the most exquisite ball-gowns. There were hats, too, for every conceivable occasion, and an irresistible riding-habit in palest green frogged with black, a trim black shako embellished with a pale green plume, and matching boots of softest kid.

The extravagance of it all was quite daunting, and Theo became seriously alarmed that what she had once considered an over-generous allowance would be totally inadequate to meet such acquisitions as the Duchess seemed to feel were necessary.

'But my dear child!' cried the Duchess when the purchase of two dozen pairs of silk stockings drove her to voice her fears. 'Your allowance is but pin-money! Edmund has given me *carte blanche* to rig you out in the primest twig, and the reckoning is to go to him, so you need harbour no fears on that score!'

Theo could only pray that her grandfather knew what he was about, or he was likely to suffer a relapse when confronted with the said reckoning!

For her first formal introduction into society she wore

a gown of orange blossom Italian crepe cut low at the neckline and falling in soft folds from a high waist. Her grace's own hairdresser did the most amazing things with her hair, weaving into a complex series of knots a rope of seed-pearls which exactly matched the ones that trimmed the neck of her dress.

The tall graceful creature who emerged at the end of it all was a revelation, but did not, she confessed laughingly, bear the least resemblance to the Theodora Radlett she knew!

'Nonsense, my love! You look charming!' exclaimed her grace, resplendent in lavender-grey silk and feathers. 'And first impressions are of the utmost importance, you know!'

The assembly was being given by Lady Shadley, a bosom-bow friend of the Duchess, who confided that the Earl and Countess of Shadley were at the forefront of the fashionable scene. Her ladyship could therefore be relied upon to have invited simply everyone worthy of note. In the event, this seemed to be no exaggeration; the *ton* flocked to it, and Theo grew dizzy from curtsying as she was introduced to this personage and that while her patroness looked on, glowing with pride.

'I hear that the Duchess is confidently predicting a *succès fou*,' said Benedict, coming upon Theo unawares in one of her brief moments of respite, and looking, she thought, quite dashing in the black-and-white formality of his evening clothes.

'You are quizzing me!' she accused him, laughing.

'Not I! I look forward eagerly to being able to bask in your reflected glory. You must know that I have already been solicited by more than one gentleman of my acquaintance for the honour of being introduced to my fascinating American cousin!'

'Fascinating?' In spite of the grandeur of the occasion, she giggled. 'Oh, now I know you are funning!'

Benedict put up his glass to survey her. 'Fascinating,'

he insisted. 'I do see what they mean, sweet coz. Very
fetching! And I am clearly not alone in my opinion.' His
glance moved to encompass a fair, rather thick-set
young man whose attention strayed continually in their
direction. 'Alverton has hardly let you out of his sight!'
One eyebrow lifted. 'You could do worse, you know—
eldest son—heir to the Shadley fortune. How would the
prospect of becoming a countess in due course appeal to
you, I wonder?'

Theo's indignation was tinged with embarrassment,
for it could not be denied that Lady Shadley's son had
singled her out with conspicuous single-mindedness. But
if Benedict thought for one moment that she had been
encouraging the young man's attentions!

She opened her mouth to refute any such accusation,
but he only laughed as her eyes kindled.

'Pax! It would never do for us to be seen brangling
here! You are moving in élite circles, my dear. Did I not
see you talking to Sally Jersey but a moment since? It is
people like Lady Jersey and Countess Lieven and their
little coterie of friends who determine what is *de rigueur*
and what is not—and you flout their conventions at your
peril!'

Theo was unimpressed. 'The Duchess was telling me
something of the sort, but I thought she was exaggerating.' A faint smile curved her lips. 'She is a little prone to
embellish the truth at times!'

He laughed. 'Nicely put, coz! But in this instance, the
truth needs no puffing up.' He looked across the room to
where her grace sat leaning forward in animated conversation with Lady Jersey. 'If I do not mistake the
matter, she is even now securing your admission to
Almack's, and that is the most sought-after accolade of
all!'

Theo privately thought it all rather silly, but it was a
most agreeable silliness for all that, and her letters to her
grandfather bubbled with amusing anecdotes about her

introduction to the *haut ton* which she guessed would entertain him as well as assure him of her pleasure in it all. What she did not tell him was of her meeting with the Comte de Varron, who had presented himself at Benedict's side during that first assembly and demanded to be introduced to his most charming companion.

Somewhat to her embarrassment, she found herself looking up into the smiling appreciative eyes of the gentleman she had encountered briefly on her illicit walk that first morning in London. Not by a flicker did he betray that this was not their first sight of one another, though his fingers exerted a subtle pressure as he raised her hand to his lips with a murmured *'Enchanté, mademoiselle.'*

Theo looked at him with some curiosity; he was older than he had at first seemed, with a faint sprinkling of silver in his curling black hair, but he was undeniably handsome, with an elegance of dress and ease of manner that might all too readily captivate any lady unwise enough to be beguiled by such superficial lures, which, she told herself severely, she was not! Though, with Benedict looking daggers, she was moved on impulse to respond with more vivacity than she might otherwise have done to the Comte's overtures.

'Yet one more charming relation,' he said with that attractive lopsided smile. 'I have already made the acquaintance of another Monsieur Radlett—Beau, is it not? And the fair Madame, also. Now, it would seem that the *pièce de résistance* is saved for the last.'

'You are too kind, Monsieur le Comte,' Theo said demurely.

'It is not a kindness to speak the truth, mademoiselle.' He appeared to be weighing his words. 'Would I be correct in thinking that *you* are the American granddaughter of Lord Radlett?' She indicated that she was. 'Then, forgive my impertinence, but as your cousin here is well aware, I desire most urgently to speak with your

grandfather concerning the whereabouts of an irreplace-
able family heirloom. It is my earnest hope that you will
be able to tell me that his lordship's health is now
sufficiently improved for that to be possible.'

Before Theo could answer, Benedict had interjected
smoothly that he feared it was not.

'Strange!' The Comte's eyes narrowed. 'Monsieur
Beau gave me to understand that he was considerably
improved.'

'Beau hasn't seen his uncle for several weeks,'
Benedict said smoothly. 'I, on the other hand, was at
Shallowford only two days since.'

'You didn't tell me!' Theo exclaimed, her eyes flying
to meet his. 'He isn't worse? Oh, you would tell me if he
was worse?'

His expression was inscrutable. 'My dear Theo, how
you do leap to conclusions! Nothing has changed, including the doctor's strict injunction that your grandfather must have no visitors.'

A great surge of relief went through her. Of course, he
was simply trying to put the Comte off! Glancing at the
Frenchman through her lashes, she thought he was not
best pleased, but Lady Shadley came bustling up at that
moment to carry her off to be introduced to yet another
important personage, and she did not see either of them
again that night.

But on the following afternoon, when she was walking in Hyde Park at the fashionable hour with Lord
Alverton and his sister, Clarissa, she saw the Comte in
conversation with Selina and another gentleman. Selina
seemed to be on excellent terms with the Comte. As
Theo watched, she threw back her head to laugh at some
obvious witticism, at the same time laying her gloved
hand lightly on his arm.

The Comte looked up and inclined his head as he saw
Theo and her companions, and a moment later the two
groups had drawn level and somehow, after the initial

courtesies were at an end, they fell into step and began
strolling in the same direction.

Selina was like a new woman: as Theo had suspected,
she blossomed in company, and in a pretty grey dress
strewn with tiny violet flowers and a villager straw hat
with violet ribbons displaying her fair curls to advantage,
she belied her years. She greeted Theo with such an
affecting display of delighted surprise that their companions must have thought them the dearest and closest of
friends.

She was, she declared with just the right degree of
wistfulness, endeavouring to take up her life again now
that her period of mourning was almost at an end. 'I have
decided that I owe it to Aubrey. The poor boy cannot be
expected to feel about my dear Geoffrey as I do . . . he
hardly knew him, after all.'

Theo suppressed a smile and asked how Aubrey
did.

'Oh, my dear, he is different boy! I declare you would
hardly know him, so many friends he has made . . . he is
forever out with one or the other of them!'

'Well, I am very glad, so long as he is happy.'

'Happy? But of course he is happy!' Selina stared at
her, a faint note of sharpness entering her voice. 'Why
ever should he not be?'

Theo said hastily that there was no reason in the
world, but something in Selina's manner bothered her
slightly. She told herself she was being absurd and put it
from her mind.

It seemed at first no more than simple coincidence that
the Comte should be placed at her side so that they at
once began to converse agreeably together. The third
gentleman in the party, a Mr Fontley, at once took pity
on the shy seventeen-year-old Clarissa, which left Lord
Alverton and Selina to make the best of one another—a
situation which did not please either of them greatly.

Lord Alverton, being already head over ears in love

with Theo, both envied and resented the ease of address and sheer panache of the older man, while Selina was piqued by the Comte's readiness to set her aside in Theo's favour, the more so as he had until that moment been paying her the most singular attention. Although he could not even be contemplated as a husband, she fancied that he would be irresistible as a lover, and she had set her heart on him.

But no one casually observing the little group as it wove its way among a growing throng of colourful ladies and gentlemen who were taking advantage of the sunshine, strolling about beneath the trees, or nodding to acquaintances from the elegant carriages that formed a never-ending procession along the carriageways, would have remarked anything in the least untoward.

Only by very inconspicuous degrees did the gap between the couples begin to lengthen as the Comte with consummate skill contrived to fall a little way behind the others until he and Theo were out of earshot. She was at first simply amused—and if the truth be admitted, not a little flattered—that he should wish to single her out in this fashion.

And then he began to quiz her about her grandfather, and she realised with a little stab of mortification the purpose of this manoeuvring. Her tone was consequently a little sharp.

'Believe me, it would avail you little to see him, Monsieur le Comte. My Cousin Benedict did broach the matter to him after his first meeting with you, and my grandfather was quite adamant that he knew nothing of the whereabouts of your necklace.'

'But then,' he continued persuasively, 'when people reach a certain age and state of health, they do not always behave rationally and can even grow a little . . . forgetful? Do you not find this to be so?'

Theo gave him a very straight look. 'If by that you mean that my grandfather is in the habit of telling lies, monsieur . . . then I can only deplore your want of judgment!'

'*Doucement, mademoiselle*,' he murmured soothingly. 'I make no accusations, and certainly I intended no disrespect. It is simply that my case is desperate! I clutch at straws! You must understand that life has not treated me well . . . the years of exile and privation . . .'

'At least you were spared the fate of many,' she said, reluctant to succumb again to his persuasive charm.

'True,' he agreed wryly. 'My father got me away to Vienna before the worst happened. He even managed to provide for me at that time.' The Comte shrugged. 'But that was more than twenty-five years ago, mademoiselle . . . such funds as he was able to salvage have been used up. And now, with the Bourbons once more back on the throne in France, I am able to return to Paris, but to what? I find myself the only surviving member of the de Varron family, with scarcely a *sou* to my name—my own home gone, and my uncle and aunt's beautiful mansion, to which I am heir, in a state of total neglect, long since stripped of all its valuables.'

In spite of herself, Theo found herself feeling for him. And though both Benedict and her grandfather doubted his credentials, his story sounded genuine enough.

'I am sorry for you, Monsieur le Comte,' she said slowly, 'but surely it was only to be expected? The mob . . .?'

'Yes, yes!' He sounded suddenly impatient, a little of his cool charm deserting him. 'However, there was an old family retainer still living like a rat in the kitchens of the hotel . . . he swears that my aunt, as she was dragged away, screamed to the English milord, who came often and had been married to her sister, to "save the *Cascade*".'

A very strong element of uncertainty, the possibility that her grandfather *was* concealing something, made her say coolly: 'And you prefer the word of a servant to that of my grandfather?'

'Not so, mademoiselle!' He was very much the aristocrat as he stared down his patrician nose at her. 'I simply seek the truth.'

She flushed, feeling rebuked—undeservedly so. 'Then is the truth not most likely to be that the *Cascade* went the way of your aunt's other jewellery . . . seized and probably broken up by the mob to be sold or hoarded against hard times?'

He was silent a moment, and then he shrugged. 'That is the voice of reason. I am loath to accept it, but perhaps before long I must do so—apply myself to some genteel occupation—or starve!' The corner of his mouth tilted suddenly, and his eyes grew softly quizzical. 'You argue most eloquently, *ma chère cousine* . . . we are that, are we not? Your *grandpère* is fortunate to have you for his advocate. He loves you very much, no doubt?'

Theo thought of all that had happened between them, and involuntarily she smiled. 'I rather think that he does—now.' There was a silence between them for a few moments, then she said diffidently: 'Have things really come to such a pass for you?'

His mouth quirked up even more, but there was a terrible irony about his smile. 'As you remarked earlier—I escaped *Madame la Guillotine*. Who knows what life may yet have in store for me!'

The little cavalcade ahead of them had finally halted and was waiting for them to catch up.

Lord Alverton looked reproachfully at Theo and made a great point of saying that the Duchess had charged him most strictly with the task of delivering Miss Radlett into her hands by six o'clock, as they were promised to Lady Sefton for dinner.

The Comte, taking the hint, made his adieux, and the others did likewise. Clarissa, who had blossomed in the company of the kindly Mr Fontley, blushed as she bade him farewell—and Selina smiled brilliantly, but with such daggers in her eyes that Theo was glad she would not be called upon to bear her company.

A short distance away, a stanhope was drawn up at the side of the carriageway. Its single occupant, a dandy of the first stare, sat watching the group, his long white fingers curled convulsively around the ribbons. An acquaintance riding towards him slowed his mount in order to exchange civilities, and surprised upon Beau Radlett's face a look that could only be described as venomous.

CHAPTER
NINE

A LETTER HAD come from Shallowford. Theo took it
eagerly from the salver held out to her by Bracegirdle
and carried it up to her room, where she might read it
undisturbed.

There were in fact two letters—a short one from her
grandfather, couched very much in his usual abrupt
style, and a much longer one from Great-aunt Minta
enclosed within it. This rambled on in very much the
haphazard way she conversed, and was punctuated with
exclamation marks and blots . . . how quiet the house
was with everyone gone away, except that Edmund was
cross as a crab and roaring at everyone fit to bring on an
apoplexy . . . and partaking of curried mutton, which, as
she had warned him at the time, was guaranteed to
overset his digestion! And it did!

Theo, reading between the lines and smiling to herself
as she visualised the two of them squabbling like children, was suddenly brought up short by the next sentence. Her eyes sped across the page and then returned
to read more slowly: *Gorton*, the old lady ran on, *has
almost recovered from the painful bump he sustained to
his head last week . . . it was all most unfortunate and
Purley says he hasn't the least idea how the intruder could
have got in, Edmund having as you know a great aversion
to fresh air so that not a window in the house can be
opened without a sustained effort by several people from
within—and none of the doors forced! However, the man
was disturbed before he was able to lay hands on anything*

of value, and Edmund's day room was soon put to rights,
though at first sight you would suppose it to have been
struck by a tempest! My brother's wrath upon finding that
the villain had been allowed to escape left the servants
feeling in very similar case!

From here the letter reverted to commonplaces, but
Theo scanned it urgently hoping for some further reference or explanation, was thwarted, and finally threw it
down upon the bed.

Her first instinct was to rush down there immediately
to find out what really had happened, but the initial
panic quickly subsided and a measure of common sense
reasserted itself. There had been nothing untoward in
her grandfather's letter—and Great-aunt Minta was
given to odd quirks at times. Perhaps she had become
confused by some tiny incident—Gorton could have had
a mishap, anything! But if it had been serious, Benedict
would have known about it, and would have told her. He
had been at Shallowford only last week.

And then she remembered his curious curtness when
putting the Comte off—more than was called for, she
had thought at the time. This set in train a whole new lot
of suppositions. What if the intruder should be somehow
connected with the Comte's missing necklace? What if
the Comte were not the Comte at all, but merely an
opportunist out to lay his hands on a valuable heirloom?
The idea of him as a burglar was ludicrous, but he could
have employed someone . . . and Selina would have
been able to direct him to Lord Radlett's apartments.
What if Benedict had suspected?

Oh, heavens! Theo caught her spinning thoughts and
steadied them. She was worse than Great-aunt Minta,
making a fanciful plot out of something and nothing.
She might as well suspect Beau! The sooner she saw
Benedict and sought his reassurance, the better.

It was at this very point in her deliberations that
Bracegirdle came to inform her that Mr Benedict

Radlett was below in her grace's drawing room and craved a few moments of her time. Mindful of her surroundings, she forced her feet to take decorous steps while her spirit wanted to soar ahead.

Benedict turned from his contemplation of the view beyond the window as she entered.

'You must be a reader of minds!' she began without preamble, hurrying forward eagerly. 'How else could you have known that I wanted so much to talk with you?'

But there was no answering smile, no feeling of rapport. His face was set in its harshest lines as he watched her cross the room towards him in all the youthful freshness of her jonquil muslin dress, her hair swept back in a simple knot and her cheeks becomingly flushed as though with some inner excitement.

'I didn't. But I wanted words with you,' he said. His voice was clipped, and he saw her falter, look puzzled, and then come on, but more slowly, with the light dying out of her eyes.

'Is something wrong?' Her mind flew instinctively to Shallowford, so that she didn't immediately register his next words.

'You were, I believe, to be observed walking alone and conversing intimately with the so-called Comte de Varron in Hyde Park yesterday afternoon?'

Theo's eyes opened wide, taken aback not so much by the unexpectedness of the question, but rather by its nature and implications.

'Have you then reason to suppose that he is not what he purports to be?'

Benedict frowned. 'I have no idea at present, nor is it relevant. Come—you are being evasive. Were you or were you not?'

Theo's temper flared then, but she kept it in check— just.

'I find your question impertinent, and I don't believe I am obliged to answer it, cousin! You have no jurisdiction over my behaviour, and I deeply resent your implication that it is in any way wanting!'

His mouth was a thin sardonic line. 'Fine words, Theo, but wasted. I daresay any one of a hundred onlookers will have marked the truth.'

'In which case we can hardly be said to have been alone!' she retorted with a tight triumphant smile.

'Thank you. I think I am answered.'

'How satisfying for you!' She began to pace the room in an attempt to assuage her annoyance. 'I suppose I have Selina to thank for this piece of interference?'

'You may not care for Selina, but she is older and has been about the world a good deal more. She knows well that a man with de Varron's reputation . . .'

'Humgudgeon!' Theo declared, standing before him in a belligerent pose. 'She was furious because the Comte preferred my company to hers! And to say that we were alone is a piece of arrant nonsense. There were six of us, including Lord Alverton and his sister, and the Comte and I fell behind a little only because he wished to talk privately . . .' She stopped, looking a trifle ill at ease. 'About his past and present circumstances, and about his need to find the Diamond Waterfall,' she finished defiantly.

'Turning you up sweet, in fact,' he said dryly.

'Certainly not!' And then she bit her lip and said with incurable honesty, 'Oh, well—perhaps. But he didn't succeed!'

Benedict continued to regard her with an uncomfortable degree of penetration for a few moments, then a faint ironic smile crept into his eyes. 'So be it,' he said. 'I was clearly misinformed. I am sorry.'

She glared at him a moment more and then grinned ruefully. 'You do have a quite maddening way of disarming one, cousin!'

He laughed.

'Perhaps I can make amends. My curricle is at the

door. Would you care to take a drive?'

Theo looked demure. 'You don't think that people might look askance?'

'Sheathe your claws, young lady! I am resolved to be pleasant to you, no matter what the provocation.'

Theo walked to the door. 'Then I shall fetch my bonnet, and tell the Duchess where I am going.'

Later, driving down Piccadilly towards Green Park, Benedict asked what it was that she had wished to talk to him about. Theo had already been reminded by the sight of the letter lying on her bed when she was getting ready, and had but awaited an opportunity to speak. He listened without interruption and then said in his most off-hand way, 'Well, you know how the old lady is prone to exaggerate.'

But this was not good enough. 'Exaggerate, perhaps—but not fabricate, Benedict.' She studied his unhelpful profile and thought inconsequentially how like her grandfather's it was—arrogantly uncompromising. 'It did happen, didn't it? And you knew about it. Why didn't you tell me?'

'It was nothing—a trifling incident . . . and no lasting harm done.'

'But . . .'

'I knew you would worry . . .' He glanced briefly aslant at her. 'And I was right. Now, just forget it.'

His tone warned her not to pursue the argument, and Theo knew better than to try at that precise moment, but she resolved to get to the bottom of it one way or another. However, for the present, the day was agreeably sunny, with a faint drifting scent of blossom on the air, and as they turned in at the park gates a scene of peace and tranquillity lay before them, temporarily lulling her fears.

On the grass beneath the trees children played under the eye of a watchful nursemaid, their voices mingling happily with the soft crunch of carriage-wheels on the path. As the curricle rounded a clump of shrubbery, a white stuccoed building came into view, which Benedict explained belonged to the park ranger—and near by, to her delight, a small herd of cows grazed contentedly in the charge of a cowman, with milkmaids in attendance appropriately dressed.

'Perhaps you would care to take a glass of milk, coz—straight from the cow?'

Theo threw him a suspicious look. 'You *are* roasting me?'

'Certainly not. It is a particular feature of the park.' He returned her look with blandness. 'I take it the idea don't appeal to you?'

She said not, and he laughed.

They drove back in a spirit of amity which Theo was loath to spoil. However, something had been on her mind since the previous day, and she very much wished to clarify it.

'Benedict, have you seen anything of Aubrey since he came to town?'

'Not a lot,' he said drily. 'But then we don't really frequent the same clubs. Nevertheless, I believe I can hazard a pretty accurate guess as to how he is passing his time!'

'Oh dear! Something Selina said did make me wonder.'

Benedict gave his attention to negotiating the turning out through the Bath Gate, and then continued, 'His behaviour is no worse than that of many a young buck turned loose on the town for the first time, though I don't care for his companions. Wild as the devil, some of them.'

Theo's heart sank. 'I had the impression from Selina that they were highly desirable.'

His mouth curled sardonically. 'What Selina means is that they are—some of them, at least—from families moving in first circles!'

'But Aubrey can't afford that kind of connection, surely?'

'True, but when did that ever stop anyone?' Benêdict glanced at her briefly. 'Don't get involved, Theo. The boy isn't your responsibility.'

If he had been looking at her at that moment he would have observed the stubborn thrust of her chin, but she was very quiet for the remainder of the journey. Only when they drew up once more at Grosvenor Square did she blurt out the question that had been on the top of her tongue.

'Benedict—how much does it cost to purchase a cavalry commission?'

He secured the reins before turning upon her with frowning severity. 'What did you say?'

'It's what Aubrey really wants to do, though Selina doesn't know about it and I promised not to tell her,' she said, rushing on before her courage failed her. 'It could be the answer to Aubrey's difficulties . . . and I thought, if it wouldn't cost too much . . .'

'No, Theo. You can't afford it.'

'I do have money,' she said defensively. 'Money of my own.'

'Fine. But don't throw it away on something that is rank foolishness!' He saw that she was about to argue further. 'The only way the army is likely to solve Aubrey's problems is in the event of a war—and that we don't have at present. Putting Aubrey in a pretty uniform with time to kick his heels would be quite as dangerous for him as his present situation.' His voice was cuttingly ironic. 'What that boy needs is a spot of hard work to occupy his time, so that he can't get into mischief!'

Theo's bosom heaved with indignation. 'You speak from experience, of course!'

For a moment she thought she had gone too far, then to her surprise he laughed, albeit a trifle wryly. 'As you say—I speak from experience, sweet coz.' Quite deliberately he turned the conversation, nodding in the direction of a gleaming phaeton which was being walked in the charge of a groom.

'You had best go in. If I am not mistaken, your ardent admirer will be kicking his heels in the Duchess's drawing room.'

Benedict declined to accompany her, saying with maddening off-handedness that he had no desire to watch Alverton making calf's eyes at her.

Theo was given little time to ponder on what Benedict had said. Lord Alverton was the bearer of an invitation from his mama, who was arranging a picnic for the following afternoon, in the woods near Merton, and begged that the Duchess and Miss Radlett would be of the party.

'Do say that you will come, ma'am,' he urged shyly, his pleasant face creased in earnest lines. 'We are to be quite a large gathering—mostly young people. It will be the most tremendous fun.' He glanced at the Duchess, who sat watching the exchange between himself and her young protégée with a happy complacence. 'Her grace is agreeable to the arrangement and awaits only your word on't.'

Theo found herself wishing that he were a little less like a good-natured puppy, but she could not hurt his feelings, and could only hope that he would not read too much into her acceptance.

'If he had a tail, I feel sure it would have been wagging,' she observed impulsively as the door closed behind him. And then, remembering how close the Duchess and Lady Shadley were, wondered if she had been injudicious.

But the Duchess only said with a twinkle, 'Yes, he is a trifle eager, my love—but so very eligible, and not an ounce of vice in him! My Henry was just such a one in his youth—and I can swear to it, they make most excellent uncomplaining husbands in the fullness of time!'

Theo murmured something unintelligible which appeared to satisfy her grace, but this passing reference to the Duke brought into Theo's mind a vivid mental image of the quietly courteous but almost timid elderly gentleman to whom she had been introduced on one of his rare appearances in Grosvenor Square. Until that moment she had supposed her hostess to be a lively widow, but the Duchess had declared playfully that Henry was of a very 'bookish' disposition, and spent most of his time at his club or in the country. And even as she accepted this explanation, a small voice inside Theo was protesting that the very last quality she would want in a husband would be meekness!

And later that night after yet another soirée, when she found sleep hard to come by, she finally forsook her bed and padded across to the window, where she threw back the curtains and curled up on the wide ledge to contemplate the way her life was going.

It would be untrue to say she was not enjoying herself; each day had still a sufficient novelty about it to entrance her. But for how long? How long would it be before the unremitting round of pleasure began to pall—before the thought of exchanging the same meaningless pleasantries with the same empty-headed people became tiresome? Even now she found their conversation for the most part to be tediously concerned with dress, social precedence and scandal—with just occasionally, if one was lucky enough to meet a fellow spirit, the chance to discuss something a little deeper.

Perhaps the fault lies in me, she thought with a sudden quirk of humour. *What overweening conceit, after all, gives me the right to think myself better than others? No, not better*, she amended stubbornly, *but different.*

Theo looked out upon the tall regimented ranks of chimney-pots outlined against the starry sky, thought of Shallowford, and sighed. Perhaps if she threw herself into the social round with renewed enthusiasm, the time would pass the sooner and then she could go home. It was strange how, without consciously willing it, Shallowford had replaced Philadelphia in her mind as home.

As she was about to close the curtains, she became aware of a light moving intermittently in the house opposite—Radlett House. But there wasn't anyone there at present—at least, so she had been given to understand, although she supposed there must be some sort of caretaker. She stood for a long time watching, unable to bring herself to close the curtain. The light finally moved from the downstairs room, and she was just berating herself for allowing her imagination to run riot when it appeared in the room above. A vague uncomfortable prickling stirred at the back of her neck. What kind of caretaker wandered the house in the early hours of the morning? *Draw the curtain*, she admonished herself sternly, *and stop leaping to conclusions!*

'Do you happen to know, ma'am,' she asked the Duchess on the following day, 'if Radlett House has any servants in residence?'

The Duchess looked up from the list she was compiling for the ball she intended to give shortly in Theo's honour. Her manner, as ever when not concerned with essentials, was vague.

'I believe there to be an elderly couple on the premises, my love. Why? Did you wish to see over it? I'm sure something could be arranged. Your cousin Benedict would take you . . . or Beau. No, perhaps not. One ought to like him, of course . . . but . . .' She shuddered delicately. 'But, now I think of it . . . I have seen Beau leaving the house quite recently . . . when was it? Still, that is neither here nor there . . . He can't be living there, for one would know, and besides, Edmund would never countenance it!' Her voice sank dramatically. 'He can't abide Beau, you know, which, one must own, is not to be wondered at . . . such a cold posturing man! But I suppose he must be invited to the ball. Now, where does he have his rooms . . .?'

Theo, only half listening, looked out across the square at the empty house, her thoughts running riot. First the break-in at Shallowford, and now lights at night where there should be no lights. Was it being fanciful to imagine a connection? Somebody searching for something . . . the Diamond Waterfall? Oh, no, she was making a melodrama out of nothing! Who knew about it, after all?

'Theo, my love?' The Duchess's tone was gently reproachful.

She pulled herself together and walked quickly across the room to stand dutifully at her grace's side.

'I thought that we might go through the arrangements one more time . . . to see if there is anything I have forgotten. We must remember to notify the officers of the watch and the link-boys, to ensure that the road is kept clear. Mellicent Graham's rout last week was such a sad scramble . . . carriages blocking the way for hours! Now, about your Aunt Selina? She is all but out of black gloves, is she not? I know she goes into company . . . more perhaps than one might consider quite . . . but then, it is not for me to be judging others, and one would not wish to be thought inhospitable! And there is that *very* charming French Comte . . .'

Selina could have learned of the necklace from him, Theo mused, her thoughts drawn irresistibly back. And he had almost certainly approached Beau. And Benedict. All of whom, with the exception of the Comte, had a perfect right to enter either house without resorting to subterfuge. Unless they did not wish to be seen to be there—or had employed someone else to search for them.

'My love . . . are you quite well?'

Oh heavens! This will not do! Theo met the concerned

eyes of her hostess and murmured something about having slept badly. The Duchess was all concern, and very conscious of feeling a fraud, Theo made a determined effort to put the whole affair out of her mind before it became an obsession.

CHAPTER
TEN

THEO HAD hoped that Benedict was exaggerating when he spoke of Aubrey's involvement with the wrong kind of companions, but she was to see for herself on her next visit to the theatre.

This was one pleasure of which she would never tire. From the moment of entering the carriage that was to take them there, she loved the clamour of the traffic when each vehicle seemed intent upon self-destruction—lamps stabbing the darkness, wheels shuddering over the cobbles, and the coachmen shouting at one another, each jostling for the best position. The closer one came to the theatre, the more did their exploits resemble some great gladiatorial spectacle worthy of a Roman amphitheatre.

And in the auditorium itself, there was a magic that encompassed her long before the play began, a shimmering, ever-moving pageant of bejewelled ladies in exquisite gowns. It mattered not one whit that her own attire, by comparison, paled utterly into insignificance, because she always had the feeling that she was an invisible onlooker, privileged to enjoy the spectacle without ever being part of it.

Lord Alverton, whose party this was, would have refuted the poor view she took of herself, had he but guessed it. As it was, he took his duties as host very seriously, ushering everyone into his mama's box while carefully reserving the prime position for Theo. And as he relieved her of her wrap and settled her comfortably in her chair, he contrived to let her know how perfectly delightful she looked.

Theo received the eager compliment with gratitude, knowing it to be partial, yet pleased none the less. She was quite unaware that more than one over-decked lady turned to look after her with something very like envy in their breasts. It was not merely the charming simplicity of her apricot silk dress with its ribbons caught high under the brief bodice by a knot of fresh flowers, matching the ones that nestled in her hair. It was the look of rapt enjoyment shining out of her eyes that really set her apart from the rest.

She became so immersed in the play that she was all the more annoyed by the increasing amount of noise that issued from the pit where all the young bucks and dandies made sport of the actors and each other. During the interval she stared down at them as though she might make them aware of her disapproval—and found herself looking into Aubrey's eyes.

Just for an instant they registered pleasure at seeing her, and then one of his companions, a bored-looking young man with extravagantly high collar points, a spotted cravat and a green coat, followed the direction of his glance and leaned forward to make some comment, obviously about her. Aubrey looked uncomfortable, but he laughed and turned away.

For Theo a little of the pleasure went out of the evening. She had not expected to see Aubrey again, but later as she was waiting with the rest of the party for their carriage, a small group of young bloods came swaggering past, their progress noisy and none too steady, and one slightly behind the rest.

'Hello, Aubrey,' she said quietly.

He stood, peering at her. The light was not good, but she thought he was flushed, his eyes red-rimmed.

'Cousin Theo.' It was the half-sulky voice she knew so well, but thicker—the words slurring a little.

'I'm sorry you didn't enjoy the play,' she said.

A youthful world-weary voice ahead drawled, 'Do come along, Radlett, dear boy—if you are with us. Unless, that is, you prefer your cousin's company to the charms of pretty Nell Beckett!'

There was a look of confusion in his young face, and she said with swift pleading, 'Don't go with them, Aubrey!'

His mouth grew stubborn. 'Course I'm going. They like me, y'see. And you're wrong about the play.' He giggled foolishly. 'We enjoyed ourselves no end!'

The encounter left Theo deeply troubled, and on the following afternoon when the Duchess had gone out to visit an elderly relation, she took a hack and directed the driver to Upper Wimpole Street.

A handsome young footman in livery—one of a pair—opened the door to her. (How like Selina, she thought drily, to surround herself with such personable servants!) She was shown first into a side parlour, and then the second footman came to take her up to a sunny withdrawing room.

It was immediately evident that she had chosen an inconvenient moment, for Selina was not alone. The Comte de Varron turned from the mirrored embrasure near the window as she entered, his fingers unhurriedly putting the finishing touches to his cravat, and plainly amused by her embarrassment as he made her his bow.

And Selina? Theo had seldom seen such a change in anyone. She wore a floating peignoir in palest blue silk which mirrored her eyes, and her golden curls tumbled over her shoulders, making her look, at first glance, like a girl. No, not quite a girl—there was something altogether too . . . ripe was the word which sprang unbidden to Theo's mind, and she blushed for its implications. She had seen already how Selina could blossom in company, but had never quite thought of her as this ravishing, desirable creature until now . . . and to see her mouth prettily pouting, one who was none too pleased at having her *tête-à-tête* curtailed.

The Comte, however, was more than equal to the situation as he raised Theo's hand to his lips and murmured compliments which, whether she believed them or not, were balm to her agitated spirits.

'But I am a most fortunate man,' he insisted, handing her to a chair. 'To find myself suddenly in the company of not one, but two, beautiful young ladies!'

Theo found it difficult in his company to broach the subject of Aubrey as she had wished, and tided over the awkwardness of explaining the reason for her visit by mentioning the Duchess's ball and hoping that they would be able to attend. Mollified somewhat by the prospect of mingling with the cream of society, Selina became more affable, and presently when the Comte showed no sign of leaving, Theo rose, saying casually that she had hoped to see Aubrey.

'One would have thought,' Selina said archly, 'that you would have little time for a mere boy like Aubrey with suitors like Lord Alverton clamouring for your company!'

It crossed Theo's mind that Aubrey would be something of an embarrassment to Selina . . . too much a reminder of her years. It was a disturbing thought, and it made her persist, until, grudgingly, one of the footmen was summoned and offered the information that Mr Fane had gone out some hour or more since.

Theo pulled on her gloves. 'Then perhaps you would ask him when you next see him,' she said casually, 'whether he would care to take a ride with me one morning.'

Selina shrugged agreement, but could not guarantee anything. 'He is always out, these days,' she said vaguely.

'Do you have a carriage waiting, Miss Radlett?' the Comte inquired politely, and when she was obliged to admit not, he insisted that he must be allowed the privilege of driving her home.

'There is no need,' she said quickly, seeing Selina's tightening mouth. 'I am sure I can procure a cab.'

But he was adamant, and she found herself presently being handed into a smart tilbury with a very handsome blood mare between the shafts. Quite a turnout, she thought, for a gentleman who was reduced to self-confessed penury.

As if interpreting her thoughts, he said drolly, 'I lodge with a most accommodating acquaintance who permits me the use of his equipage.'

'You are fortunate in your friends, monsieur,' she returned politely. And then, because his easy acceptance of what amounted to charity seemed so inexplicably at odds with someone of his supposedly proud aristocratic origins, her doubts rose up once more.

'Do you mean to remain long in England?' she asked impulsively, and immediately wished she had not, for a note of austerity entered his voice.

'The answer to that lies partly with you, mademoiselle.'

'Oh, come!' she exclaimed, irritated as much with herself for permitting him the opening as with his intransigence. 'I thought we had settled all that.'

'How can one consider such things to be settled when no conclusion is yet reached?' He looked aslant at her. 'I had hoped you would have given the matter further thought.'

'There is nothing more that I can do, Monsieur le Comte,' she said flatly. 'I thought I had made that very plain.'

'*Eh bien*—that is a pity.'

That was all he said, but with such a curious inflection in his voice that an involuntary little *frisson* of unease crawled up Theo's spine. She tried to dismiss it, but her mouth felt dry and she could think of nothing to say.

They were moving through the streets at a fairly spanking pace, and as she was still unfamiliar with the layout of London's thoroughfares, she had no way of knowing where they were.

'Was the Duchess aware that you intended to visit the ravishing Selina?' he asked presently, breaking the silence.

It was on the tip of her tongue to say No, but instead some instinct led her to prevaricate. 'I believe I may have mentioned it.'

'She would not, I think, have countenanced your coming alone.' He smiled at her, but there was a reckless glitter in his eyes that was deeply disturbing. 'So—only consider, *chère mademoiselle*, how simple a matter it would be to arrange that you disappear!'

Theo drew a breath and strove to remain calm. 'Kidnap, monsieur?' she said lightly, as though discussing an interesting hypothesis. 'How very melodramatic! And so difficult to carry through single-handed, for you may be sure that I would not submit willingly to such Turkish treatment!'

She thought she saw a momentary glimmer of appreciation, but it was not reflected in his voice.

'Then one would be obliged to render you senseless—it would be but the matter of a moment.'

'How very . . . unpleasant!'

'*Vraiment*. It would naturally grieve me greatly to cause you pain, but necessity can occasionally drive one to take disagreeable measures!'

Theo was by now almost convinced that he meant it; they were in a part of London that she didn't recognise, the streets had grown progressively seedier, and there would seem little chance of summoning anyone to her aid. Her only hope was that he had evolved the idea on the spur of the moment, for if this were so, she might yet talk him out of it.

'Well,' she said as humorously as she could manage,

'I'm sure that your sentiments do you credit, though I fear they will do little to console me for my broken head, or whatever other gruesome fate you may have in store for me!'

It was clear that her attitude puzzled him, but his driving still hadn't slackened pace, and soon they would be out of town. It took every ounce of will-power she possessed to keep the tell-tale tremor of fear from her voice.

'Am I allowed to know where you would take me, or how you mean to make use of this abduction, kidnapping, call it what you will?'

She thought at first that he would not answer. Perhaps he hadn't given the matter that much thought; perhaps, she concluded with a rather disagreeable hollow feeling, it might have been wiser not to prompt him now to do so. She stole a glance at his profile and was not reassured.

'You are pleased to jest, my dear young lady,' he said with some deliberation. 'But I can arrange a place quite simply—and then, as I see it, there are at least two options for me.'

Theo held her breath.

'On the one hand, I think your grandfather might of a sudden become much more . . . accommodating, were he to learn that your life was in jeopardy. Do you not agree?'

She let her breath go on a little sigh. 'He might,' she agreed gravely. 'In which case, always supposing that he has your Diamond Waterfall, you could conceivably get it back, though I should warn you he is a man who hates to be bested!'

'He is not alone in that!' came the swift reply.

'No.' She frowned. 'What is much more likely, however, is that the shock will kill him.'

He was silent for a moment.

'Well, I should be sorry for that,' he said in a clipped voice. 'But I can hardly be blamed if he chooses to hold what does not rightfully belong to him. *Diable!*'

From nowhere, an urchin dashed out into their path. It seemed that nothing could save him from being mangled, and indeed, as the Comte, hauling back on the reins and pulling frantically to the off, brought them to a plunging halt, one of the hooves struck the child's body a sickening blow.

Theo was thrown against the Comte with considerable force, and by the time they had untangled themselves and climbed down, a small crowd had gathered.

The Comte's angry protestations that he could not have avoided the boy brought dark mutterings of 'bloody Frogs, wild driving', and 'fancy swells as didn't give a cuss for folks worse off than themselves'.

Theo ignored the veiled threats and ran to kneel beside the two women already at the boy's side. The Comte muttered a Gallic curse, seized the youth nearest to him, pressed a coin into his hand, and promised another if he minded the tilbury. Then he strode away to stand at Theo's shoulder.

'Dead, that's what the little bleeder is, all on account of you!' shouted one of the women, glaring accusingly up at him. He gave her his most austere stare, and after a moment her eyes slid away.

'Does the boy still live?' he demanded tautly of Theo.

She made no answer, being intent upon seeking a pulse. At last finding a thin thread, she began to run her hands gently over the child's emaciated body.

'Is either of you his mother?' she asked, as pressure on his ribs drew a faint moan.

'' is mam's dead, more'n a year now,' offered one of her companions.

'And the father?'

The woman shrugged.

'Well, the child isn't dead, but he does need a doctor.' Theo looked up, conscious of a lack of response. 'Who is responsible for him?'

'Reckon 'e fends for 'imself,' someone muttered. 'Thievin' mostly.'

'Well, he can't fend for himself now.' Theo stood up, the light of battle in her eyes. 'So, who among you is willing to take him in?'

The crowd melted away with surprising suddenness, until only a few women remained.

'The Widow Brodie'd most likely take 'im,' said a large rough-looking woman, wiping her hands on a none-too-clean apron. 'But as for doctors . . .' She shrugged.

Theo looked at her uncertainly, but there was little choice. 'Where does this Widow Brodie live?' she asked quietly.

'End house—that side.' The woman jerked her head.

'I shall take him,' said the Comte, lifting the boy with surprising gentleness as Theo urged him to have a care for his rib, which she was fairly sure was broken, as was his left wrist.

If there was something incongruous in the sight of the suave, elegant Frenchman striding down the mean street with his ragged and undoubtedly lousy burden, he seemed unaware of it, and Theo was too preoccupied to notice.

The gaunt, middle-aged woman who opened the door to them was not upon first encounter an encouraging sight, but though sharp-tongued, she bade them to come in and lay the boy on a sagging couch against the back wall. Theo observed that though the room was shabby, it was spotlessly clean.

She explained briefly what had happened and the extent of the boy's injuries as far as she could determine them.

'I'll see 'im right,' said Mrs Brodie. 'The wrist's a clean break, and as for his ribs . . . well, I reckon I can bind them up as good as any doctor.'

'You will need money,' said the Comte, who had

stood aloof from the discussion. He tossed a handful of coins on to the window's table, and looked a little helplessly at Theo. 'For food and . . .' He shrugged.

'It is enough,' said the widow dourly.

'*Merci.*' He bowed formally.

'Well, then . . .' Theo smiled and moved to the door. 'We are very grateful to you.'

'Can't hardly let the little perisher snuff it, can I?' come the sharp retort. 'He's not a bad kid, for all that 'e thieves! Reckon it en't his fault.'

'No,' said Theo.

She walked rather blindly out into the sunshine and back up the road a little ahead of the Comte. The boy into whose charge he had entrusted the tilbury was still at his post, valiantly defending it against a horde of inquisitive children, and upon receiving his promised reward, ran off, with the rest in hot pursuit.

It was very quiet when they had gone. Theo stood with one hand resting on the gleaming panel of the tilbury feeling suddenly weak with exhaustion. She was very much aware of de Varron standing near by, and presently lifted her eyes to meet his.

'Well!' she exclaimed on a faint sigh.

He was regarding her with a look—part bewildered, part quizzical. 'I am asking myself,' he said in a wondering way, 'why are you still here?'

She returned his look steadily. 'I am waiting for you to take me home, monsieur—if you will be so kind as to help me up?'

He came forward then, and with his hand firm beneath her arm, stood very close staring down at her with a fierce intensity.

'You had every chance to escape me—why did you not attempt it?'

Theo studied his face. At such close quarters it showed a myriad of fine lines that lent the handsome features their particular stamp of distinction and

maturity—and, for added measure, just a fascinating hint
of decadence. His eyes, narrowed in frowning concentration, were very blue—and clearly puzzled by her lack
of fear. She was a little puzzled herself.

'I'm not sure,' she said with quiet deliberation.
'Perhaps I saw something in you just now that made the
thought of flight unnecessary. You see, it seemed to me
that a man who could show so much concern for an
unknown child could not be half so callous as he was
endeavouring to paint himself to me.'

Having thus effectively deprived him of speech, she
added with the ghost of a smile, 'So please—may we go
now? The Duchess will be wondering where I am.'

He shook his head as if in a daze. '*Incroyable!*' he
murmured, and without another word, handed her up
into the seat.

The equipage swayed on its springs as he leaped up
beside her and took up the reins. Just before he gave the
patient mare the office to start, he looked at Theo again
with the glimmer of a smile.

'I wonder,' he mused. 'But for the accident—would I
have gone through with it?'

'That, thank God, we shall never know, monsieur,'
she replied with devout sincerity, and leaned back with
closed eyes.

They were well on their way when she opened them
again.

'You know,' she mused thoughtfully, 'I guess that if
Grandpa does have that necklace, his main objection to
admitting it lies in his fear that you are an impostor.'

'But you do not think this?'

She considered. 'There was a time when I wasn't
sure.'

'And now?' He could scarcely keep the urgency out of
his voice.

'Now? Oh, now,' she concluded, 'I am inclined to
believe you.'

He laughed, and gave the reins a slap that sent the little mare dancing faster. '*Merci bien, ma chère Mademoiselle Théo!* And you will help me, yes?'

'I will do what I can,' she said, smiling at his sudden, almost boyish, ebullience. 'Though I'm not sure how much help I *can* be, other than to write to Grandpa.' She thought a moment. 'What will you do with the necklace if it should be found?'

He cast her a speculative look. 'Nothing is certain, but this acquaintance with whom I stay—he also has an acquaintance—not of noble family, you understand, but a man of immense wealth—he has, I believe, many factories!'

Theo was shocked. 'You would sell it, monsieur? And to such a one?'

'Ah, no,' he assured her. 'Not unless all else fails. The wealthy factory-owner has a daughter—a plump little pudding. *Eh bien*, this child, upon learning of the beauty of the *Cascade*, longs to own such a prize—and papa would like for his daughter to be a Comtesse . . .'

'So you would sell yourself,' she said, disappointed.

The Comte shrugged. 'So what would you, mademoiselle? In France, a *mariage de convenance* is commonplace. The little pudding will be content to be a *grande dame* with her *Cascade Diamant*, papa will be puffed with pride and will pay handsomely for the restoration of the de Varron fortunes—and I shall thus take my rightful place once more in society.'

'I suppose so,' Theo said reluctantly. 'But it all sounds very . . . unromantic.'

He put back his head and laughed. 'Ah, *chère mademoiselle*, in France we seldom confuse romance and marriage!' He gave her a droll look. 'Now I have really shocked you!'

'Not at all,' she said primly, and turned her thoughts once more to the main stumbling-block to the realisation of his expectations. 'Would papa not agree to the marriage without the necklace?'

'Perhaps,' said the Comte a little austerely. 'But one has one's pride. With the *Cascade*, at least I am not empty-handed!'

'Have you any idea how many people here know about the Diamond Waterfall, apart from the girl and her papa?'

'It is hardly the kind of information one bandies about, you understand,' he said in his droll way. 'Such questions as I have ventured to ask have been confined solely to members of your family.'

'So Cousin Beau knows about it. And Selina?'

He nodded. 'And your cousin Benedict, of course. He was the first to know.'

'Yes.' She thought about the mysterious intruder. 'Did you ever visit Radlett House in Grosvenor Square?'

'No—because he—your cousin Benedict—informed me that my lord was ill and living in the country.'

A further unpleasant thought crossed her mind. 'Did Aubrey know about the necklace?'

'That I cannot vouch for.' The Comte glanced at her ruefully. 'Such an interrogation! Where does it all lead, I ask myself!'

'I'm not too sure,' Theo admitted. 'But we shall see.' She noted with relief that they were approaching Hyde Park. From the number of people about, she guessed that the hour must be late. 'I hope the Duchess hasn't set up a hue and cry,' she said with a half-nervous laugh.

'It is not too late to turn back,' he suggested pro-vocatively. 'I could then pursue the second of my alternatives.'

'Oh yes,' she exclaimed. 'I never did discover what that was?'

He threw her a glance brimming with mockery. 'I thought to seduce you.' And as her eyes opened wide and faint colour stole into her cheeks, he continued, 'You would then be obliged to marry me, your *grand-*

père must perforce accept the situation, deliver to me my property and his grandchild also—a much more agreeable prize than the little pudding, *hein?* And romantic!'

The sheer effrontery of it was too much for Theo. She succumbed to laughter which was part relief, part appreciation.

'But not anything like so financially rewarding!' she gasped. 'No, Monsieur le Comte, I think you had better hold to your original plan—you have many irresistible qualities, but I don't think I would be very comfortable having you for a husband!'

His eyes twinkled. 'But then I had not thought to make you comfortable, mademoiselle!'

His comical expression sent her into fresh whoops, and she was still laughing as they passed a small group of people talking beside a drawn-up carriage, and she found herself looking down into Benedict's eyes.

CHAPTER
ELEVEN

THE REPERCUSSIONS of that afternoon were to cast a
shadow over the days that followed. Theo arrived home
to a gentle but firm reprimand from the Duchess for
disappearing without telling anyone where she was
going.

'Independence may be all very fine, my love, but too
much of it can lead to misunderstandings!'

Her eyes had opened wide at the sight of her somewhat dishevelled charge, but a carefully edited account
of the afternoon's events, although it had her tut-tutting,
appeared to satisfy her. Theo, however, was left with an
annoying sense of guilt that she had been less than
honest, which in turn left her in no mood to deal with
Benedict when he came.

That he would come she had no doubt; but her hope
that she might have gained the safety of her room had
been foiled by her interview with the Duchess, so that
they were crossing the hall together when he was admitted. The sight of the Duchess stayed him momentarily.
Then he bowed punctiliously and came on, the lines of
his face harshly drawn, his voice dangerously clipped.

'Servant, ma'am. Permit me, if you will, the favour of
a few words with my cousin.'

Her grace, from several steps up the staircase, looked
down on the two young people; the antagonism between
them was almost palpable.

'Oh la!' she exclaimed comically. 'Very well, sir—if
dear Theo is agreeable! But do not keep her, I beg of

you—and do not put her in bad humour, for you will
remember that we go to Almack's this evening!'

Theo, with one hand already on the banister rail,
toyed with the notion of denying him his few words and
taking to her heels, but there was a look about him at
that moment which gave her pause. He was just careless
enough of the conventions to make his reaction uncertain (vastly unjust, she railed inwardly, when he
expected complete conformity from her!), and she
had no wish to embarrass the Duchess in front of her
servants.

So she tossed her head at him and led the way across
the hall to the small saloon.

'Well?' she demanded, when the door had closed
behind them. The yellow sparks were very much in
evidence in her flashing eyes. 'I give you fair warning
that I am in no mood to listen to a tirade of abuse!'

'Perhaps you would have preferred the veiled ridicule
of the people I was with as you drove past?'

Theo drummed the little bureau at her side with
impatient fingers. 'If people choose to make ill-
mannered comment, that is their misfortune.'

'And yours, believe me! For if the patronesses of
Almack's come to hear of it, do you suppose they will let
you through their doors again?'

'I don't give *that*'—she snapped her fingers angrily—
'for the patronesses of Almack's—or for anyone else
who cares more about social niceties than about people
themselves!'

His mouth was a thin line. 'And what of the Duchess,
who has gone to so much trouble on your behalf? Do you
snap your fingers at her also?'

Immediately she was stricken with conscience, which
served only to make her the more angry. 'Oh, this is
ridiculous!' she said in a low trembling voice. 'Of what
do I stand accused? Of driving in a perfectly acceptable
fashion with a gentleman who is a distant cousin? I have

done so with you more than once, and quite fail to see where the difference lies.'

'My dear good girl, there is every difference in the world! Have you seen your appearance?'

With little regard for her feelings, Benedict seized her by the shoulders and dragged her across to a pier-glass set in one of the room's several alcoves. She saw, with something little short of horror, that the skirt of her green redingote was dusty and streaked with dirt where she had knelt in the road. Her close-fitting hat, still slightly askew from the accident, had permitted a tangled strand of hair to escape its confines, and a further streak of dirt disfigured her face. No wonder her grace had stared. A sorry sight, indeed! The reflection did little to assuage her temper.

'And as for acceptable behaviour,' he drawled with withering sarcasm, 'there was little of it apparent in the unseemly display of mirth which I was witness to!'

'So I was laughing? I had not realised that that, too, was a crime in society's eyes! It seems to me that the sooner I return to the country, the better we shall all be suited!' Theo made a futile gesture, her eyes stinging. 'As for my disarray, it has a cause, but there is no earthly reason why I should divulge it to you. You have absolutely no authority to censure me!'

'Very true.' He ground the words out. 'And you may thank heaven for it, for if I had, you would get more than a verbal dressing-down, believe me!'

'Oh, you are insufferable! I will hear no more!'

She pushed blindly past him, but his hand shot out to grasp her wrist, staying her flight.

'Keep away from the Comte de Varron, Theo. His kind are not for you!'

'He is more of a gentleman than you, cousin!' she cried, quite forgetting how short a time since she had had cause to doubt it. Her eyes glittered with unshed tears so that she could not see his face, and, unable to free herself, she fell to goading him the more; there was even a strange kind of excitement in seeing how far she could push him. Her voice broke on a wild laugh as she concluded: 'If the idea were not so preposterous, one might conclude that you were jealous!'

She heard his breath sucked in. The next moment he had pulled her hard against him, and his mouth on hers was like a punishment, compelling her surrender with an angry, almost brutal intensity that invaded every fibre of her being. She couldn't breathe, and yet she seemed full of rushing air, and though her senses spun with the force of some violent emotion, she knew that it wasn't fear, or even anger.

When he at last released her, she made a small incoherent whimpering sound—and as his face swam into focus, she saw that his eyes were strangely glittering. As she ran for the door, she heard him say with a kind of groan, *'Oh, damn!'*

It was some time before Theo could compose herself. Never in her wildest imaginings could she have dreamed of anyone treating her as Benedict had done. It was an assault in every sense of the word—and, worst of all, the thing that shamed her to her very toes, was that somewhere in the middle of it she had lost all desire to fight him.

Maddie watched with troubled eyes as her young mistress paced the bedchamber in a state of great agitation until at last she sank on to the stool in front of the dressing-table with her head in her hands.

'Will I be taking a message to her grace, Miss Theo? For you'll not be wishing to go out this night, I'm thinkin'. All this gadding and such . . . I never did hold with it!'

Her words seemed at first to have gone unheeded, but just as Maddie was about to take the matter into her own hands, Miss Theo uttered a deep shuddering sigh, lifted her head, and then, as though coming to from a great distance, sprang to her feet.

'Heavens, we must hurry!' she cried, almost as though nothing had happened (though not quite), and at once began to pull impatiently at the fastenings of her redingote—in which she might well have been tramping through a midden, from the look of it, thought Maddie.

With the shedding of the dress, Theo resolved to put all that had happened out of her mind.

'I promised the Duchess most faithfully that I wouldn't be late,' she said as Maddie fastened her into a gown of peach-bloom crepe with tiny ivory flowers scattered across the brief bodice. 'She has set so much store by this evening, and in the circumstances I must do all I can to please her!'

This last meant little to the maid, but she reckoned that if looking well was anything to go by, she'd never seen Miss Theo look better, a sentiment echoed by Monsieur Henri, the Duchess's hairdresser, who proclaimed with great enthusiasm that the delicate hue of mademoiselle's gown was *ravissant*—and set off her beautiful hair to perfection.

Peach satin slippers and a pair of pretty ivory gloves strewn with peach flowers completed an elegant toilet which made the young American much admired at Almack's that evening. It seemed to those who knew her that Miss Radlett sparkled as never before. She certainly made a determined effort to be at her best, and the knowledge that one or two unkind comments were circulating about what were being termed her 'colonial manners' only served to put her even more on her mettle.

'If only you are not censured by those who matter, my love,' whispered her grace. 'We can, of course, count on dear Lady Sefton for support, and I believe I can convince Lady Jersey that it is no more than spiteful tittle-tattle. Thank goodness Mrs Drummond-Burrell is not here tonight . . . she is a very high stickler indeed! Ah, see . . .' She let her breath go on a little sigh of relief. 'Here is Lord Alverton arrived . . . and he has eyes for no one but you, so I believe we may be easy.'

Lord Alverton was indeed so smitten that he could think nothing Miss Radlett might do worthy of censure. When his mama had ventured in the most amiable way to remark on her occasional free and easy ways, he had pokered up at once and declared that it was her very lack of pretension which he found most engaging.

For once Theo was really pleased to see him, and she treated him with a degree of partiality that, had she but known it, gave him increasing cause to hope. But he had to compete with many other gentlemen who wished to know her better, and when, half-way through the evening the Countess Lieven condescended to smile on her, the Duchess pronounced the evening to be an unqualified success.

Theo was glad for her sake that all had gone as her grace wished, though for her part she found Almack's a sad let-down. The rooms were spacious enough, but the refreshments were meagre and lacking in variety— nothing so far as she could see but bread and butter and cake, to be taken with tea or lemonade—and so many restrictions governed what one might or might not do that she quite failed to understand why so much store was set by being there.

However, she was wise enough not to voice her opinion, asserting instead with conviction that she had enjoyed herself prodigiously. And if her glance had strayed to the door every time a tall figure dressed in the obligatory knee-breeches decreed by the patronesses of Almack's entered, she was quick to convince herself that she was heartily relieved that Benedict had not seen fit to put in an appearance.

Over the next few days there were sufficient callers to make her cousin's non-appearance pass for the most part unnoticed. Theo was in the highest spirits, with Lord Alverton in regular attendance, and on the occasions when she and Benedict did meet, he behaved with a kind of casual mocking politeness that was not so far removed from his usual way as to occasion comment.

For her part, she strove to emulate him in the casual acceptance of his approach. She knew that the Duchess looked at them strangely once or twice, but since Theo did not appear to be in the least cast down, she refrained from comment.

She could not know the thoughts that teemed through her young protégée's mind and heart—the sensation of loss that persisted and would not be quenched. Theo did not herself understand how it was possible to miss someone when he was quite often there at one's side, but that was how she often felt now.

She missed being able to share with him her appreciation of the ridiculous—there was no one else she knew of in the whole of London to whom she could confide those moments of pomposity, of pretension, of sheer absurdity which they had both enjoyed so much.

But it was evident that Benedict suffered no such pangs. When they attended the same function, as frequently happened, he was never without a beautiful companion on his arm, and though he seemed to favour no particular one, they all quite clearly doted on him.

And so things continued until the night of the midsummer masquerade at Richmond. This event, arranged by friends of Lord and Lady Shadley, had for some time been the subject of much excited discussion and preparation, especially among the younger members of society.

The masquerade was to begin at dusk and continue until dawn, and the road between London and Richmond was choked with traffic from early on in the evening of Midsummer's Eve. Owing to a mishap involving one of the wheels of the Shadleys' coach, their party was late setting out. The sun had gone and only a few faint streaks of pink still lingered across the clear washed sky, but the air was yet warm from the heat of the day and a feeling of eager anticipation prevailed.

The coach itself contained Lord and Lady Shadley, the young and very excited Lady Clarissa, and the Duchess of Bury, while Theo and Lord Alverton drove on ahead in his lordship's phaeton.

Theo had mixed feelings about the arrangement, for although it was very pleasant to be driving in the open air instead of in a stuffy coach, Lord Alverton had given her such warm looks as he had handed her into his phaeton that she was almost convinced that he was on the verge of a proposal.

It irked her even more to know that the fault was, in part at least, her own, for she had been so eager to demonstrate to Benedict how little she cared what he thought of her that she had encouraged Lord Alverton quite shamelessly, and must now do her best to fend him off.

It was already dusk by the time the party came within a mile or so of their destination, with the phaeton by now well out in front along the winding road, so that to Theo, looking back, the lights of the coach appeared and disappeared among the trees with a curious air of unreality.

'Have I told you, dear Miss Radlett, how beautiful you are looking tonight?' said Lord Alverton in a rushed, oddly stifled voice.

'Yes, sir—you have, several times.' Theo endeavoured to keep her voice light. 'It is very kind of you to be so complimentary. I was afraid that all these flowers and draperies might be a little much.'

'Never!' he declared vehemently, stealing a quick impassioned look at her. 'Persephone—sweet harbinger of spring—it is you to the life, my dear!'

She was about to point out in some desperation that

Persephone spent much of the year in Hades, when sounds of an altercation came from behind them.

'Oh, do stop, Lord Alverton!' she cried. 'Something is wrong, I know it!'

He pulled up at once and secured the reins to the low branch of a tree. 'You had best stay here,' he cried, leaping down.

'No, no! I must see what has happened!'

They turned the corner in time to see three masked figures on horseback ranged about the Shadleys' coach, with one felon in the act of thrusting his pistol in through the window that had been let down against the warmth of the evening.

'Devil take it!' raged Lord Alverton. 'I don't have a weapon! Miss Radlett, for God's sake, retreat, I beg of you!'

The highwayman nearest to them heard what he said, and his attention was momentarily distracted. Then several things seemed to happen at once. The sound of his sister's screams reacted powerfully upon his lordship, and without further thought he rushed forward; at the same moment another carriage could be heard approaching, coming quite fast from the London direction, and the ruffians, in danger of being attacked from both directions at once, panicked. One of the two holding the coachman at bay shouted to the third to abandon his work and run for cover, and without waiting to see if he had heeded the warning, turned tail and made off while his companion still hovered uncertainly. In the general confusion a volley of shots rang out as the coachman, seizing his opportunity, reached under the seat for his spare pistol and loosed both barrels, while the new arrival also fired on the fleeing men, hitting one of them.

Theo, pressed tightly against a tree as they crashed past, saw that the man bringing up the rear was clutching at his shoulder; in all the confusion his mask had slipped,

and for one split second of time she was transfixed—
staring into Aubrey's terror-twisted face. Before she
could move or speak, he was gone, and she was running
towards the coach.

Lord Alverton was already helping the ladies down,
assisted by a familiar tall figure.

'Good God! Benedict!' she exclaimed faintly. 'Is it
really you?'

'And in the nick of time, sir!' declared Lord Shadley,
who emerged from the coach at that moment, supporting his prostrate daughter. Benedict relieved him of his
burden until he was safely down the steps, before turning to Theo.

'Are you all right?' His voice sounded abrupt, almost
as though he were angry with her, but she was too
preoccupied to wonder why this should be.

Alverton was quietly comforting his sister, whose sobs
were gradually subsiding, while Lord Shadley, having
reassured himself that his family and the Duchess were
suffering from no more than shock, was counting the
cost of the hold-up, and giving vent to his spleen.

'I'll see to it that the devils are strung up if we can
only run them to earth!' he spluttered. 'Ye winged
one of 'em, Radlett—so it's likely we'll have *him* at
least!'

Theo's heart lurched with fear. She must get Benedict
alone. But for now there was the Duchess to be reassured . . . she had suffered the loss of a sapphire necklace and bracelet, but after the initial shock, had proved
surprisingly resilient and declared that she was quite
ready to drive on.

Lady Shadley too had lost a necklace. She was less
sanguine than her friend, but Benedict pointed out
calmly that the sooner they completed their journey, the
sooner might they all rest and recover.

'Very true,' grunted Lord Shadley. 'I'm much in-
debted to you, sir—I shan't forget it.'

Benedict disclaimed any credit other than that of being in the right place at the right time.

It was while they were all busy reassembling that Theo seized her chance to draw Benedict aside and confide in him.

'Are you sure?' he said, swearing softly.

She drew a shuddering uneven breath. 'Yes, of course I'm sure! It was Aubrey. Oh, Benedict—what are we going to do?'

He shrugged. 'There's little we can do.'

'How can you be so callous!' she whispered, her eyes flashing angrily in the darkness. 'You heard Lord Shadley . . .' Her voice faltered for an instant. '. . . what he intends shall be their fate! Would you let that happen to Aubrey?' And when he didn't immediately answer: 'Doesn't it concern you at all that you are responsible for his injury?'

He gripped her arm none too gently, and his voice was very low and contained. 'Stop it, Theo! If you mean am I sorry that I hit Aubrey, then yes—of course I am. But if the boy indulges in dangerous games, he must take the consequences.'

He fell silent as Lord Alverton came towards them.

'We are ready to continue now, Miss Radlett,' said his lordship, and then with a rather pointed glance at Benedict, who still held Theo by the arm, 'My thanks to you, sir. You were remarkably quick off the mark.'

Benedict stepped back. 'Not at all, my lord,' he said politely, his eyes on Theo. 'It was the purest chance.'

CHAPTER
TWELVE

By MIDNIGHT the revelry was in full swing.

The Elliotts, in whose Palladian mansion the masquerade was being held, had spared no expense in their attempt to outdo all other entertainments in a season of entertainments. The extensive grounds ran down to the river, and hundreds of lanterns illuminated a scene of enchantment. Against a mountainous backdrop of startling reality which incorporated a full-sized rushing waterfall were scattered a number of Chinese pagodas vying with each other for magnificence, and all set beside winding man-made streams crossed every so often by ornate little bridges.

It was linked by acres of greensward that stretched like dark emerald velvet in the lantern-light, and was cooled by the sound of splashing fountains. There were hothouses carpeted with moss and filled with exotic fruit and flowers, and lush dimly lighted conservatories where delicate ferns drooped their fronds in the warm moist air.

And everywhere one looked there were people in frivolous mood, all masked and clad in a riotous mixture of historical costumes and flowing dominoes—some romantic, some amusing, but all colourful.

After a brief rest, the Shadley party—the younger members in particular—were able to put their distressing experience behind them. Indeed they found the magic impossible to resist; even Theo, troubled though she was, found herself being swept along with the rest and was soon enjoying it all immensely.

So light-hearted did she become that even when Lord
Alverton lured her into a pagoda and attempted to
propose to her in passionate fashion, she was able to
fend him off without giving offence.

'I can't contemplate marriage to anyone this evening.'
She laughed irrepressibly. 'Only consider, my lord, how
impossible it would be to have a wife who must spend six
months of every year in the bowels of the earth with
another man!'

'Miss Radlett—Theo—be serious a moment, I beg of
you!' he pleaded, seeking to imprison her hand. But she
eluded the trap.

'No, no! This is not a night for being serious! Dance
with me instead.'

Formal dancing was going forward in the ballroom,
but for the romantically inclined a small group of mu-
sicians had been sited in a corner of the shrubbery, and
the novelty of waltzing in the garden under the stars with
the moon hanging low like a Chinese paper lantern
proved an irresistible attraction for many couples.

'It is just like heaven!' sighed Lady Clarissa dreamily,
as they stood on the terrace looking down.

Theo laughed indulgently—pleased that the child had
recovered from her fright and was able to appreciate the
many compliments that had been showered upon her in
her pretty shepherdess gown. A young and eager cavalier came to carry Clarissa off for a country dance about
to begin in the ballroom, and Theo was left alone.

But only for a moment. A tall figure in a black domino
was at her side, and there was no way that a mask or a
flowing cloak could conceal her cousin's identity. Her
heart stirred and skipped a beat.

'This is my waltz, I think,' he said, imprisoning her
hand.

Perversely she held back. 'I don't remember granting you a waltz, sir,' she returned demurely, quite forgetting their estrangement, how angry she had been

with him so short a time ago.

'You didn't, but you would have done, had the opportunity arisen—which it now has,' he concluded smoothly.

A gentle tug on her hand was all the coercion that was needed to draw her down the steps and into his arms. *It is the night*, she told herself weakly, surrendering her spinning senses to the sweet sensation of being whirled around the garden in his arms while his cloak, billowing about them, seemed to set them apart. *Nothing tonight is real . . . his arm encircling my waist, his hand warm and intimate through the thin silk of my dress and feeling so right!* Lord Alverton's hand didn't feel at all like that!

Benedict looked down into her eyes, unreadable behind the flower-trimmed mask, and loosing one hand so that he held her only by the waist, he lifted the offending obstruction carefully over her hair and hung it on his arm.

'That's much better,' he murmured, silencing her protests with a kiss, and as she looked up at him, silent now, her eyes dark and slumbrous, his own pulse quickened, his voice grew deep. 'You look like a nymph—a goddess who has wandered out of those woods yonder.' He circled her slowly towards the trees until they were in their shadow. 'And one must salute a goddess with due reverence . . .'

It wasn't like the last time. Now his mouth was caressing, sweetly probing, persuasively demanding . . . she was drawn closer until her body was no longer under her control but melted exultantly into his . . . wanting . . . needing . . . she knew not what. A soft moan escaped her as his lips caressed her eyes, trailed down her jawline to explore the pulse beating wildly in her neck—exquisite torture until they returned once more to claim her mouth.

And then a young lady almost crashed into them as she came shrieking past, wildly pursued by her would-be swain—and the fantasy was pricked like a bubble.

But still he was slow to release her, and Theo was incapable of accomplishing it alone.

'Oh, goddess!' His voice was curiously vibrant in her ears as he ceremoniously replaced her mask. 'This is midsummer madness, indeed! I hope you won't demand that I apologise—for one should never seek to excuse perfection!'

She walked back across the moonlit lawns with his hand under her arm, in a complete daze. She had no notion of what she said or did, or when he finally left her, with a mocking bow, in Lord Alverton's charge. She took supper without knowing what she ate, and, she supposed, conversed with reasonable sense, since her companions appeared to accept her behaviour as normal for the occasion, though the Duchess chided her playfully on her want of appetite.

'But then as a gel I was always wont to toy with my food whenever I was in love!' she sighed with an arch glance in Alverton's direction—and when her protégée blushed prettily crimson, she was sure she had hit the mark.

As soon as she might do so without drawing attention to herself, Theo begged to be excused and escaped to the terrace to calm her teeming emotions. It was blessedly quiet outside, the gardens almost deserted, most people being still at supper, and she was able to wander along the terrace at will, pausing at the far end to lean against the balustrade, her face pressed to one of the cool stone supports.

She stood for a long time—or so it seemed—looking out across the herb gardens which ran along the side of the house. Here there was only moonlight and the mingled perfumes that rose with pungent sweetness on the air. She drank them in greedily, and they acted like balm, stilling her disordered senses. Midsummer madness—was that all it was? Combined of the magic and the moment? She had certainly never felt that way before. Her fingers stole to her face as she remembered how shamefully she had abandoned herself—whatever must Benedict have thought? How could she face him again?

A sound penetrated her agonised reflections. As she listened, it came again from somewhere close by in the shadows at the corner of the building—half cough, half groan, and in spite of there being so many people close at hand, Theo found the hairs on her neck lifting.

'Who is there?' she said in a soft calm voice, mastering an urge to flee.

There was a moment of skin-crawling, breath-holding silence, followed by a despairing sob.

'Cousin Theo! Can it indeed . . . be you?'

'Aubrey!' She ran swiftly to where the shadows concealed a deeper shadow—one that shivered with faint movement.

A hand, trembling violently, came out to touch her. 'It is you . . .' he sighed. 'I'm . . . not raving.'

Theo caught him as he half-fell towards her, a gasp of pain wrung from him.

'Oh, my poor boy—you need help!'

'No!' He ground the word out. 'You know . . . what will happen!'

'But I can't just do nothing!'

Aubrey's teeth were chattering, though the night was still warm, and she saw that one shoulder was stiffly held. 'See—put your good arm round my neck so that I can support you.' Slim as he was, he was almost a dead weight as they staggered upright. 'Can you walk a little way, do you think?' she urged. 'Manage a few steps?'

'I'll try,' he muttered through his teeth.

'There is a small pagoda just below here,' she explained. 'If you can make it as far as that, at least you will be under cover while I consider what to do next!'

Theo saw that the mask he had used in the hold-up was still hanging about his neck. She managed to work it back up into place.

'There! Now, if anyone sees us, we are but a couple of revellers under the influence of a little too much wine!' She tried a few experimental steps and was much encouraged. 'Perhaps we might even contrive to sing a little. Do you know "Cherry Ripe"?'

Aubrey sank his head on to her shoulder. 'Oh, Cousin Theo . . . I did so *hope* that I should find you!' he sobbed, and it was like the cry of a lost child.

'Well, now you have,' she said in a matter-of-fact voice, swallowing the lump in her throat. 'Come along now . . . together—"Cherry ripe, cherry ripe— ri-ipe . . ."'

They staggered along the terrace, Aubrey's voice little more than a croak, and half-fell down the steps. 'Whoops!' she exclaimed, laughing as they almost bumped into a couple coming the other way. They laughed in return.

'Only a minute more and we are there,' she urged, for Aubrey was growing so heavy that she feared he must be losing consciousness. 'Don't—oh, please don't faint!'

Somehow she got him inside the pagoda, then paused, out of breath, to take a look round. The light from the garden illuminated the interior, picking out the little bamboo sofas and chairs and spindly tables—and towards the far corner a delicately worked bamboo screen. After a moment's consideration, this was where she made for, and as she lowered Aubrey to the ground, he slumped against the wall in a most alarming fashion. She looked closer and saw that his eyes were still open, though barely focusing.

'They . . . left me . . .' he was muttering in a puzzled way. 'Wouldn't wait. I . . . didn't know what to . . . where to go . . . followed the way you'd gone . . .'

'Don't try to talk! All that isn't important now.' Theo bent close. 'Listen, Aubrey—I have to leave you for a few minutes.'

His head lifted. 'Mama ain't here?'

'No,' she said, troubled. 'No, I'm afraid not.'

'Good. Don't . . . want her to know . . . go all to pieces!'

'Yes,' Theo agreed, surprised by his perspicacity. 'But hush now!' She put a hand over his mouth. 'I mean to see if I can find some brandy, and something with which to bind up your shoulder. Listen—it's just possible that someone may come in, so I shall put this screen around you. But you must be very quiet! Do you hear me?'

'Very quiet . . .' He slurred the words, and she could only hope that he understood.

She arranged the bamboo screen, and after a last anxious look, turned and sped back across the lawns and into the house, making at once for the supper room, whence came the muted strains of the Pantheon Pipes hired for the entertainment of the supper guests. With any luck, the room might by now be thin of people.

'Miss Radlett! There you are.'

It was Lord Alverton. Theo could have screamed with vexation.

'I could not think where you had vanished to,' he chided with a fond familiarity that sounded suddenly irksome. 'The dancing is to begin again soon. I hope you will honour me with the first quadrille?'

'Well, I'm not sure . . .' Thankful for the concealment of the mask, she put a hand to her head as though she might thereby be granted divine inspiration.

He at once exclaimed in some distress: 'My dear ma'am, you have injured yourself! No doubt you are feeling faint! Pray sit down!'

She looked, and saw with horror that her hand was liberally smeared with Aubrey's blood. Oh, good God! What to do now—what to say? She muttered something incoherent about having slipped.

But fortunately he was not interested in explanations for the present.

'You must allow me to call someone—Mrs Elliott. Yes, she will know just what to do—where to procure bandages . . .'

Theo protested that it was not at all necessary . . . a mere scratch! A handkerchief would suffice.

He at once produced his own—large, sensible and, he assured her, quite unused.

'And a little brandy, perhaps? Do let me persuade you to take a little brandy? Ladies do not in general care for it, I know, but I do assure you that its effect can only be beneficial!'

Brandy was certainly one of the things she had come for, but if he should wish to stand over her while she drank it . . .?

'Yes, brandy—the very thing, Alverton. I should fetch it on the instant. My cousin is looking distinctly faint!'

It was Benedict, of course—his sardonic voice calm, practical, immensely reassuring. Quite the old Benedict, in fact. Had he forgotten so soon what had happened in the garden? Perhaps for him what had happened was an everyday occurrence! She subdued a sudden sick feeling—no time now to think of that—no time to think of anything except Aubrey, and how best to help him.

As Lord Alverton hurried away, Benedict said urgently, 'Right—where do you have him hidden?'

She looked up, startled, her mind racing. Was he omniscient? If only she could be sure how he would act. What was it he'd said? *If the boy plays dangerous games, he must take the consequences* . . . but surely he couldn't have meant . . . She tried to gauge his expression, cursing the stupid masks they wore. She said: 'I don't know what you mean.'

'Yes, you do.' His mouth curled. 'You were seen, my dear—in the dubious company of a drunken highwayman, singing bawdy songs!'

'"Cherry Ripe" isn't bawdy!' she protested, and knew

she had given herself away.

Lord Alverton returned with the brandy and a large white napkin.

'Splendid,' said Benedict, taking them from him and putting one hand firmly under Theo's arm, inexorably lifting her to her feet. 'My thanks to you. I am taking my cousin outside. She is feeling a trifle faint—the sight of blood, you know—but with a breath of fresh air she will soon feel much more the thing. Come, Theo!'

'Oh, but I . . .' Alverton began, and found that he was talking to himself.

'I am not squeamish!' Theo protested as she was bundled willy-nilly out on to the terrace. 'How dare you take such liberties!'

'Would you sooner I had told the truth?' Benedict said harshly. 'That you are harbouring the man who robbed his family? Now then, quickly—where is he?'

Theo hung back. 'You won't give him up to the law?'

'You do have a charming opinion of me,' he drawled, and she immediately wished the words unsaid.

'I only thought . . .' she began miserably. 'But of course you wouldn't do such a thing! I'm sorry.'

She led him quickly to the pagoda, and called softly to Aubrey. There was no reply. Benedict put the brandy and the napkin on a table and moved the screen aside. Aubrey lay slumped in a heap, motionless.

'Oh, dear God!' she whispered. 'I shouldn't have left him. Is he . . .?'

Benedict was already on his knees, feeling for a pulse. 'It's not too good, but I expect he's lost a lot of blood. Look—if I lift him up, can you get his coat off?'

Between them, the task was soon accomplished and the wound was exposed, still seeping blood steadily.

'Devil take this poor light! I can't tell whether the bullet is still in, but with any luck, it's too high to have touched any fatal spot. Pass me that napkin and I'll bind it up as best I can.'

Theo didn't move at once. Unbidden, the memory of her father came back, the bullet lodged in a place where it could not be removed . . . the agony and heartbreak that had followed. Her head began to swim.

'Theo!' Benedict's voice was like a whiplash. 'Pull yourself together, for God's sake! The napkin . . .'

'Sorry.' She stumbled to the table and passed him the cloth. 'It was just . . . remembering . . .'

He uttered a soft curse. 'You'd better drink the brandy yourself,' he said tersely. 'The boy has no use for it at present.'

'I'm all right now,' she insisted, but she took a sip just the same.

Benedict ripped the lining out of Aubrey's coat to bind the napkin in place and stood up.

'Look—I'm going to get him into the curricle and drive back to London with him as quickly as possible. He'll need a doctor.'

'He doesn't want Selina to know,' Theo said quickly. 'He's afraid she'll panic.'

'I'd no idea the boy had so much sense,' said Benedict approvingly. 'I shall take him to my rooms for the present, until we see how things go. I doubt Selina will even miss him!'

'I ought to come with you,' Theo said distractedly. 'He'll get awfully shaken up.'

Benedict got to his feet. 'Don't cast aspersions on my driving, young lady!' He took her face in his hands. 'It's your job to go back and join the merriment as though nothing had happened.'

'Oh, but I couldn't!'

'Oh, but you must! And we don't want to arouse any suspicion, so keep that hankerchief tied round your wrist, and I'll get rid of this coat of Aubrey's somewhere along the way.' As she looked up at him uncertainly, he dropped a kiss lightly on her forehead. 'You know I'm right, sweet coz. I shall not be missed, but you most certainly would be!'

CHAPTER
THIRTEEN

IT WAS now three days since the masquerade, and not a word from Benedict other than a brief enigmatic note from him on the first morning stating that their mutual friend had arrived safely and was in good hands.

Theo told herself repeatedly that if anything had gone wrong he would have contrived to let her know, but worry still overshadowed all she did, and her state of mind was not improved by a visit from Lord Alverton, who had refused to take her behaviour at the masquerade seriously and came to make a formal offer for her hand. It grieved her to reject him, the more so since she was aware that she had perhaps been guilty of encouraging his attentions more than she ought.

'You have been looking decidedly peaky ever since that night in Richmond,' said the Duchess, all unknowing, and eyeing her with a troubled frown. 'Of course, there was that alarming business on the road—Lord Shadley is determined that something shall be done about it, you know—and indeed it was enough to set anyone's nerves all on end.' Her glance fell upon the bandage which Theo still wore on her wrist, more to conceal what was not there than what was. 'You are sure that scratch is not paining you, my love?'

Theo, consumed with guilt, said hastily that it was not. But her grace's somewhat ghoulish fears were not so easily lulled to rest.

'I cannot help but wonder whether we should not have had Dr Baillie to look at it . . . one does occasionally hear of seemingly trivial injuries turning quite putrid, with the most dreadful consequences!'

'My dear ma'am, there is no such danger in this case, I promise you!' Theo exclaimed, not knowing where to look. 'But, in truth, I am a trifle tired, and if you would not mind, I think I will not come with you to the musical soirée this evening.'

'Very sensible, my love,' approved the Duchess. 'An early night will not come amiss. And you must recruit your strength for our own ball, which is not more than a week away!'

Theo had not expected that it would be so easy to dupe the Duchess, and guilt once more threatened, but the prospect of having a whole evening to herself quite lifted her spirits, which had suffered a reverse thanks to a letter that morning from her grandfather which had been full of splenetic utterances.

He had, he said, been obliged to suffer a visit from Beau—*driven from Town by the duns and expecting me to go bail for him*, scrawled the crabby hand. *But I vowed I'd not do so ever again, though almost anything is preferable to having him about the place like a damned parasite!* There followed a whole string of querulous complaints so that she could almost see him sitting before her, shoulders hunched and head thrust aggressively forward. A feeling of homesickness overwhelmed her.

This Frenchie you're so taken up with—sounds a deuced havey-cavey character! Got a damned unhealthy obsession with that necklace, seems to me—can't think what that great-nevvy of mine's about, letting the fellow sit in your pocket, and so I shall tell him when I see him . . .

Oh well, she thought. At least I tried. The Comte would have to be told, but she didn't feel like going out of her way to do so just now.

*   *   *

The doctor took his leave, and Benedict stood for a moment in frowning thought. The report had been satisfactory, more so than might have been hoped for, in fact—but then Aubrey did have youth on his side, and once the bullet had been removed there had been no complications barring a little fever and the weakness caused by his loss of blood.

With the doctor's parting words still fresh in his ears, Benedict concluded his meditation and walked briskly through to his dressing room, which had served as Aubrey's bedroom for the past three days. His man, Robinson, was quietly clearing away the soiled dressings and scraps of lint left by the doctor, but at a nod he collected them together and left the room.

Benedict went across to the bed and looked down at the patient. Aubrey was lying propped against the pillows, his pallor rather more marked than usual as a result of the recent ministrations of the sawbones. And from the set of his mouth, he was probably in considerable discomfort, though he had more bottom than Benedict would ever have suspected.

'Mauled you about a bit, did he?' he asked sympathetically.

'I shall do,' came the terse, ungracious response.

Benedict smiled faintly and settled himself in the chair beside the bed, stretched out his legs, and folded his arms across his chest.

'Of course you will. In fact, my boy, I'm told that you are making excellent progress.'

Aubrey eyed him warily. When Benedict used that smooth-tongued approach, it was usually a prelude to something damnably unpleasant.

'I still feel weak as a cat, though,' he muttered, hastily back-tracking.

'Yes, well, that's only to be expected. But the doctor assured me that talking wouldn't tire you too much.'

There was a palpable silence. Aubrey looked down at

his hands until he could bear it no longer. He met Benedict's eyes and found them not hostile, but quite implacable.

'We do *have* to talk, you know.'

'Yes. I daresay I haven't . . . that is, I am aware that I owe you a great deal . . . my life, most probably . . .'

'I am flattered that you should think it,' drawled Benedict with extreme dryness. 'But I fear my part has been a modest one. Theo and Sir James are due the greatest share—Theo most of all, for without her prompt action you would most assuredly be dead by now, or in prison—or both.'

Aubrey flushed. 'Yes, well, I am grateful! I know that what happened . . . what I did must seem . . .' He was groping for words.

'Lunk-headed?' suggested Benedict succinctly. His voice hardened. 'Or criminally stupid?'

'It wasn't meant to be!' said the boy miserably. 'We just thought it would b-be a bit of a lark . . . like boxing the watch, you know . . . p-pick on a lone coach, relieve the revellers of their jewels. It d-didn't seem like stealing . . . they said we'd return the booty later . . .'

'How very magnanimous of you! What a pity your victims weren't privy to your exceeding generosity of purpose. The ladies in particular would not then have been frightened half out of their wits!'

'I d-didn't think . . .'

'Didn't think, or didn't care,' said Benedict harshly.

'No!' It was an indignant cry. 'Only . . . talking about it beforehand, there d-didn't seem to be any harm in it!'

'No harm?'

As though cornered, Aubrey moved on the pillows and winced. 'Well, you know! I thought you of all people might understand!'

Benedict sat forward suddenly, his voice softly cutting. 'You know, I sometimes get a little tired of having my past thrown up at me. I did some rackety things in my youth, and had my hair combed for them in no uncertain manner, but by God! I stopped short of going on the High Toby!'

There followed a long silence. Then:

'What do you mean to do with me?' Aubrey's voice was subdued.

Benedict sat back again, crossed one leg over the other, and regarded his gleaming toecap thoughtfully. 'That rather depends on you. The doctor tells me that you will be fit enough to be moved in a day or two'—he saw alarm flicker in the boy's eyes—'in which case I mean to take you down to Shallowford to recuperate. But before that,' he continued as relief flooded Aubrey's face, 'you will write to your so-called friends, informing them that if all that was stolen is not immediately returned, I shall be obliged to inform on the lot of you.'

'But you don't know who the others were!' Aubrey cried in some agitation.

'Don't count on't, my boy,' said Benedict softly. 'I am confident that I can name them without the least trouble.'

There was sufficient conviction in his voice to stem any further argument. Beads of perspiration stood out on Aubrey's forehead, and Benedict knew that he could press the matter no more for the present.

Without hurry, he rose and went across to a near-by table to wring out a cloth in cool water. He sponged Aubrey's face with surprising gentleness.

'There—I'll tease you no more for now.' He poured a measure of the composer prescribed by Sir James and obliged Aubrey to drink it. 'Later, when you feel more the thing, I have a suggestion you may care to consider—concerning your future.' He removed one of the pillows and laid the boy carefully back. 'That should be more comfortable.'

Aubrey's eyes were already clouding. 'I was wrong about you. You're a . . . great gun!'

'How very discerning of you!' drawled his host.

The boy chuckled drowsily and closed his eyes.

Theo practically threw herself upon Benedict when he arrived in Grosvenor Square. She was in her room trying to read Mr Scott's *Marmion*, and not taking in a word, when Bracegirdle came to tell her that Mr Benedict Radlett was below in the gold drawing room.

'Oh, if you only knew how I have longed for news!' she cried, holding out her hands to him. 'It has taken every ounce of my resolution not to rush to your rooms.'

'Which would have been most improper,' he said in mock reproof while taking hold of her hands.

'I suppose so, though I doubt *that* would have been a consideration, only I suddenly realised that I didn't properly know your direction—and could hardly discover it without occasioning comment.'

'You don't change at all, I see.' But he laughed and led her to a sofa near the window where the setting sun cast an aura of flame about her head. 'I wasn't sure when best to call. You are so seldom at home.'

'No, but Lady Bellingham was having one of her boring musical evenings—and I felt quite unable to sit through it.' She looked at him eagerly. 'How is Aubrey?'

'Better than he deserves. Still weak, of course, but making excellent progress. Sir James is very pleased with him.'

'Sir James?' Theo's eyes grew round. 'Benedict—you didn't approach *Sir James* to remove the bullet from Aubrey's shoulder?'

His smile mocked her. 'Why should I not? He's a sawbones, and a good one—and I'm not exactly *au fait* with the present standard of London doctoring.'

'But—well, he's a terribly high stickler! However did he react?'

The smile became a grin. 'Devilish sticky at first! Gave me that thin-nosed stare. But I talked him round. Followed your example—poured the butter-boat over him!'

Theo burst out laughing. 'That I *don't* believe! He would never succumb to flattery. But I don't care how you did it so long as Aubrey is the better for it!'

'Unscrupulous wench!' he said. 'Would you dare as much for me, I wonder?'

Theo blushed and looked quickly away—down at his hand, which still enclosed hers. 'Perhaps. But you are not so young and . . . and vulnerable as Aubrey, and do not need to be rescued from your folly.'

He lifted her hand to his lips. 'Oh, sweet coz—you know nothing of my needs!' he said softly.

It would be so easy to respond in kind, she thought as her pulse began to quicken, but no—he should not so easily play havoc with her emotions again. Determinedly she drew her hand away.

'We are discussing Aubrey,' she said firmly, praying that no trace of a tremor was discernible in her voice. 'Does Selina know yet what has happened?'

He shrugged, accepting her rebuff with equanimity. 'Not to my knowledge.'

'I doubt she has even missed him,' said Theo, unable to keep a note of waspishness out of her voice. He raised an eyebrow.

'You could well be right. But she will have to be told something. I have it in mind to take the boy down to Shallowford at the weekend. He should be strong enough to manage the journey by then.' Benedict sipped a glass of Madeira thoughtfully provided by Bracegirdle.

'Oh, yes. That will be just the thing for him!' Theo sighed. 'I only wish that I might come with you!'

His look was uncomfortably searching. 'Tired of the *beau monde* already?'

'Does it make me sound too ungrateful if I say yes?' She grimaced. 'I don't wish to be. It's simply that an unremitting round of pleasure seems such a totally meaningless exercise—for me at any rate. There are so many ways in which I can be useful at Shallowford.' She sighed even more heavily. 'But I can't come. The Duchess's ball is next week, and as she is giving it for my benefit I can hardly leave her to complete the arrangements alone, even though she is much better at it than I am.'

'A pity.' Benedict stood, and set down his glass.

'Will you stay in the country?' she asked, hoping very much that he would not.

'That rather depends,' he said. 'On Aubrey's condition, among other things.'

She gave him a considering smile. 'I believe you care rather more for Aubrey than you would have one think.'

'"Care" is coming it a shade strong,' he drawled. 'But I'll allow the young rip don't want for pluck. He's been in considerable pain these past few days and has borne it like a good 'un. He has time enough to put all this behind him and make something of himself.'

The tone of his voice made her look up at him more closely. 'Did you have a particular something in mind?'

'I might—if he has the wit to seize his opportunities. It did me no harm.'

Theo stood up, too—taken aback. 'You mean India? Oh, Benedict, he is very young to go so far away?'

'Nonsense.' There was faint exasperation behind his eyes. 'True, I was a trifle older—but you said the lad was hot to join a cavalry regiment, and the East India Company can offer him excellent opportunities for advancement. I will engage to purchase a commission for him, and have friends enough out there to keep him under their eye—see he doesn't come to harm.'

'You appear to have it all worked out,' Theo said, still not entirely convinced. 'Have you put the proposition to Aubrey?'

'No. I'll wait until he's more fully recovered.'

'And Selina? She won't care for it.'

Benedict's lip curled. 'Do you think not?' he drawled.

'It's my belief she'd dab her eyes a few times, sigh a little, and wave him farewell with no more than a slight pang!'

On reflection Theo thought that this was probably true, and it made her feel a little sad for Aubrey's sake. She thought again of Shallowford.

'I do hope Aubrey's presence won't upset Grandpa,' she said. 'I had a letter from him today and he sounded decidedly fractious.'

She told Benedict what Lord Radlett had said about Beau, but carefully omitted the rest.

'Is Beau really so badly in debt? I confess it isn't the first time the idea has been put into my mind.'

'My dear child, Beau has been in debt for most of his life, to some degree or other, but if you mean is he more than usually squeezed at present, then I would hazard that he is.' Benedict's tone grew sarcastic. 'Gambling over the odds on his expectations, no doubt!'

'But that's awful!' Theo exclaimed. 'He's going to feel utterly betrayed if he discovers what Grandpa is contemplating! Will he have told him, do you suppose?'

'Not unless his temper got the better of him. I fancy your grandparent's warped sense of humour would derive more satisfaction from the thought of allowing Beau to hope, and then dashing his expectations when they are beyond recall.'

Theo was shocked and disappointed. She had accepted that her grandfather was difficult, crabby, even wildly unreasonable; but that he could be so vindictive hurt her more than she could express, for she had in a curious way grown to love him and found it hard to believe that she could not, if she really tried, reverse his attitude before it was too late.

But she was to be denied that opportunity.

Two mornings later, when Theo and the Duchess were about to set out on a shopping expedition, Benedict arrived—striding into the room with a lack of ceremony that betrayed a degree of urgency above the usual, his face set in lines of such grimness that Theo's mind immediately flew to Aubrey—he had taken a turn for the worse. But before she could frame the question, Benedict had come forward to take her hands.

'I'm very sorry, my dear,' he said, and she saw in a detached way that his eyes were bright with compassion. 'It is your grandfather. He died quite suddenly, late last night.'

CHAPTER
FOURTEEN

'MY DEAR child, such a sad homecoming!' Great-aunt Minta folded Theo in her arms as soon as she entered the library, and then led her to the sofa near the fire, looking, Theo observed, more frail than she remembered. 'It came as such a surprise in the end, you know. All was much as usual last evening, except that Edmund was more crotchety than ever! I rebuked him, I remember, for drinking too much port—"It ever made you blue-devilled!" I told him roundly . . .' Her voice trembled.

Theo begged her not to upset herself, but it seemed as if she wished to talk, and thinking that perhaps she needed to do so, the girl let her continue.

'And then, this morning quite early, Gorton found him . . . just as if he had gone to sleep and slipped away. Well, you will see for yourself how peaceful he looks, only . . . well, I know it is fanciful of me, but already the house seems quite empty without his presence!' She cleared her throat and sat up very straight. 'You know that Beau has arrived already? Hardly seems five minutes since he was here before! So much upheaval as there will be!'

Theo wondered with a sinking heart whether Aunt Minta had the least idea how much of an upheaval was likely.

Already it seemed much longer than a few hours since she had first heard the news from Benedict. While the Duchess had exclaimed and commiserated and shed a few tears, she had stood quite still in her grief, white-faced and silent, only the tightness of the skin stretched across her knuckles as she gripped a chair-back betraying the extent of her distress.

She had been ready to leave on the instant. The Duchess had put her coach at their disposal, and, drying her tears, had begged Theo not to be considering any inconvenience her going might cause, but to recruit all her strength for the ordeal ahead.

But there were other matters to be considered. Benedict had seen the lawyer and informed Beau, but the question of Aubrey remained. He must risk removal to his mother's house in Upper Wimpole Street, or make the journey to Shallowford a little sooner than had been expected.

By then, of course, Selina knew of Aubrey's folly and its unhappy outcome. She had been by turns angry and tearful, the distraught mother wounded by an ungrateful offspring, for all the world, Theo complained indignantly to Benedict, as though much of it had not been due to her own lack of guidance.

Now that he was in trouble, her concern seemed to centre as much upon how people would react towards *her* if the truth should come out as upon the possible fate of her son. Lord Shadley was still breathing fire, and in spite of the mysterious return of both his wife's and the Duchess's jewels, Bow Street was known to be pursuing the most diligent investigations, encouraged by the discovery of a coat with a bullet-hole in it thrown in the bushes some way from the scene of the crime, which seemed to confirm that one of the felons had been hurt.

'Why the devil could you not have picked on someone other than Lord Shadley to rob?' Benedict had berated his young charge in some exasperation when the affair did not die down. 'Not only a magistrate, but one committed to stamping out this particular kind of offence!'

Selina had already acquiesced eagerly to Benedict's suggestion of moving Aubrey to Shallowford the moment he could travel, but the Viscount's death had now precipitated matters, and her alarm lest she should be obliged to have Aubrey at home, with all the attendant possibilities of questions being asked, was so apparent that a hasty consultation with Sir James had ensued, and he had given his consent for the boy to make the journey.

Theo realised that her great-aunt was still talking, and she hadn't heard a word. As if the old lady could read her thoughts, she said suddenly, 'But there—I daresay you won't want to be listening to me prosing on just now . . . such a journey as you must have had!'

Theo assured her that they had been very comfortable in the Duchess's coach and that although Aubrey was looking a little frail, Benedict had taken him straight up to his room, and was hopeful that he had taken no lasting harm. From the blank look in Great-aunt Minta's eyes, it was evident that some kind of explanation was required.

'The poor boy is recovering from a rather nasty accident,' she said simply. 'Benedict had intended to bring him down here later in the week, but in the circumstances . . . well, it seemed rather silly to make two journeys, and the doctor pronounced him well enough to travel.'

To her relief the old lady accepted the explanation as it stood, saying merely, 'Quite so. Very sensible. Is his mama come also?' And she seemed to accept without surprise that she was not.

'But I can't possibly just drop everything at a moment's notice!' Selina had cried plaintively. 'And really I cannot see any reason why I should. There will be nothing at all for me to do. You and Benedict between you can minister to Aubrey's needs far better than his poor mama!' A slight note of waspishness here. 'I suppose I must come for Lord Radlett's funeral, though God knows I have little enough cause to mourn that man's passing . . . and whatever else I may be, I am not a hypocrite!'

While she could not admire Selina's sentiments and found her frankness harmful, Theo acknowledged that there was an element of truth in what she said, enough perhaps to enable her to accept if not condone the older woman's behaviour.

Feeling a sudden need to wash and change, Theo hugged the old lady and stood up. 'You know, I believe I will go to my room, just for a little while.'

Upstairs she met Benedict coming away from Aubrey's room. The boy was already asleep, he told her, and with any luck would be none the worse for his experience.

'You look tired,' he said abruptly. 'I hope you mean to rest?'

'A little. I am more travel-weary than anything else.' She hesitated. 'I thought perhaps I might freshen up and then go along to my grandfather's room.' She heard him draw in an exasperated breath. 'Well, you know I like to get things over with . . . and Aunt Minta says that Gorton is very cut up. I wouldn't want to add to the poor man's distress by appearing to neglect to pay my last respects. Gorton, you know, sets great store by such things.'

'The devil with Gorton!' said Benedict softly. 'I am more concerned with your distress!'

'I don't mind,' she insisted. 'Oh, did Purley tell you that Beau is already here? Now, the thought of facing him *does* bother me!'

He touched her cheek briefly. 'You needn't let it touble you, my dear. I will handle Beau.'

He was called upon to do so almost immediately. He had hardly left Theo when Purley came hurrying along the corridor to meet him. The old butler was badly out of breath and showing his years.

'Oh, sir—would you be so good as to come? Only it's
Mr Beau . . . oh, dear . . . I suppose I must learn to call
him his lordship . . .' His mouth quivered uncontroll-
ably, and it was some moments before he could continue: 'In his . . . in the late master's sitting room, he
is . . . and driving Gorton into a fit of the shakes,
demanding the keys to all the cupboards.'

Benedict swore and, without waiting to hear more,
strode away in the direction of Lord Radlett's
apartments. He heard Beau's voice before he
reached the open door, its languid tones clipped with
fury.

'Perhaps I have not made myself clear, dolt! Or else
grief has addled your wits. But I will tell you one more
time. My uncle is dead and you now take your orders
from me—and I am ordering you to surrender to me all
the keys my uncle possessed—for this room, the bedchamber, or any other room where there may be locked
drawers or cupboards, and don't tell me you have no
knowledge of their whereabouts, or I shall lose all
patience!'

Benedict pushed the door wider and stepped in, unnoticed.

'But then patience never was noticeably one of your
virtues, was it, Beau? I fear it is something you may now
be obliged to cultivate.'

The dandy swung round at the sound of the familiar
sneering drawl, something very like a snarl on his lips.
'You!'

Benedict acknowledged the greeting with a sardonic
bow, only his eyes betraying a cold anger. It was not
apparent, however, as he turned to the pale, shaking
valet.

'I'm sorry I was not here sooner, Gorton. I fear you
have been obliged to suffer more than you should.' He
heard Purley come panting up behind him, and said with

a brief glance in his direction, 'Perhaps a restorative might be in order?'

The butler nodded, averting his gaze from the new Lord Radlett, whose raddled face was red as a fighting-cock with suppressed rage.

'You come along of me now, Mr Gorton,' he said, made bold by Benedict's presence. 'We'll take a glass of something together in my sitting room as'll maybe put a bit of a spring back in your step.'

'That's the barber!' said Benedict approvingly, as the two elderly servants left the room, supporting one another. 'Take your time. No need to hurry back.' He closed the door firmly behind them and waited for Beau to unleash his wrath.

He was not disappointed. Gone was the languid dandy as Beau launched into a tirade of abuse, which included, among other accusations, that Benedict was attempting a persistent subversive undermining of his authority, culminating not a moment since in a deliberate attempt to institute a brawl in front of the servants in order to provoke him beyond what was bearable. Benedict watched him with a curious air of detach-ment—the bored face, held rigid within the confines of that ridiculous high collar, transformed by the hatred spewing from the normally fastidious mouth.

Only when the older man finally paused for breath did he intervene with cool precision. 'Had you not overstepped the bounds of decency by invoking your so-called *authority* almost before our uncle was cold, none of this would have happened. Panic, my dear Beau, and greed are responsible for your present discomfort.'

'What the devil are you on about? It is my right . . .'

'You have no rights here until Great-uncle Edmund's wishes are made known—and that won't be until after the funeral, when Cartwright reads the Will,' said Benedict harshly. 'Until then, you will touch nothing.'

Beau was very still suddenly, staring at him through

narrowed lids. 'And who gave you leave to be so damnably officious of a sudden?'

'Not officious. Simply exercising my authority as one of the executors of Uncle Edmund's Will.'

The silence screamed with unspoken obscenities.

'Oh, how clever you have been, Cousin Benedict,' Beau said at last, his voice low and full of venom. 'And I wonder just how unspeakably cunning. No doubt, having wormed your way into that old cretin's confidence, you will have arranged matters exactly as you want them.'

'I hope so,' said Benedict without expression.

'And will we all be expected to jump to your tune?'

'We shall just have to wait and see, shan't we? And now, if *your lordship* will be so good . . .' He turned to open the door, and in so doing saw that the door from the bedchamber was open and Theo was standing there, her expression frozen somewhere between misery and horror.

Beau looked from one to the other with arrogant loathing and swept from the room without a word.

'How long have you been there?' Benedict asked harshly.

Theo stared at him as though uncomprehending. She had come in by the door leading from the corridor to the bedchamber as she had always done, and finding Gorton not there, had been drawn to the bed, where her grandfather was laid out in stately simplicity under a white satin sheet, his aggressive features softened in death. Great-aunt Minta was right—he did look at peace—but Theo missed that surging unpredictability of temperament that had smouldered beneath the surface even when he was so ill, and knew exactly what the old lady had meant about the empty feeling.

It was only gradually that the sound of voices had penetrated her reflections. She moved to the door between the rooms in time to hear the last part of the

exchange between the two men. That they should be
arguing at all with her grandfather's remains hardly cold
was bad enough, but as to *what* they were saying . . .

'*Have* you arranged things exactly as you want them?'
she asked tonelessly.

He made again that sound of exasperation. 'Don't you
be idiotish, Theo, for God's sake! It is quite enough to
have Beau ranting like a lunatic! And before you start
leaping to conclusions, I suggest you reserve judgment
until you have spoken to Gorton.'

'Gorton?' Theo shook her head as though ridding it
of unworthy thoughts. 'Yes—where is Gorton? He isn't
ill?'

'Not precisely,' drawled her cousin sardonically.
'Though he isn't exactly in prime twig either! A condition not improved by Beau's haranguing him for
refusing him access to your grandfather's effects!'

'Oh, the poor man! I must see him. Where is he?'

One of Benedict's eyebrows lifted faintly. 'At present
Purley has him in hand, and is I hope plying him with
enough small libations to make him feel much more the
thing!'

'I hope so. Perhaps,' she said uncertainly, 'I'll come
back and see him later.'

'As you wish—but he may not be too coherent!'

Dinner that evening was attended by an air of unreality. Beau, to everyone's relief, declined to be present.
He had taken himself off, according to Purley, soon after
the unfortunate incident earlier, without a word as to
when he might return. And Great-aunt Minta was in a
very strange mood, acting for all the world as though
nothing had happened and eating her way steadily
through every course as it was presented to her and
chattering non-stop throughout. Benedict behaved with
great solicitude towards the old lady, and Theo desperately tried to keep her own demeanour cheerful,
though she could eat little, and she was very doubtful

if her great-aunt would have noticed one way or the other.

Nevertheless it was something of a relief when the old lady announced her intention of retiring to her room at once, so that Theo was not obliged to continue the charade in the drawing room. She visited Aubrey briefly, but found him weary after the journey and disinclined to talk, so she retired early herself, though for a long time sleep eluded her.

The air of unreality continued throughout the following day, and Theo suspected that nothing much would change until after the funeral. Beau had returned late on the previous night, but he kept to his room and did not trouble anyone. Benedict was preoccupied with affairs of business, spending much time closeted with the estate manager in preparation for Mr Cartwright's visit.

Great-aunt Minta, too, kept to her room for much of the day, and so Theo was thrown very much on her own resources. She rode for a while, visiting one or two of the estate cottages, where to her surprise she found much grief over the Viscount's demise, and much apprehension concerning the future, for whatever faults her grandfather may have had, and they were many, he had never neglected those in his charge.

When she returned, she visited Aubrey again and found him much more alert. For some reason best known to herself, Maddie had elected to take him in charge, and although he made faces about her bluntness, Theo guessed that Maddie's curious mixture of outspokenness and rough kindness might be just what he needed.

Aubrey was almost embarrassingly grateful for all she had done in his behalf—'Benedict says that I would be dead but for your resourcefulness!'

Theo protested that her part had been grossly exaggerated, but it was clear that he was determined to see her surrounded by haloes of angelic light—and she would have to suffer it until she could give his thoughts a new direction.

'I've been an awful fool, I know,' he admitted awkwardly. 'Benedict says I was the biggest cawker ever, and must lie low here until my shoulder is completely healed, as the Runners aren't above finding me even now!'

Theo was to find the phrase 'Benedict says' cropping up quite frequently in the conversation, and she suspected that he too was marked down for adulation.

'But I've learned my lesson,' Aubrey continued ingenuously. 'And when I *am* fit again, I mean to make a new start.' He looked sideways at Theo, a half-eager light behind his eyes. 'Has Benedict said anything to you about the possibility of my going to India?'

'He did mention it,' she said cautiously.

'Well, I wasn't sure at first, but the more I think about it, the more sure I am that it would be just the thing for me! Benedict says that I could *really* fulfil myself out there!'

'India!' cried Selina. 'Oh, no—that's quite out of the question!'

She had arrived late that afternoon, reluctant and clearly ill at ease in the house she had always hated, and was regaled by Aubrey with the news rather sooner than might have been considered propitious.

To Theo's dismay, she had been accompanied by the Comte de Varron, but he had dismissed her fears by assuring her in his most engaging way that he had not the least intention of intruding upon a time of grief—and would rack up for the present at that charmingly rural hostelry they had passed some way back. He gave no reason for his presence other than as escort to Selina, but Theo feared that his motives might be rather less altruistic than he would have her believe, and it was with a degree of unease that she watched him depart.

'But why India of all places?' Selina had demanded of Benedict. 'Aubrey's case cannot be so desperate that he must needs be dispatched to some barbaric outpost at the other end of the world!'

'Strange as it may seem, I had not originally conceived the idea with any such object in mind,' said Benedict impatiently. 'Your son, my dear Selina, wishes to be a soldier—and I happen to have the means at my disposal to gratify his wish. I had made enquiries before ever he landed in his present predicament.'

'You seem to know a great deal more about my son than his own mother!' she snapped.

'And whose fault is that, pray?'

'Benedict!' Theo threw him a reproachful look and went to sit beside Selina. 'You know, I felt just as you do at first, but Aubrey really is keen to go, and it could be the very thing for him.'

'I might have expected you to take Aubrey's part,' said the other ungraciously.

'Oh, good God!' Benedict exploded with soft vehemence. 'Would you rather the boy continued his aimless existence, getting into more trouble? Always supposing we can bring him off safe from this scrape! Or are you willing to allow him a chance to make something of himself?'

'There is no need to make it sound like an ultimatum!' But it was evident that Selina was beginning to see the advantages in the idea.

'Benedict has a friend—a colonel in the Indian army who is here on leave at present,' Theo pressed home the idea. 'He and his wife are agreeable to taking Aubrey with them when they return in about six weeks' time. He should be fit by then.'

'And in the meantime I shall use my influence with the East India Company to buy Aubrey his commission and put in a good word for him.' Benedict looked sanguine. 'Incidentally, India is not all barbaric. Life out there can be highly civilised!'

Selina looked from one to the other. 'Well, I suppose I must give way.' She gave a little sob, dabbed at her eyes with a scrap of embroidered cambric, and gathered her wrap about her. 'No one,' she concluded tragically, 'shall accuse me of standing in my son's light!'

It was quite late that evening, when Theo had already gone to her room, that Purley came to knock softly on her door. He begged pardon for disturbing her so late. 'It's Gorton, Miss Theo. I wonder if you would come and have a word with him. He's been properly on edge all day, but I took it as he was working himself up to the funeral tomorrow.' The old butler shook his head. 'Howsoever, it must be something more that's troubling him, for he's just come to me saying he must see you, miss—and right away! I did suggest Mr Benedict might be more proper, considering the hour and Gorton's state of mind, or better still, that he should wait until morning, but he was quite adamant—it had to be you and it had to be now.'

'Then I had better go and put him out of his distress,' she said.

'You'll find him in his late lordship's sitting room, miss.'

She entered the room quietly. It was softly lit, and Gorton was sitting thin and tense on the edge of his chair. He saw her and came to his feet, his sparse figure sternly erect from long years of habit.

'It is very good of you to come, madam,' he said with the quaint formality that was so much a part of him. 'I fear you will think my behaviour exceedingly odd . . .'

Theo smiled reassuringly. 'I am certainly intrigued, Gorton, but I know that you wouldn't do anything without good reason.'

'Thank you, madam. The matter is one of great delicacy, and I have given it considerable thought before coming to a decision.' He indicated the chair he had just vacated and begged her to be seated. 'If you will bear with me for a few minutes . . .'

Theo made herself comfortable and hoped he wouldn't take too long coming to the nub of his peroration.

'Perhaps I should explain at the outset, madam, that the relationship between a gentleman and his valet, especially when of long duration, is a very singular one—indeed, it would not be over-fanciful, I think, to attribute to it a confidentiality not dissimilar to that of the confessional.'

Theo resigned herself to a long wait.

'Thus I had been aware for some weeks before his passing of a conflict raging within his lordship's mind concerning a certain item of considerable worth which, many years back, had been consigned to his care.'

She was suddenly all attention.

'The Diamond Waterfall!'

'Just so, madam. I believe it came as something of a shock to his lordship to be reminded of the necklace, reviving as it did unhappy memories—and he was at first quite adamant that no one in the de Varron family could have survived the Revolution, so that when a claimant did come forward, he convinced himself that the man was an impostor.'

'He continued to think it, so far as I know,' Theo said, recalling his most recent letter.

'Not with anything like so much certainty as time passed, madam. His lordship did go so far as to have his lawyer institute enquiries, though at the time of his death nothing was proved, to my knowledge. And his lordship being a man very set in his opinions'—Gorton paused, looking apologetic, but Theo waved him on impatiently—'he regarded the claimant, even if genuine, as being much too coming, and therefore unworthy of the name. He seemed to see the case'—now

Gorton really did look uncomfortable—'as a parallel with his own, madam, if you follow me?'

'I follow you perfectly, Gorton,' she said drily. 'But I still don't see why you asked me here.'

'Ever since your last letter, madam, his lordship had brooded even more, and a few nights ago—almost as if he had a presentiment—he said to me, "Gorton, if anything happens, I want you to give that troublesome gewgaw to my granddaughter! No one else, mark you"—he grew quite heated about that. "She'll know the right thing to do," he said.'

'Oh dear!' Theo said, but she was consumed with a desire to see at last this precious bone of contention. 'Well, then . . .'

'Quite so, madam. If it wouldn't distress you to come into the other room?' He led the way into the bed-chamber, lit only by two candles at the head of the bed. At a place near the bed where the rococo panelling was at its most riotous, Gorton moved one of the acanthus leaves to the right and pressed the centre of a flower head, and a panel slid silently back to reveal a dark recess.

He took from it a flat oval case, carried it almost reverently into the other room, and set it down on a table beneath the lamp. The case was of soft padded leather, beautifully tooled and worked with gold.

The elderly valet shakily released the ornate clasp and raised the lid.

'Oh, Gorton!' Theo breathed softly.

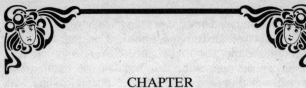

CHAPTER
FIFTEEN

'"... AND THAT the house and estate known as Shallowford, together with all its attendant assets, shall become the property of my grand-daughter, Theodora Elizabeth, for her absolute use, conditional only upon her willingness to take up permanent residence in England. It is further my earnest hope that she will in due course have the good sense to marry her cousin, Benedict Radlett, but in no way do I stipulate this as a condition of . . ."'

'No, by God!' Beau was on his feet, his chair scraping back, the flat of his hand landing with a resounding crash upon the polished table-top. The library echoed to its reverberations, and the Cavalier Radlett glared down in disapproval.

So he had done it! Theo could not bear to look at Beau's face, knowing full well the extent of his rage.

'I knew that the evil old fool hated me, but that he should thus deprive me . . . it is not to be borne!'

'Be quiet, Vincent, and sit down!' ordered Great-aunt Minta from the depths of her armchair near the fire. 'You were a greedy little boy, and you haven't changed. If you cannot be satisfied with Grosvenor Square and that very pretty house in Warwickshire, not to mention the Radlett sapphires . . .'

'Which should be mine by rights!' interposed Selina hotly.

'No, no, dear. That is to say, you ought to have had the use of them until poor Geoffrey's death—and my brother was lax there—but you could not have kept them, you know. They are part of the estate.'

'The estate!' Beau almost choked on the word, his normally sallow face almost puce. 'There is no damned estate, my dear aunt—or at any rate no income to speak of, without this place!' He pointed a shaking finger at Benedict, who was sitting unmoved with his chin sunk in the folds of his neckcloth. 'And he knows it, devil take him! He devised the whole infernal scheme to serve his own ends!'

Mr Cartwright, shocked into silence by Beau's tirade, shuffled his papers uneasily. He had expected trouble, of course—it was a hazard frequently encountered upon such occasions—but there was a malevolence in the air here which went beyond all his worst fears.

Benedict straightened up, his tone uncompromising. 'Be so good as to let Mr Cartwright finish, Beau—the objections can come later.'

The dry voice began again: '"Should my grand-daughter decline to fulfil the condition of residence, the house and estate shall be sold in its entirety, and the monies derived therefrom shall be divided in equal parts between my nephew, Vincent Radlett, my great-nephew, Benedict Radlett, and the above-mentioned Theodora Elizabeth Radlett . . ."'

Theo hardly heard the rest of what was said. To be squabbling over his fortune so soon after her grand-father had been laid to rest seemed little short of indecent.

It had been a simple funeral, attended only by the family and servants, and the workers on the estate. 'Edmund had few friends,' her great-aunt had said, 'and those there were are mostly gone before him.' The Duchess had sent a great basket of flowers, but had a self-confessed abhorrence of funerals, and so had declined to come. For the rest, only Gorton apart from herself seemed to exhibit any real signs of grief.

Mr Cartwright's voice droned on, tidying up the few final bequests and solemnly bringing the Will to its conclusion.

Was Beau's accusation justified? Theo remembered his quarrel with Benedict only yesterday—the one she had interrupted. And much further back, when her grandfather had first announced to her his intentions— had it not crossed her mind at that time that there was some collusion between her grandfather and Benedict? And yet, surely, if Benedict wanted the money, he had only to guide the ailing Viscount's thoughts in that direction?

Theo felt slightly sick. Wasn't that exactly what he had been doing until she came on the scene? Selina had been convinced of it. And perhaps, cleverly, he had changed tack when he saw the closeness developing between herself and her grandfather, and decided that there were other ways of achieving his objective.

Mr Cartwright was gathering his papers together, clearing his throat. Benedict rose from the table without a word and crossed to the massive sideboard, dispensing ratafia for the ladies and returning to the table with a decanter in one hand and a clutch of glasses in the other. He poured the wine and pushed a glass across the polished surface towards the perspiring attorney.

'There—you have earned that, I think,' he said drily, and took his own drink across to the fireplace, where he stood staring down, deep in thought.

Beau had himself in hand now, but as he reached for one of the glasses and began to sip the contents, Theo decided that she had rather he ranted than looked at one in that unnerving way.

'So—now we know,' he said, and one might have been deceived into thinking it the old languid Beau, were it not for the narrowed glittering eyes. 'A very pretty piece of work! But it's a cock that won't fight! I shall, of course, have the Will overset.'

'I don't advise it, my lord,' said Mr Cartwright in some trepidation. 'There are no grounds . . .'

'You think not? An old man whose wits were clearly addled by illness, gulled by a devious little American interloper into believing she had brought him back from the dead—oh, she had him tagged and tied in no time at all!' His words, low and vitriolic, cut Theo to the heart, and any lingering sympathy she might have entertained for Beau in his misfortune vanished.

Benedict was across the room in a flash, leaning across the table, his clenched knuckles on the polished surface betraying his anger.

'You will withdraw that scurrilous accusation at once, or answer to me for it, though you are almost twice my age!'

'Benedict, don't! There is no need,' Theo said.

'Gentlemen, I beg of you!' pleaded the harassed lawyer. 'Sir, I saw his late lordship myself not above two weeks since, and there can be no question that he was of sound mind!'

'Of course not!' declared Great-aunt Minta with a snort. 'Most idiotish thing I ever heard! Edmund was cantankerous, cross-grained, and obstinate as Satan, but queer in his attic he was not!'

The two men were still glaring at one another. Theo touched Benedict's arm. He turned to look down at her, and when she shook her head, he shrugged, the fire dying out of his eyes, and flung himself into a chair. Beau continued to sip his drink.

'Well, then, my lord . . .' A note of relief crept into Mr Cartwright's voice. 'That concludes our business, I think.'

'Not quite, Mr Cartwright.'

They all turned to look at Theo, who had pushed back her chair, and stood up, motioning them all to remain seated.

'I have a small ceremony to perform. I think everyone

here, with the exception perhaps of Aunt Minta, is
aware that there has been a great deal of mystery and
speculation recently concerning the existence and
whereabouts of a certain diamond necklace.'

The atmosphere was again charged; Selina looked
more animated than she had done throughout the whole
proceedings so far.

'My dear Theo . . . never tell us that you have found
it?'

'What necklace?' demanded the old lady.

'So the old man did have it all the time!' said Benedict
softly.

Only Beau did not speak.

Theo began to wish that she had chosen a less conspicuous way of setting matters to rights, but having
begun, she drew a deep breath and continued, explaining briefly for her great-aunt's benefit the history of the
necklace, and the Comte's claim to it.

'Well, bless me!' she said. 'Still, Edmund was ever
close about his affairs!'

'Mr Cartwright has been making enquiries about the
present Comte de Varron, and he tells me that his agent
has been able to find no evidence disproving his rights to
the title . . . and therefore, to the necklace.'

Mr Cartwright nodded agreement.

Benedict was looking distinctly quizzical. 'You didn't
answer Selina's question, my dear coz, but may we
assume that the said necklace is now in your possession?'

'Grandpa left instructions with Gorton that he was to
surrender it to me in the certainty that I would do with it
what I thought right.'

'There you are!' crowed the old lady. 'If that ain't the
act of a sane man . . .!'

'So it seemed to me,' Theo continued, speaking with
more confidence now, 'that as the Comte de Varron
is at present in our midst—indeed, he was so good
as to attend the funeral this morning—it would be

appropriate if his property could be returned to him before he leaves for London.'

She walked across to the door. 'I sent him a message asking him to call here at about three o'clock.' She glanced at the clock on the mantelshelf, which was about to chime. 'Purley?' The butler was hovering in the hall, and Gorton stood close by in the shadows, holding the case. 'Has the Comte de Varron arrived?'

'He has, Miss Theo. I showed him into the small saloon as you said.'

'Good. Then perhaps you would bring him along to the library now.' She beckoned Gorton into the room with her. It was quite extraordinary, she thought, how all of a sudden she felt quite calm and in command of the situation.

When the Comte came in, he bowed over her hand with his usual gallantry, his lopsided smile very much in evidence.

'What is all this about, mademoiselle?' he murmured. '*Vraiment!* Such mystery! To be advised to make myself ready to return to town at once!'

'You will see,' she said and introduced him to Great-aunt Minta, who was charmed by him.

Theo took the case from Gorton and laid it on the table. 'I asked you here, Monsieur le Comte, in order that I might return to you formally something which is rightfully the property of your family.'

A gleam of expectation dawned in his eyes.

As she released the catch, Selina rushed up to the table, eager for her first glimpse of the much-sought-after heirloom.

'Oh lud!' she breathed.

The Diamond Waterfall lay on a bed of black velvet, shimmering in the light—swathe upon swathe of diamonds linked at intervals, and down the centre front, by pear-shaped stones of incredible size and brilliance.

'Bless my soul!' exclaimed the old lady, who had been slower to reach the table.

The Comte was silent for a moment, though his long fingers caressed the stones lovingly. '*Dieu!*' he said at last. 'I had no idea!'

'It is quite exquisite, isn't it?' Theo said, still somewhat in awe of so much beauty.

Mr Cartwright, after his initial surprise, was arranging his papers swiftly but neatly into his case and snapping it shut as though he could not wait to be gone, and talking very earnestly to Benedict as he did so. Both Selina and Beau had excused themselves very quickly and left the room, and when the Comte expressed a desire to be on his way, Theo walked with him into the hall. As he waited for his tilbury to be brought round, he looked down at her, smiling and indicating the case which was held possessively close beneath his arm.

'My dear Mademoiselle Théo, I do not know how I am ever to thank you.'

'No thanks needed, monsieur,' she said. 'Once I knew where the necklace was, there was only one thing to be done.' Her eyes twinkled. 'It was fortunate that you happened to be so close at hand!'

'Was it not?' he agreed. 'I will not deny that I hoped. But, *sapristi!* I had no idea that the prize was so great!'

'I confess that I shall be happier when I know that you have got it safely to London, which is why I suggested that you be ready to leave immediately.'

'But . . . there is no danger, surely? Who will know what I carry, after all?'

Beau knows, said her instincts—just as they told her that Beau was behind that attempted burglary. Common sense persuaded Theo that he would not be so stupid as to try anything in this case, but she had seen his eyes when they had looked on the necklace; his mood was unpredictable, and she was uneasy.

She passed it off, however, by saying lightly, 'No one

will know if you go at once, but it is astonishing how
quickly these things become public.'

'Such a Miss Prudence!' he murmured, kissing her
hand and lingering over the salutation. 'But I shall be
guided by you.' He sighed regretfully. 'A pity we cannot
pursue our acquaintance to a different conclusion! My
Cascade Diamant is worthy of a more elegant neck than
that of the "little pudding", *hein*?'

'But puddings are very necessary to fend off starva-
tion,' she said, dimpling. 'I wish you *bonne chance*,
Monsieur le Comte.'

He laughed and released her—and looking past him,
she saw Benedict coming from the direction of the
library, his face set in something very like a scowl.

Then rushing feet sounded on the staircase and Selina
appeared, a bandbox in each hand, her shawl slipping
from her shoulders. She looked like a girl, eager and
breathless.

'Jules, oh Jules . . . I feared you might have gone!
Please, oh, please, take me with you!'

The Comte looked at first taken aback and then
amused.

'As you wish, *chérie*,' he said with a droll glance at
Theo.

'But Selina!' Theo exclaimed. 'What about Aubrey?'

She pouted prettily, but there was determination in
the wide china-blue eyes. 'My dear, you know that I am
not really needed! Aubrey pays far more heed to you
than he ever did to me, and one can see that he is
stronger with every day that passes! I have asked him,
and he does not mind, truly.'

'Well then . . .' Theo shrugged helplessly. 'You will
keep in touch, I suppose?'

Selina promised and was gone.

Benedict said curtly that Mr Cartwright was ready to
leave, and Theo, her chin lifting slightly, walked past
him back to the library. The lawyer assured her as he

departed that he would be down again in a week or so, by which time it was his fervent hope that they would all have settled their differences.

Great-aunt Minta was established once more in her chair, looking rather confused by all that had gone on, and Theo sat with her for some time talking quietly until finally the old lady dozed off. Benedict did not come back when he had seen Mr Cartwright on his way, and she remained where she was, lulled by her great-aunt's gentle snores, until Purley came to say she was wanted.

Beau stood in the hall looking the epitome of studied elegance in his caped coat, his face a mask of cool disdain as his valet assembled a steadily mounting pile of baggage around him.

'I assume you will not object, Theodora, if I have *your* travelling coach put to.' The emphasis laid on the possessive pronoun did not escape her. 'I wish to go as far as Long Winton, where I have friends. From there I can travel post to London at my leisure.'

'Yes, of course.' Theo knew she was meant to feel uncomfortable, and bit her lip. 'But this isn't necessary, surely? You are very welcome to remain for as long . . .'

'You are too kind, but I think not.'

His voice had a clipped finality, and she could not but be relieved that her gesture had been rejected.

She wandered upstairs to the drawing room and curled up on one of the sofas, trying to come to terms with the fact that this house was now hers, and that decisions would have to be made. But not now.

There was a sound at the door, and she looked up to see that Benedict had followed her.

'An eventful afternoon,' he said pleasantly, closing the door and coming towards her. 'Your grandfather wasn't alone in springing surprises! How long have you been keeping that particular one up your sleeve, I wonder?'

He was leaning over the back of the sofa now, so that

she was obliged to screw her neck round in order to see him. He was at his most sardonic, and she—feeling both guilty and aggrieved on top of everything else—was not disposed to humour him.

'Nothing like so long, I fancy, as you have known about that ridiculous clause in Grandpa's Will,' she retorted.

Benedict's eyebrows lifted in mock surprise. 'About us marrying? But I thought we both knew that his mind was travelling that particular road. He wasn't exactly subtle about it at times! Though I confess I could wish he hadn't voiced his expectations quite so blatantly on this occasion.'

Theo looked away quickly, putting up a hand to ease the crick in her neck, and very much aware that he was still regarding her with some intentness.

'You don't think the word "ridiculous" a little excessive?' he said persuasively.

'You know perfectly well what I mean!'

He had moved closer. 'Do I? You have something against the married state, perhaps? Or maybe you have accepted Alverton's proposal and omitted to tell me?'

'No!' His breath was warm against her cheek, and she was in serious danger of being unable to think straight. She evaded him and jumped to her feet, moving away out of reach, and was provoked beyond measure when he made no immediate move to come after her.

She picked up a small porcelain swan from the near-by table and absently stroked its head with one finger. 'I have been wondering,' she said a little unsteadily, 'whether I ought not to consider Grandpa's alternative— you know, about my going back home, and the house and estate being sold and divided.'

'How interesting,' he drawled. 'And what conclusion have you reached?'

'Well, I hadn't really got very far. But it does seem very unfair to both you and Beau . . .' She was floundering. 'I mean, I don't know exactly how much the place would realise . . .'

'Something in excess of three hundred thousand pounds, at a rough guess,' he supplied helpfully.

'Oh, glory!' she stared down in blank dismay at the little swan, whose neck she had snapped in two, conscious only of the shock of his revelation. 'You must be mistaken!'

He came across, took the poor decapitated creature from her nerveless fingers, and laid the pieces on the table.

'Was it valuable, do you suppose?' she said, distressed to see what she had done.

'I haven't the slightest idea, but it's yours now, anyway—or had you forgot?'

'No, indeed, how could I?' She put up her hands to cover her flushed cheeks, her mind working furiously. If he was right . . . 'That settles the matter, then. Shallowford will have to be sold! I couldn't possibly . . . that is, no wonder Beau was so incensed!'

'The devil with Beau!' he said. 'Do you want to sell it?'

'It isn't a question any longer of what I want—it's more a matter of what is right, and it can't be right for me to have all that while you and Beau . . .' Theo turned to pace the floor and found him blocking her way. Instinctively she took a step back. 'It isn't even as though I need a home—I have a perfectly good one in Philadelphia.'

He was smiling, and she couldn't for the life of her tell why.

'Very well,' he said equably. 'If you are so set on Shallowford being sold, I shall buy it.'

'You!' She almost squeaked the word.

'Well, it would be a pity if it went out of the family, don't you think? And there is Aunt Minta to be considered.'

'Oh, dear, I had quite forgotten her!' If only he wouldn't stand so close. She was trapped between the table and the sofa, and there was no way of escape without an ignominious loss of dignity. She fixed her gaze resolutely on one of his coat buttons. It was mother-of-pearl and had a particularly luminous sheen. 'But you couldn't afford . . .' She stopped suddenly, realising with a jolt how very little she really knew about his years in India. She had simply assumed that he had frittered them away. She lifted her head and looked him full in the eye. 'Could you?' she demanded, her spirits soaring to think that he did not need her money after all.

'Well,' he mused, 'I won't pretend that I am able to find such a sizeable amount tomorrow, but with a little judicious juggling of funds, I foresee no insuperable difficulty. And in any case, nothing could be done immediately, you know. The Will has yet to be proved, and there are all the legal niceties which one must observe. But a few weeks should suffice to clear everything up.'

Theo waited for him to say more, but he didn't. She knew that she ought to have felt relieved that the house would stay in the family, but all she was conscious of was a great hollow void of disappointment and loss that brought an unpleasant constriction to her throat and a prickling behind her eyes, and made it incredibly difficult for her to say brightly, 'Then I shall be back in Philadelphia before the winter.'

Benedict uttered a little exclamation at this, and a moment later she was being gathered close.

'No, you won't, my idiotish, darling girl! You will stay here and marry me—and there will be no more nonsense about selling up and going to Philadelphia!'

From the depths of his coat Theo said unsteadily, 'Such a charming proposal! How could any girl refuse it!'

He put a hand almost roughly under her chin and forced her head up. Her face was wet with tears, and he exclaimed and kissed them away, and then his mouth was sweet on hers and she melted into his embrace.

'Did you really imagine for one moment that I would let you walk out of my life?' he murmured, his breath warm against her skin.

'I haven't known quite what to think for a long time now,' she sighed. 'On Midsummer Eve I was almost sure, but then it seemed that I had mistaken a temporary madness for something more, and there was Aubrey and everything . . .'

He stopped her mouth with kisses. 'I have been a fool! I vowed that I would let you have your visit to London without any ties, and then I was as jealous as hell of every man who looked at you, scared out of my wits that you might succumb to one or other of them!'

Later, when they had told Aunt Minta and Aubrey and received their wholehearted congratulations, they ate a quiet dinner together and then walked in the garden until the pink of the sunset faded from the sky, and made plans for the future.

'About Shallowford,' Theo said dreamily.

Benedict smiled down at her in gentle mockery. 'You don't really want to sell it, do you?'

'It would be rather silly,' she admitted. 'Though I wish there were something one could do about Beau. Grandpa does seem to have been rather hard on him.'

His eyebrow lifted. 'Don't waste too much sympathy on Beau, my love. He wouldn't do as much for you, believe me.'

'No, but it must be dreadful to expect so much and then get practically nothing!'

'I wouldn't exactly call what Beau has ended up with nothing! The house in Warwickshire has about nine hundred acres of prime farming land. The tenants' rents from that alone would keep any reasonable man in comfort.'

'Oh, well, I shan't worry about him any more.' She

looked aslant at him. 'Would you really have bought Shallowford?'

'I might. But I'd as lief be kept by a rich wife!'

'Indeed?' she said, laughing.

The next few days were sheer bliss for Theo; even the loss of her grandfather could not dim her happiness. Aunt Minta had taken a slight cold and kept to her room (though Theo did wonder if she was being tactful), and with Aubrey mending nicely and sitting up for longer each day, so that they had no need to worry about him, she and Benedict spent long hours out of doors, riding over the estate so that Theo could familiarise herself with all that had now become her responsibility.

Maddie quite obviously approved, and said bluntly that she had more colour in her cheeks now than she'd had in all the time she'd been here.

'I've certainly never slept so well,' Theo said.

So what it was that woke her that night she couldn't at first decide. Then, with a slight shiver of apprehension, she heard a noise. Someone was in the room. She was suddenly wide awake, nerves tingling.

'Maddie?' she called sharply. 'Is that you?'

The darkness was less black now as her eyes grew accustomed to it, and in the silence she was sure that someone other than herself was breathing.

And then a shadow loomed in front of her, and before she could cry out it seemed to rear up. There was a blinding flash of pain—and then oblivion.

CHAPTER
SIXTEEN

MADDIE WAS a woman not given to hysterical outbursts, but she came as close as she was ever likely to on that morning when she went in to wake her mistress and found her gone and all in disarray.

'Lawks-a-mercy!' she cried, and without further thought lifted up her skirts and rushed along to Mr Benedict's room, to hammer on the door until he opened it.

She had never seen anyone move so fast. He had his dressing-gown on and was striding down the corridor before she had drawn her first breath, and she was left half-running in his wake.

'She didn't go of her own accord, sir, that I'll swear to . . . though some of her clothes *have* gone from the closet. Well, you'll see for yourself!'

Benedict stood, one hand supporting him against the doorpost, surveying the tumbled bedclothes, the general disorder, with an expression that made even Purley hesitate before approaching him.

He had been summoned by one of the servants, several of whom had collected, drawn by the general air of something amiss. He watched Mr Benedict move quite unhurriedly, but rather as if he were in a dream, to the side of the bed and then reach out to run a reluctant finger along an ominous dark streak that stained the sheet.

'Dry,' he said tonelessly. 'It must have happened some time ago. In the early hours, I'd guess.'

'But . . . how, sir?' Purley's distress showed in the shakiness of his voice. 'No one could have got in, let alone taken Miss Theo out, without *someone* hearing!'

'They got in and out once before,' Benedict said. He brought his hand down with sudden force on the bed rail. 'Dammit! Of course!' He rounded on the butler, and it was as though he had come out of a trance. 'Purley, do you recall anything about a concealed passage? Miss Theo's father told her about one they used to use.'

'Lord save us, sir! I had clean forgot about that! Yes, indeed, the boys used it often . . . only I'm blessed if I can remember how they operated it.'

Benedict brushed aside his agonised indecision with an impatient movement. 'That doesn't matter. What I want to know is, who else knew about it?'

'Well, most of the family would, I reckon.'

'I didn't.'

'No, well, you never came here much as a boy, sir, as I recall. But your father, now . . . he would have known, and Mr John and Mr Geoffrey, of course, and . . .' He stopped, his eyes growing wide.

'And Beau,' Benedict supplied softly.

'Oh, sir! You'll never be thinking . . .' He seemed unable to voice the thought.

'We shall see.' Benedict was suddenly brisk. 'Purley, send to the stables at once. I want to know exactly where our newly-fledged Viscount was taken when he left here the other day.'

'I say, what's going on?' Aubrey had wandered in sleepily in his nightgown in the middle of the excitement and was now wide awake.

Benedict berated him soundly for being out of bed. 'I have enough on my mind just now without you threatening a relapse!' he snapped.

Aubrey was undismayed. 'Lord, I shan't do anything so ninny-hammered as that! But you can't expect me to go meekly back to bed without knowing.' He added with sudden truculence, 'Is it true that Cousin Theo has been kidnapped?'

'So it would seem,' Benedict said without emotion.

'Well, you don't seem very concerned,' the boy charged him accusingly, and then rather wished he had kept silent, for he surprised a momentary look of such naked agony in Benedict's eyes that it pained him to see. 'I'm sorry,' he muttered.

Benedict brushed his apology aside. 'Go back to bed, there's a good fellow.'

'Very well.' Aubrey's eyes brightened. 'But as soon as I feel more the thing, can I look for that secret passage? It's the most famous thing ever! Fancy it having been here all this time!'

Long before Maddie had first made her discovery, Theo was facing Beau across a small breakfast table in a pretty parlour, she knew not where. Her head still throbbed abominably, though the first blinding pain, the sickness, and the feeling that the top of her skull was pulsating on and off had thankfully diminished.

Beau sipped tea and regretted that she had no appetite. 'My apologies, Theodora,' he said in that polite, languid fashion she now knew so well. 'I fear my man hit you rather harder than I had intended.'

With tentative fingers she probed the area on the side of her head where her hair was matted with fast-caking blood, and immediately wished that she had not. Beau lifted his quizzing-glass as she winced.

'A nasty contusion,' he admitted, his heavy-lidded eyes quite pitiless. 'It will, of course, be attended to the moment our business is completed.'

Such generosity! Theo's mind, though clearing slowly, was still refusing to function with any degree of alertness. How she had come and why she was here at all (wherever here might be) were questions that required a greater degree of concentration than she could, for the present, summon.

More than anything else she wanted to lie down in a cool darkened room—and sleep. But since that luxury was clearly not to be granted to her, she must at least be grateful to find herself in agreeable surroundings and with a change of clothes. It would not be fanciful in the circumstances to imagine a far worse fate.

She said wearily, 'I am probably being very stupid, but I am not aware that we have any business to conclude.'

His smile was a travesty, and as such was anything but comforting. 'That is probably because you have been too complacent in your good fortune to give the matter serious thought. Had it been otherwise, my dear Theodora, you surely must have realised that I would not permit you and Benedict to deprive me of my rightful inheritance!'

Not for the first time she found something curiously menacing about his rather posturing dandyism. He was probably a little mad, she decided, and wished desperately that she felt less befuddled and more up to the task of dealing with him. If only Benedict were here!

'Well, I am truly sorry if you feel cheated, Cousin Beau,' she said placatingly. 'It must seem a little hard, I'm sure; though to be fair, your rightful inheritance is exactly what you did get—and since it isn't so little as I had at first thought, I suppose Grandpa had a perfect right to leave Shallowford as he pleased.'

Beau had turned a rather unpleasant shade of red, and she had the distinct feeling that what she had intended as reasonable comment had fallen some way short of its mark. His mouth tightened.

'I do not concern myself with legal quibbles, nor do I intend to let the matter go unrectified.'

'But . . .'

He cut her short. 'Pray, let me finish, Theodora. We do not have a great deal of time, and I wish to explain to you exactly what you are going to do.'

Theo's inclination to argue was not matched by a corresponding effort of will. The early sunlight slanting low through the window hurt her eyes, and she frowned and closed them, putting up a hand to shield them from the glare.

'You had better attend me, my dear,' said the petulant voice. 'It would not please either of us if I were obliged to summon my man to persuade you!'

'I am listening,' she muttered.

'Good.' He nodded. 'Well then, to business. I have had a document drawn up in which you voluntarily decline the terms stipulated by my uncle's Will, and thereby request formally that Shallowford be sold. Furthermore, with commendable generosity, you relinquish your portion of the monies thus obtaining in my favour.'

Dimly Theo recollected how close she had come to implementing at least a part of what he now demanded, and wondered that she should have considered him worthy of so much consideration.

'Fustian!' she said faintly.

He continued as though she had not spoken. 'When you have signed this document, and it has been properly checked over and witnessed by my lawyer, you will write to Cousin Benedict, explaining that you have experienced a crisis of conscience and could not rest until all was made right.' He ignored Theo's sharp intake of breath, and concluded blandly, 'And that you intend to return to America at once. You will then be conveyed with all speed to Falmouth, where there is a ship due to sail tomorrow on the morning tide. Your passage is booked.'

A slow anger had begun to burn in her as she listened to him calmly arranging to rob her of all she held most dear. The sheer effrontery of his assumption that she would meekly submit to his evil machinations brought

with it an added indignation which made her head throb
unbearably.

She opened her eyes and stared at him across the
table.

'You are quite mad,' she said distinctly. 'I have no
intention of doing what you suggested.'

For some reason this seemed to amuse rather than
annoy him, and for the first time fear crawled insidiously
along Theo's spine. He was too confident. She began to
pray desperately that Benedict would come.

'Perhaps you would care to read this.' He slid a sheet
of paper across the table towards her. She dragged her
eyes away from his heavy-lidded smile that seemed
already to reveal a hint of triumph, and looked down at
the closely written page, without at first focusing on the
actual words.

And then Aubrey's name leaped out at her, and she
narrowed her eyes against the agony of focusing and
began to read what was in effect a succinct and damn-
ingly accurate indictment against Aubrey, giving the
most precise details of his part in the recent hold-up of
Lord Shadley's coach on the road to Richmond. It
further informed the reader exactly where Aubrey could
be found, still nursing the injury which would most
surely clinch the matter of his guilt.

The letter was addressed to Sir William Roach, pre-
siding magistrate at Long Winton. Theo's heart stopped
beating for a long moment, and then began again with a
painful thud. She looked up, reluctant to meet Beau's
eyes, which seemed to gloat.

'Did you imagine I hadn't guessed the cause of
Aubrey's little indisposition?' he said, his voice like silk.
She shut her eyes, but the voice went on remorselessly.
'So you do see, don't you, my dear Theodora?
Unless you co-operate at once, this letter will go straight
away to Sir William—who is, incidentally, a friend of
Shadley's—and within the hour young Fane will be

in custody. And you *do know* the penalty for highway robbery?'

'You wouldn't be so cruel,' she whispered, knowing full well that he would.

'If I had managed to get my hands on that accursed necklace, I might have been more disposed to be generous,' he said with sudden venom. 'But you *had* to do the *right thing*, did you not? Just as I feel that I should do likewise in Aubrey's case and deliver him up to the law—unless you can persuade me to change my mind!'

Benedict was in his curricle and his horses eager to be off when Theo's letter arrived. He swiftly secured the reins and sprang down with orders to the groom, 'Hold 'em ready.'

The hapless messenger was then marched indoors to be left standing nervously twisting his hat while the decidedly grim-visaged gent read his letter. It must have been bad news, for when the said gent looked up at last, it was like staring into the pits of hell!

Then came a regular inquisition, and the man had ample cause to regret his own impetuosity, for 'not until after nine o'clock' had been his instructions, which if he'd stuck to 'em instead of wanting to get an hour ahead of himself, he wouldn't have fallen foul of this flash cove whose piercing grey eyes dared you to speak less than the truth.

No, he hadn't known the man who paid him to deliver the letter, but yes, he had seen him the odd time coming out of a perticler house in Long Winton recently bought by a rich merchant—name of Brady . . .

It was all Benedict needed to know. The house was the one that Beau had been taken to when he left Shallowford. He tried not to think as he drove there what pressure must have been put upon Theo to make her write such a letter.

At the house in Long Winton the servants were at first

uncooperative, but the butler, sizing Benedict up at a glance, informed him reluctantly that, yes, Lord Radlett had been staying there for the past three days. Mr Brady had gone north more than a week ago, but was in the habit of allowing *carte blanche* to his friends. The practice did not appear to please him.

'Is there a young lady with his lordship?' Benedict demanded.

The butler was clearly embarrassed. A young lady had arrived very late on the previous evening—so late, in fact, that he had not known of it himself until this morning. 'A very genteel young lady, sir—rich brown hair—but sickly-looking on account of having suffered a fall . . . nasty contusion on the head.' He misliked the look in the eye of his interrogator. 'Not fit to travel, in my opinion,' he concluded.

'They've left already, then?' Benedict said sharply.

'More than an hour since, sir, in a post-chaise, and his lordship's man riding with them. I believe Falmouth was mentioned,' he added by way of being helpful, and not having taken overmuch to Lord Radlett.

Benedict waited to hear no more. If he was to overtake them, every moment was vital. At every posting station along the way he asked questions—Beau was not, after all, an inconspicuous figure—and it was not long before he began to get answers, and reckoned that very gradually he was gaining on them.

At Chicklade he was informed that a couple answering his description had stopped for refreshment and had left again less than a half hour ago. The landlord's impression of the young lady, as being passive and uninterested in anything, almost inclined him to wonder if he had mistaken his quarry, but Beau was described too accurately for there to be any mistake, and the thought of Theo reduced to such uncharacteristic behaviour drove him on with renewed fervour. He stopped only to down a pint of ale, and the landlord's wife obligingly put a thick slice of beef between two rounds of bread so that he could eat it as he travelled.

He drove through the night and into a watery dawn, and five miles short of Falmouth he was almost following in the dust of their wheels. He went straight to the harbour to seek out the American packet *Delaware*, where all was bustle, in order to reassure himself that no one answering Theo's description had yet gone aboard. She hadn't, but with little more than one hour to sailing time if the wind held, he knew he must find her quickly.

Fortunately Falmouth was no great size, the harbour set in a small basin surrounded by a circle of gentle hills, and many of the houses huddled on the water's edge with seaweed-encrusted steps leading straight up to their doors. Benedict sought out the most likely hotel and to his immense relief learned that a couple such as he described were at that moment resting in a small private parlour. Further discreet questioning elicited the information that the gentleman's servant was refreshing himself in the taproom.

When a short time later he opened the parlour door, he did so with infinite care, so that at first neither occupant of the room heard him, and he was able to observe how despondently Theo lay back with closed eyes in a wing chair, her bonnet removed so that he could clearly see the matted patch of hair—no doubt concealing a lump that would be hurting like the devil.

There was a red mist of fury before his eyes as he heard Beau, who stood at the window, say in his most finicky way: 'If you are sufficiently recovered, Theodora, I believe we should go now. I have arranged for a man from the hotel to take your valise down to the harbour.'

Benedict closed the door with a firm click, and Beau swung round, his eyes for once so wide that they almost bulged from their sockets. 'The devil!' he exclaimed.

'Something like that,' Benedict agreed softly.

Theo looked dazed for a moment, as though she could not believe what she saw. Then she was out of her chair and across the room to him, a stifled sob breaking from her.

'Oh, how like you to come, my dearest love, but indeed you ought not to have done so!'

With his arms tightly about her, he stared down at her poor head.

'So you endeavoured to convince me, my dear, in that very curious missive you sent me.' His voice lost all gentleness as he looked towards the dandy, who still stood transfixed. 'Perhaps Cousin Beau would care to explain himself before I settle with him?'

Theo cried, 'No, you must not! He has that brute of a man with him . . . and besides, there is nothing you can do. I have to go . . .' Her voice broke.

Benedict held her away a little, frowning down.

With Theo's desperately voiced plea, some of Beau's old arrogance returned.

'You see, Benedict, your interference has got you nowhere, and will simply earn you a broken head.' His tone was almost gloating as he moved in mincing fashion towards the bell-pull. 'You really should have taken the hint!'

Benedict put Theo from him, crossed the room in a few loping strides, and hit Beau flush in the mouth. The dandy went down without a sound and lay motionless, a thin trickle of blood oozing from a cut lip.

'I've been wanting to do that for a very long time,' he said with satisfaction.

Theo came suddenly to life, running to kneel by the prostrate form, her headache forgotten. 'You haven't killed him?'

'No such luck,' Benedict said grimly, and lifted her to her feet. 'And now, my dearest Theo, will you tell me what the devil all this is about? Why *did* you consent to this nonsense?'

She told him then about Beau's threat against Aubrey. 'I read the letter and had no doubt whatever that he would do as he said. He has it with him now—in case I should prove difficult.'

'So that was it.'

'He stood over me as I wrote to you, so I couldn't tell you; but I knew that, desolate as I was to leave in such a way, it wouldn't be the end for us, as I meant to write again the moment I was free of Beau.'

Benedict had gone to kneel beside Beau, and was searching methodically through his pockets. 'This looks like it.' He read the letter without comment and tore it into little pieces.

'Yes, but he can easily write another,' Theo pointed out. 'And unless you can get Aubrey to safety before then . . .'

'He can't if he isn't around to do so,' said Benedict with sudden decision. He picked up Theo's bonnet from the floor, where she had cast it upon first seeing him, and grinned to see her growing bewilderment. 'My dear love,' he said, 'I fear your poor head must ache quite abominably.'

She put up a hand to caress his face. 'It is growing less painful by the minute,' she asserted tremulously.

He caught her to him and kissed her with sudden ardour, and then resolutely put her away from him.

'Nevertheless,' he said, placing her bonnet gently on her head and tying the ribbons with loving care, 'I think that you should seek an apothecary as quickly as possible—we'll ask the landlord to send someone with you to the nearest one. And be sure that he gives you some laudanum to help you to sleep, because of the dreadful pain!'

Theo stared at him in growing suspicion. 'Benedict— what are you plotting?'

'Later,' he said, 'There isn't much time.'

'But what about Beau—and Beau's man? He'll never let me leave!'

'Oh, don't you fret about him—he was called away rather unexpectedly,' said her cousin off-handedly. He refrained from adding that it had taken only a word, reminding the man what penalty he might expect for his role in the kidnapping, to make him disappear. 'And as for Beau . . .' There was a curious gleam in his eyes. 'There is nothing wrong with him that a nice long sea trip won't cure!'

Theo stopped in her tracks, staring at him in awed disbelief. 'Benedict—you wouldn't!'

'Why not?' He grinned. 'There's a passage booked in the name of Radlett. It would be a pity to waste it, and it would get him out of our hair for a while!' His voice hardened. 'It's no more than he would have done to you.'

'But . . . you'd never get him to go on board!'

He took her by the shoulders and propelled her towards the door. 'Why do you think we need the laudanum? Now do hurry, there's a good girl. There isn't a lot of time.'

Theo went.

When she returned, Beau was slumped in a chair, his head in his hands, looking something less than elegant. Benedict perched on a near-by table, arms folded, keeping him under observation.

'Do you have it?' he asked, straightening up briskly.

'Yes.' She glanced at Beau. 'But I'm still not wholly convinced that what we are doing is right.'

'Trust me,' he said.

Beau had heard Theo's voice. He looked up, his eyes bloodshot and heavy, but glinting with malice. When he spoke he lisped, and it became obvious that he had lost a tooth. 'You may think yourthelf mighty clever, my dear—but I'll have that boy in jail before you can thave him, just thee if I don't!'

Theo, close to hysteria, wasn't sure whether to laugh or cry, but his threat decided her. She handed Benedict the phial.

He approached Beau with unusual solicitude. 'Now, don't try to talk,' he said. 'Just take this—it will ease the pain.'

Before Beau properly realised what had happened, he had swallowed the draught.

'Damn you to hell! It'th laudanum!' he cried, and struggled to get up, but Benedict held him, and soon he grew quiet.

'I hope I didn't give him too much,' Benedict muttered. 'I don't want him totally unconscious!'

A few minutes later, a small procession could be seen approaching the harbour. Theo, leading the way, carried Beau's small overnight valise, and Benedict followed with a servant from the hotel, supporting between them the sagging figure of a rather sad-looking dandy. 'Poor fellow, just had a tooth removed . . . been given something for the pain,' Benedict told the servant with perfect truth.

The story was repeated to the master of the *Delaware*, who was none too pleased to have his arrangements set at naught, even for a lord.

'I have a *Miss* Radlett on my way-list,' he said austerely.

'That's me,' said Theo quickly, throwing all caution to the wind. 'I'm afraid that my uncle's man made the silliest mistake when he booked the passage.' She gave her most winning smile. 'It really is most awfully urgent that my uncle get to Philadephia as soon as possible.'

After a certain amount of judicious haggling and formalities, involving a customs official who became enmeshed in the proceedings, proof of identity was produced from Beau's valise, together with sufficient guineas to sweeten the deal, and the matter was concluded, and the master, being in some fear of losing the tide, allowed Beau to be helped on board.

Theo watched, with Benedict's arm close about her, as the packet glided through the choppy waters and under the walls of Pendennis Castle, which stood on a mound near the mouth of the harbour. A light mist which had hung over everything had lifted in the brisk breeze, which began to fill the sails under a pale blue sky.

'Well, that's settled,' Benedict said with considerable satisfaction.

'How odiously complacent you are,' said Theo, trying to sound reproving. 'I suppose you will have considered the possibility that Beau might prevail upon the Captain to put back to port once he has recovered himself?'

'Certainly. But he is hardly in an ideal bargaining position, and I doubt the good captain would be swayed by any but the most persuasive arguments.'

For a moment Theo felt a pang of sympathy for Beau, but the recollection of what he had intended to do soon banished all but relief that they were rid of him.

'You really are quite ruthless, aren't you?' she nevertheless reproached her beloved.

His arm tightened. 'Only when those most dear to me are threatened.' He bent his head, his mouth finding hers and exploring it with a thoroughness that banished all argument and occupied her to the exclusion of all else for a considerable time.

'Now we are going home,' Benedict said huskily, punctuating the words with kisses in a way that made her shiver with delight, 'and I am going to procure a special licence with the utmost speed—and no one is ever going to take you away from me again!'

Theo had little quarrel with this prospect, but as they turned away from the sea, she spared a last glance for the diminishing outline of the ship.

'Oh, poor Beau!' she exclaimed suddenly.

'And if you say "poor Beau" just once more . . .' he threatened.

She laid a finger over his mouth and began to chuckle. 'But my dearest, only consider—an overnight bag and no valet! He will be quite overset!' A fresh thought occurred to her which sent her into fresh mirth. 'Oh, and he will have m-my . . . valise!'

The piquancy of the situation brought an answering echo of appreciation to Benedict's eyes.

'Serve him right!' he said unsympathetically.

Mills & Boon

Your chance to step into the past Take 2 Books FREE

Discover a world long vanished. An age of chivalry and intrigue, powerful desires and exotic locations. Read about true love found by soldiers and statesmen, princesses and serving girls. All written as only Mills & Boon's top-selling authors know how. Become a regular reader of Mills & Boon Masquerade Historical Romances and enjoy 4 superb, new titles every two months, plus a whole range of special benefits: your very own personal membership card entitles you to a regular free newsletter packed with recipes, competitions, exclusive book offers plus other bargain offers and big cash savings.

AND an Introductory FREE GIFT for YOU. Turn over the page for details.

Fill in and send this coupon back today
and we will send you

2 Introductory
Historical Romances
FREE

At the same time we will reserve a subscription to
Mills & Boon Masquerade Historical Romances for
you. Every two months you will receive Four new,
superb titles delivered direct to your door. You
don't pay extra for delivery. Postage and packing is
always completely free. There is no obligation or
commitment – you only receive books for as long as
you want to.

Just fill in and post the coupon today to MILLS & BOON
READER SERVICE, FREEPOST, P.O. BOX 236, CROYDON,
SURREY CR9 9EL.

Please Note:- READERS IN SOUTH AFRICA write to
Mills & Boon, Postbag X3010,
Randburg 2125, S. Africa.

- -

FREE BOOKS CERTIFICATE

**To: Mills & Boon Reader Service, FREEPOST, P.O. Box 236,
Croydon, Surrey CR9 9EL.**

Please send me, free and without obligation, two Masquerade Historical Romances, and
reserve a Reader Service Subscription for me. If I decide to subscribe I shall receive,
following my free parcel of books, four new Masquerade Historical Romances every two
months for £5.00, post and packing free. If I decide not to subscribe, I shall write to you
within 10 days. The free books are mine to keep in any case. I understand that I may cancel
my subscription at any time simply by writing to you. I am over 18 years of age.

Please write in BLOCK CAPITALS.

Signature _____

Name _____

Address _____

_____ Post code _____

SEND NO MONEY — TAKE NO RISKS.

Please don't forget to include your Postcode.

Remember, postcodes speed delivery. Offer applies in UK only and is not valid
to present subscribers. Mills & Boon reserve the right to exercise discretion in
granting membership. If price changes are necessary you will be notified.

4M   Offer expires December 31st 1985

EP9M